It Only Takes One Bite

By Sheryl C. D. Ickes

Special Thanks and Much Appreciation to my husband, Ken, and my daughter, Sarah for supporting my writing and also for computer help. Thank you to Sharon H. for some editing advice.

This story and all characters are of my own making and are fictitious. Any errors are of my own doing.

Cast of Characters

Alexandra Jean Applecake "Alex"- owner operator of Slice of Life Cake
Shop and Bakery

Caitlin Farrell "Cat"	- friend of Alex and employee of Alex
Maggie Marchetti "Mags"	- friend and employee of Alex
Joyce Hentzel "Jo-Jo"	- friend and employee of Alex
Didi Gambini	- friend and employee of Alex
Detective Thomas Baker	- detective
Detective Johnathan Whitamyer	- Tom's regular partner
Detective Clifford Taylor	- temporary partner to Tom
Mike Porter	- Cat's boyfriend and a truck driver
Jake Marchetti	- Maggie's husband
Carlos Gambini	- Didi's husband
Rick Hentzel	- Joyce's husband
Bevirly Jordan	- bride
Matthew Abrahms	- groom
Ben Gifford	- Alex's lawyer and friend
David Darr	- Alex's ex-husband
Cassandra Victorio "Cassie"	- Alex's friend and pet store owner
Cyrus Mendelhoffer	- Alex's handyman, older gentlemen
Veronica Waters	- manager of Jacob's Hope reception hall
Mrs. Johnson	- employee at reception hall
Connie Hibsman	- friend of Alex, owner of the restaurant Eats Galore
Dr. Eric Chadsworth	- doctor at hospital
Aunt Gertrude	- Alex's favorite aunt, deceased
Willow Wolf	- one owner of a florist shop

Cast of Characters conti.

Heather Grove	- one owner of a florist shop
Iris Eaton	- one owner of a florist shop
Daisy Eaton	- one owner of a florist shop
Micky	- Alex's red point Himalayan
Georgy	- Alex's sun conure
Officer Bernelli	- Police officer
Brian	- Police officer in the crime lab

Chapter 1

"Let's go, Cat! We're running late!" Alex called out. Alex grabbed the top tier of the Jordan wedding cake and headed out to the van. Cat grabbed the pillars and the decorator patch-up kit and quickly followed. Everything else they needed for the cake was already in the van. They got in and headed for the Jordan reception hall.

I'm glad that this is the last cake to be delivered," Cat sighed. "When we get back, we'll have just enough time to get ready for George's party. You are going, aren't you?"

"Are you kidding?" Alex chuckled. "Of course, I'm going. George would kill me if I didn't. Besides, I have the cake." She replied with a big grin.

Cat smacked her forehead with a hand and laughed. "I can't believe I forgot. You've kept that cake a big secret. I can't wait to see it. Can't you give me just a little hint about the design?" Cat raised her right hand and pinched her thumb and index finger together for emphasis as she said "just a *little* hint."

"No way, babe. You've been trying to wheedle that info out of me for more than two weeks. You really think I'm going to tell you now? You'll see it later tonight." Alex looked over at Cat and smiled, "Besides, haven't you heard? Patience *is* a virtue." Cat, as ladylike as never, snorted her reply to that comment as Alex asked her if she was bringing her boyfriend Mike with her to the party.

"Of course!" Cat replied. "Are you bringing someone?"

Alex shook her head. "Nah. No one interests me all that much right now," she answered with a determined look in her eyes.

"I don't know why you don't date more. It's been four years since your divorce. You know what they say about all work and no play." Cat looked over at Alex with a mischievous grin and started to reply "I could bring a friend with me tonight for you and..."

"No way!" Alex half screamed back at her friend. "I can't forget the last friend you supplied for me. You ought to know after twenty-some odd years of friendship that punk yellow hair and earrings is not my type."

"I told you that Joey was just going through a phase" Cat answered back laughing.

"*Kids* go through phases, Cat. When the time comes, I want a *man*. Someone older than me, at least by a few years anyway. But right now, I'm just too busy with my cake business to get involved in a serious relationship with a man."

Before Cat could reply to Alex's comment, Alex pulled the van into "Jacob's Hope." Bevirly Jordan's reception hall. "Stay in the van until I find out exactly where the cake goes." Alex jumped out of the van. She entered through the front door and saw an elderly woman opening an inner door. "Excuse me, do you know where the Jordan's wedding reception is being held? I have her wedding cake."

The old woman gave Alex a sharp look, nodded her head toward the front of the room, and replied, "Right in here. The wedding cake table is to the right of the wedding party table."

Alex said thank-you, but the woman had already disappeared out a side door. Alex then headed out to the van, and she and Cat carried the wedding cake inside. Since it was a little dark in the room, Cat went over and increased the lights over the cake table. The Jordan wedding cake was one of the more simple set-ups. It consisted of a single cake tier at the top, a stacked two tier base, and pillars in between. Since the florist had dropped off the flowers earlier in the day, Alex and Cat set about placing them in their proper spots. They put a small prearranged flower bouquet in the pillared area, and ferns and baby's breath around the base of the cake. Alex placed the porcelain wedding couple on top of the cake. They scanned the wedding cake briefly and decided that icing touch-ups were not necessary. After taking a few pictures of the cake, Cat reduced the lights to the point they were earlier and they left. The whole set-up took about fifteen minutes.

On the way back to the store, they agreed to meet at George's at five twenty. They would be only ten minutes early for the party, but still plenty of time to sneak the cake into the backyard for a surprise.

Chapter 2

Alex pulled into George's driveway at five twenty sharp. Cat was already there, waiting beside her car. "The coast is clear, Alex. Let's get the cake and take it around back. Its best we don't go through the house," she half whispered.

"Sounds good to me. It's in the back. Let me pull the hatch release." As Alex walked around to the back of the van, she asked Cat where Mike was.

"He's inside making sure Carla and George are distracted and don't look out the window." Cat looked in the van and beamed. Wide-eyed she exclaimed, "Ooooh, I love it! Let's go set it up."

Alex and Cat each grabbed an end of the large sheet cake. It was a very heavy cake. They slowly sidestepped to the backyard and set it on the cake table. The cake would be cut after everyone was done eating. Since the party was a pool-engagement island-type party for two of Alex's closest friends, she tried to outdo herself in creativity. The cake was not an ordinary flat cake with a picture drawn on it. The base of the cake was a rectangle measuring 33" by 17." Cake was stacked to make a three-step waterfall which began in the middle of the cake and continued to the right edge of the cake. A river ran from the base of the waterfall to the other edge of the cake. An icing-made jungle scene surrounded the river. Green trees and colorful fauna covered the mountain around the waterfall and ground on either side of the river. A man and a woman in bikini bathing suits stood at the top of the waterfall. They were made from chocolate. The couple was holding hands and gazing into each other's eyes. Because her friends were animal lovers, Alex made sure there were plenty of icing-made animals, such as monkeys, lions, tigers, jaguars, snakes, and various other animals lying among the vegetation and in the water.

In about fifteen minutes, there were so many people in the backyard, it seemed they were coming out of the woodwork. Everybody seemed to be having a good time. Alex was surprised to find that even she was really enjoying herself. Normally, she didn't have good times at big parties. She preferred smaller ones. Alex mingled with a lot of the people, finding again to her surprise that she actually knew most of those gathered here pretty well. She estimated that there were about one hundred people milling around. Alex caught up with Cat and Mike at the huge luau buffet table. They were piling up mounds of food on their plates while waiting for burgers to come off the grill. Shortly afterwards, two more of her friends and employees, Maggie and Didi joined her with their husbands, Jake and Carlos respectively. She looked around for her other employee and friend, Joyce and husband Rick, but couldn't locate them.

After everyone ate, George and Carla called everyone's attention to the cake table for a toast and the cake cutting. People were oohing and aahing over the cake until Mike rapped a spoon on his glass to get the crowd's attention. Everyone raised their glasses and Mike gave a short but amusing toast. While all her friends were laughing, Carla put her glass down and approached Alex. With tears in her eyes, she hugged Alex and thanked her for such a beautiful cake.

George and Carla had just cut into the cake when there was a commotion by the back door of the house. Alex turned to see what was causing the commotion. After some twisting around, she noticed two gentlemen asking people questions. Everybody seemed to be pointing in her direction and the men started her way with a purpose. Alex took note that the taller of the two was a really good-looking guy. He was about six feet tall. His brown hair was cut short, just shy of the collar, but still had somewhat of a wave in it. A mustache and a trim short beard finished out his ruggedly handsome face quite nicely. He was really sharp looking in blue jeans, a light blue shirt, and a brown leather jacket. The other man was a few inches shorter than the first. His black hair looked like it needed a haircut and a good shampooing. He was wearing black pants, white shirt, gray tie, and a black suit jacket. For some reason, Alex didn't know why, the shorter guy reminded her of a weasel. As they approached her, the brown haired man asked if anyone knew an Alexandra Applecake.

Alex stepped forward and stated that she was the person in question. Even though she felt some apprehension stirring in her gut about these strangers, she couldn't help notice that the taller man was even better looking up close, than at a distance. He had the darkest brown eyes that she had ever seen in a human.

"Is there somewhere we could talk that is a little more private?" tall, dark, and handsome asked.

Alex replied, "Yes. But first, may I ask who you are and what this is all about?"

"We can discuss that in private, if you don't mind."

Alex hesitated, but then said, "Sure, I guess so. Follow me."

As the small group started toward Carla's house, Cat and Mags followed. The taller man stopped and turned toward the two. "I'm sorry, but we want to talk to Ms. Applecake alone. If we decide we need to talk to anyone else, we'll let you know."

Before the group even turned around, Cat said in a voice loud enough to be heard over the surrounding party, "I don't know who you think you are, mister. But I'm not going to let Alex go anywhere until I see some identification."

A hush came over the crowd and all heads turned toward Alex's group. The tall man sighed, looked at Cat and said, "I'm Detective Baker and this is Detective Taylor. We just want to ask Ms. Applecake a few questions." After showing Alex, Cat, and Maggie his badge, he turned, raised his eyebrows at Alex and gestured with his arm for her to proceed to wherever she was leading them.

Alex swallowed nervously, cops always made her nervous, and said to Cat, "Its OK. I'll just be in the living room." When Cat showed no sign of moving, Alex added, "If there's a problem, I'll scream, alright?"

Cat hesitated and stated with reluctance, "Okay. I'll let you go in, but if I don't hear anything soon, I'm coming in." As the door closed, Alex heard her add, "I'm staying right outside this door until you come out!"

Alex rolled her eyes. She was nervous alright, but sometimes Cat could be a pain in the rear. Detective Baker half-smiled and said, "That's quite a pit bull you have there." He could see some anger flash into Alex's eyes and quickly continued, "It's nice you have such a devoted friend. However, you can relax, we're only here to ask some questions."

Once they reached the living room, the detectives took a quick look around to make sure they were alone. Detective Baker suggested everyone sit down. The room was decorated in a cozy country style. There was a single couch with two recliners all in a U-shape layout in front of the stone fireplace. The walls were an eggshell white. The carpet and most of the furniture were a slate country blue. Accent pieces were done in wild rose, harvest brown, antique white and blues. Alex sat in the recliner closest to the couch. The two detectives took the couch. Both detectives were angled toward Alex with notepads out and ready for notes. Detective Baker was the closer of the two detectives to Alex.

Alex couldn't wait any longer. "What's going on?" she asked as she looked slowly from one man to the other.

"I take it you haven't heard the news?" Detective Baker asked.

"What news? What exactly do you both think I know?"

With a smirk, Detective Taylor snidely said, " Let's cut the niceties. We're here to talk about a murder. One that we believe you committed, so you can cut the innocent act."

Alex's face went pale when she heard the word murder. She looked at the officers with incredulity and stammered out, "M-m-m-m-murder?"

"Yes, murder." Detective Taylor replied.

Alex felt a distinct chill go down her spine as she asked, "Whose murder and why do you think I had anything to do with it?"

Taylor looked at her with hatred and contempt. He spit out, "Because lady, he died after eating a piece of your cake. That's why."

As that piece of information and all its implications hit home, Alex turned pale and started to shake. She thought it was a good thing she was already sitting down or else she'd be on the floor looking up. She fought to control her emotions as she looked at Taylor. Thinking he was the most repulsive person she had ever seen, she looked at Baker. This gave her a little more time to compose herself. Baker just seemed to be observing her, which did nothing but unsettle her more. She found her voice and with a quiver in it she asked, "Who exactly is it that I'm supposed to have killed?"

Before Taylor could speak, Baker edged a little closer and replied, "A Mr. Abrahms."

Alex's mind went blank and she just looked at them for a minute. "I don't know a Mr. Abrahms."

Taylor scoffed, got up and leaned down in her face. "Like hell you don't. You made his wedding cake today. We know you made it. We know you delivered it." He paused very shortly and continued talking

12

while only inches from her face, "You must think we're dumb. I can assure you that this is not the case lady. You killed a man today and we're going to prove it. The only reason you're not at the police station this minute is because we're still gathering evidence. But I can guarantee you one thing, it's only a matter of time."

Alex had frozen at Taylor's verbal assault. She could see herself in prison and hear the metal door slamming shut, just like she had seen on cop shows on TV. Again she had to fight down a rising panic, she had to find out exactly what was going on. She felt foolish with this man in her face, she never thought of herself as a mouse and now was not the time to start acting like one.

Alex felt the anger build in herself and decided to put it to good use. With daggers shooting out her eyes, she hissed at him "What in the world are you talking about? I didn't kill a Mr. Abrahms or anyone else for that matter! I especially wouldn't purposely hurt someone with one of my cakes. It's not only my business, it's my livelihood." She paused briefly for a deep breath and continued yelling at Taylor, "And for the last time, I did not deliver a cake for any Abrahms. I had five cake deliveries today and their names were Deimler, Davis, Brenhart, Jordan, and Miller." Alex had finished with a smug sneer on her face, but one look at the detective's facial reaction changed it quickly to one of deep concern. She turned and looked at Detective Baker. "What did I say wrong?"

Detective Baker was observing Alex during the preceding conversation. He had a feeling that she really did not know what was going on, however, he couldn't let her know that was how he felt. Besides, cases were won and lost on proof, not feelings. She could be an excellent actress for all he knew. Detective Baker's conscience was telling him that if he was going to be totally honest with himself, Alex's good looks could be screwing with his thoughts and his feelings.

13

"Nothing really," Baker answered. "It's just a tad interesting that you say you didn't deliver the cake that allegedly killed Mr. Abrahms," he paused slightly for effect, "however, that's exactly what you did do."

One more time, Alex took a deep breath. Shaking her head, she replied, "I don't understand. I did not deliver a cake with the name of Abrahms. Could you please explain what it is exactly that you want from me." With a slight hesitation, she continued, "Am I under arrest?"

Baker decided honesty was called for as he answered her questions. "At the moment, Ms. Applecake, you are not under arrest. We came here on a fact finding mission. We have one dead man and we're trying to find out who did it and why. A Mr. Matthew Abrahms died immediately after ingesting a piece of his wedding cake. We are still waiting for the autopsy report. He may have died of a totally natural cause, however, people-in-the-know believe he may have been helped out of this world. We would appreciate it if you would answer a few questions, and then, we will move on to other things." He tried not to sound too abrasive and thought he failed miserably. So with a slight smile he asked her to run through everything she did earlier that day.

Alex thought about what he said. "O.K., sounds like a plan. My day probably won't sound all that fascinating when compared to what one of your days must be like, but here goes. I got up about six thirty, showered, dressed, ate, and fed the animals. I left for work around seven forty-five. I got to the shop about eight o'clock. Eight to four thirty was spent getting the store open for customers, preparing the cakes for final delivery, and for the delivering of cakes. At four thirty, I went home and got ready for the party. I got back to my store about five. I dawdled around for about five minutes, loaded the engagement cake into my van, and came to this party. I have been here ever since. End of story." Alex ended with a shrug of her shoulders, and looked at Baker for a response.

14

Baker carefully listened to everything Alex had said and calmly started to ask her some questions. "Did you do anything out-of-the-ordinary to Mr. Abrahms cake?"

"Would you please explain just who Mr. Abrahms is, and exactly what happened to him?"

Detective Baker put a hand out to keep Detective Taylor from saying anything. "Of course, Ms. Applecake. Mr. Abrahms married a Bevirly Jordan today at three o'clock. The happy couple arrive at their reception hall around four thirty. The cake cutting took place after dinner. Pictures were taken as the couple cut the cake. They shoved the cake into each other's mouths. Within seconds, Mr. Abrahms was choking and starting to convulse. 9-1-1 was called and CPR started, but to no avail. Within minutes of eating your cake, Mr. Abrahms was dead."

Alex didn't know what to say and so said nothing in response. She could, however, feel the blood drain from her face.

Detective Taylor looked at her and did know what to say, "What's wrong Ms. Applecake?" he sneered. "Nothing to say?"

Fire flew out her eyes as she turned on him. "I have plenty to say. I'm also quite sure that you don't want to hear what I'm thinking at this very moment. You pathetic, lower-life…"

Baker raised his voice to drown her out. "Enough! I suggest we continue this conversation elsewhere."

"Such as?" Alex asked as visions of bars filled her head.

"Such as …" he paused briefly, "your bakery."

"Why there?"

"If you are as innocent as you claim, you shouldn't mind. We can look around a little while we talk. Maybe even decide that you are indeed innocent."

Alex didn't hesitate. She knew she didn't kill anyone, so she agreed,

Before they left, she talked to Cat. She explained that she was going with these two guys to the bakery. That a mistake had been made and that she would clear things up. Cat allowed her to go without further questions only after extracting a promise from Alex to call her later and explain in detail just what in blue blazes was going on. Since she wasn't under arrest, Alex drove her car with Detective Baker as a passenger. Detective Taylor followed her in their unmarked police car. They drove in silence. During this drive, Alex came up with a series of questions to ask when they arrived at her bakery.

Alex pulled up to the side entrance and parked. The detectives insisted on entering before she did. Detective Taylor turned on the lights and they all walked into the decorating area. Detective Baker suggested they all take a seat and take care of a few more of the details before looking around the store.

Alex didn't hesitate. She asked the first question while dreading the answer. "Did anyone else die from eating the cake?"

"Just wait a minute, little lady. We will ask the questions and you will answer." Detective Taylor angrily replied. He didn't like this woman, nor did he enjoy his new partner's attitude toward him. He was an equal partner after all.

"It sounds like a fair question to me, Clifford," Detective Baker said. "No, Ms. Applecake, no one else died. The bride understandably spit her piece of cake onto the floor. No one else had touched the cake yet."

"You said he died with just *one* bite of my cake. How is that possible?" Alex questioned.

"*That,* we do not know. And *that's* exactly what we are trying to find out. Now if you will permit me, I would like to ask you a few questions."

Alex reddened, she was about to say something. She had even started to speak, but instead closed her mouth with a quiet snap. Alex settled with just nodding affirmatively.

"O.K., then. You say you didn't know this Mr. Abrahms. Why not? Didn't he pay for the cake?"

"No, he didn't……..at least not that I'm aware of. All my cake orders are in the bride's name unless otherwise requested. Usually the groom doesn't come in to place the cake order. Either just the bride does or she brings a friend or her mother or some such relative. Even if the groom does show up, many don't say much, and even fewer give me a name or insist it be on the order form. The cake is not usually paid on the day that it is ordered. At that time, only a twenty dollar non-refundable deposit need be paid, and that's usually cash. The entire balance must be paid at least two weeks before the date of their wedding. Whenever a payment is made or the balance paid, someone comes into the store and gives the clerk the bride's name and date of the wedding. My clerk looks up the order form and makes a note of whatever amount is paid. The name of the groom is not needed. In fact, sometimes this causes confusion, because the groom's name is given and my clerk must re-ask for a name because she can't find the order. This is a common way of handling wedding cake orders in this business, I assure you."

"Don't worry, we'll check up on it." Taylor paused for 'dramatic' flair and then finished, "I assure you."

Baker mentally rolled his eyes and shook his head. He couldn't believe what a cretin Taylor was. He turned toward Alex and continued his questioning. "Is there some tradition as to where on a wedding cake the first piece is cut?"

"No, not really. At least not that I have ever heard," Alex replied with a slight shake of her head to the left and right. "Though, I lay odds that there is an etiquette book somewhere that would prove me wrong." She looked at Detective Taylor as she said this. "In my experience, sometimes the design of the cake or the photographer will dictate where the first slice should be made. Sometimes the bride and groom decide once they pick up the knife or while the photographer gets ready. So, as you can see, there are an infinite number of places to cut the cake. That said, I will add that the one place that is not usually cut is the top tier. Almost everyone saves that tier and freezes it for their first anniversary celebration."

"Did you make the entire cake in this room where we are now sitting?" Baker asked with a quick look around the bakery.

"Yes. Cakes are baked, cooled, iced, and decorated in this room. It sat on one of these tables until it went out to the van for delivery."

Baker stood up and said, "Please stay in this one spot while we look around."

"Sure, I'll just sit on this stool and watch. Do you know what in particular you're looking for?" Alex asked with curiosity.

Taylor curtly replied, "We'll know it when we find it. Unless, of course, you would like to save us all some time and just tell us what 'it' is."

"Hey, don't bite my head off. By the way, if you make a mess, I expect you to clean it up. But first…." She hesitated until both detectives looked at her, "I want you both to wash your hands."

Taylor snarled, "What for?"

"Because I run a clean place and heaven knows where your hands have been. The sink, soap, and towels are over around the corner to your right."

"Well, actually, we'll be using gloves," Detective Baker almost apologetically replied.

"Oh, okay." She shrugged her shoulders. "I'm alright with that."

As Alex sat and watched the men separate to start their look around, a thought suddenly popped into her head. She didn't know exactly to whom she should state her question, so she addressed the general room, "How long were you two in here earlier?"

Both men stopped in their tracks and looked at her. Taylor seemed startled and asked with irritation evident in his voice, "What do you mean?" Alex looked at Baker, she was surprised to see amusement on his face mixed with what she thought was respect. This gave her added confidence that she was correct. She looked Taylor straight in the eyes and replied with a tad of smugness, "You just walked in here and turned the lights on."

"So what?" he asked, turning slightly red as he remembered his own cursing and fumbling over the light switch the first time he had used it earlier.

"That light switch is not a typical one, as I'm sure you've already noticed. It's located farther over on the wall than what one would expect. It's also shaped just a tad uniquely, don't you think? She finished her comment with a little sarcasm. Alex's light switch is in the shape of Garfield the cat. It slides up and down, it doesn't flip up and down, to turn on and off. When you turn the light on, the light plate shows scratch marks from Garfield's claws as he slides down the plate. When you turn the light off, you push Garfield up and he covers the "scratch" marks. Alex loves cats and she decided on a whim to order Garfield out of one of the "junk" magazines that she always seems to get in the mail. "Normally people fumble on that switch, but you didn't." Alex finished pointedly. "So how long were you two in here earlier? Is this just a cursory look, intended to intimidate or scare me? Hoping I'll say or do something incriminating?" As Alex finished, she looked at Detective Baker because she wanted him to answer her, *not* his dweeb partner.

As she hoped, he spoke before his partner. "Yes, Ms. Applecake, you're quite correct, we were here earlier." He raised his hands, palms toward her, and continued, "before you say anything or get mad, we had a search warrant. You weren't here, but after a quick search, we found your appointment book and knew where you'd be. We decided that we would rather have you here for any kind of search, so there would be limited questioning afterwards by everyone concerned."

"Then, may I ask, why didn't you show me this search warrant?" Alex asked.

Baker smiled, showing a full set of beautiful white teeth, Alex appreciated a nice smile, and said, "because we preferred to keep things friendly. Since you gave us permission to search, we didn't need to give or even show you the warrant. However if you wish, we'll gladly provide it for your perusal."

"Yeah, I think I do. Since you went to all the trouble of getting one, I might as well take it. I have nothing to hide, but I'll feel better if I take the warrant. By the way, are you done with my place?"

"No, we just started." Detective Baker than asked Alex if he could see the order form for the Jordan cake. Alex got up and went to her desk. She casually flipped through a few papers in her "in" box. She hesitated for a moment with a perplexed expression on her face, and then unceremoniously dumped the box's contents on her desk. Alex carefully checked each paper before putting it back in the box. Baker watched Alex's face carefully and quietly asked if there was a problem. "Well, I don't know if I would exactly call it a problem." Alex slowly responded in a somewhat distracted manner.

"But?" Detective Baker added to help her continue.

"Well," Alex continued as she looked on the floor, behind her desk, and around in general. "Usually, after we get done delivering a cake, on our return into the bakery, we throw the cake order on my desk or in the box. On occasion, we misplace or lose one, so this is not really out-of-the-ordinary, so-to-speak, however….."

"However, it seems kind of coincidental to misplace this one, doesn't it?"

Alex quickly looked up at the detective to see what he was implying, but saw nothing nasty or threatening on his face. "Yes, it most certainly does. I have found in the past that while coincidences supposedly do occur, in the real world, there's usually nothing coincidental about them."

"I agree." Baker quietly added.

"Did you guys pick it up on your earlier visit by chance?"

Detective Baker shook his head, "Sorry, afraid not."

Alex scrunched up her forehead for a few seconds and then continued, "This is weird. I remember throwing the order on my desk when I got back."

"You seem sure about that."

"Oh, I am. You see, when I'm in a hurry, I find that even the simplest acts seem to be complicated. I threw the order on the desk and it wafted over to the far edge and continued onto the floor. I picked it up and threw it on the desk again. It landed on the crack where the desk and wall meet and somehow fell through it. I was getting ticked and grabbed it again. However, that irritatingly true cliché came to mind, and I took my time and carefully placed it into the box."

"What cliché are you talking about?"

"Oh, you know! Haste makes waste."

He nodded his head and chuckled. "Yeah, I know that one a little too well I'm afraid. Unfortunately, that doesn't help us here."

Alex knew she had to agree, but where in the world did that order go? All of a sudden she smiled. Detective Baker couldn't fail to notice and asked her about it. "Now I *know* I'm tired and upset. I totally forgot that I have another copy of the order."

Baker glanced around the room briefly and asked where. Alex

21

patted her computer softly. "In here. I have a scanner. In order to protect myself from lost orders, I scan all orders into the computer. So let's see what 'Aggie' has to say." As Alex sat down at the computer and started it up, Detective Baker asked, "Aggie?"

"Short for Agamemnon. He was a person in Greek mythology," Alex responded as she started typing on the keyboard.

"Yes, I know who he is. As I remember, there was a lot of mayhem in his life," Baker stated, "violence and murder too."

"Well, I can't argue there. It's not like I live my life according to his story or its principles. I just happen to really like mythology. And, I think his name is really cool. As Alex brought up the proper file she said, "Here it is."

Alex could feel the heat emanate off Baker as he leaned over her shoulder to look at the screen. "Can you print me a copy?"

"Sure." She leaned over to turn on the printer and typed in the proper commands. Afterwards, she gave the copy to Detective Baker.

Detective Baker perused the form for a minute and then asked Alex to run through her routine for making and decorating her cakes. "Please, walk around the room and show us where each step of your routine is completed. Detective Taylor will take samples as we go."

Alex's bakery is called The Slice of Life Bakery and Supply Shop. It consists of two big rectangular parts of approximately the same size with a smaller rectangular area sandwiched in between the two. The front part is referred to as "the shop." The shop is where the public is allowed. People come in to order cakes or buy all kinds of supplies to make and decorate their own cakes or make chocolate candies. The back part is called "the bakery." The public is not usually allowed in the bakery. All the work areas are against the walls of the bakery. In the center of the room are two long tables. Except for decorating classes or demonstrations, work is not usually done on these tables;

22

however, cakes in various stages of completion usually sit there. The area between the shop and the bakery is about half the size of those two individually. A hallway splits this smaller area in half. As one walks the hallway from the shop toward the bakery, one passes a large supply closet and a bathroom on the left, and a door to the basement and Alex's office on the right. Alex's office has a door that leads to the outside. Deliveries come in and go out this door.

Alex said that the planning for this Saturday's wedding cakes actually started the past Saturday, when she pulled all the orders for this week's cakes and reviewed them. She double-checked that each cake was totally paid for and they were. If any would have been unpaid, then phone calls would have been made. Next, she checked for set-up parts and made sure she had everything she needed and she did. She then made up the delivery schedule and double-checked for any conflicts, which there weren't. Each bride's name was then written on a tablet. By each name, she indicated the amount of flowers that needed to be made for their particular cake design. After she completed the prior steps, she put everything away until Monday.

Alex walked over to her decorating corner of the bakery and continued to tell the detectives her routine on cake decorating. She said on Mondays she makes her flowers for her wedding cakes. She showed them where she got her icing, colors, and other materials needed to make the flowers. The Jordan wedding cake had only white flowers, so no coloring was needed. She turned around and showed them where she stored the flowers until needed. Icing flowers must set up for a few days and get hard. This is so they can be handled and put on the side of the cakes. This particular cake's flowers also had edible glitter put on them. Edible glitter is made from gum Arabic or vegetable gum.. It adds a glisten or shine to the cakes. If done right, it has the same diamond sparkling that fresh snow does when light shines on it. The glitter was put on the same day as the flowers were created. Alex had relaxed a little as she was talking, but tensed right back up again as she watched Detective Taylor collect samples of everything she had pointed out. She had known he was going to do it, but the reality of watching him try to collect evidence against her chilled to the bone.

Detective Baker watched Alex as she watched Taylor and noticed her tense up. He didn't want her to freeze up, so he caught her attention and asked her to continue. Alex took a deep breath to try to relax and continued with her routine. The cakes are actually baked on Thursday if the wedding is set for Saturday. Cat does all the baking unless the amount of baking is extremely heavy or she is sick. You two met Cat at the party tonight. "I believe you called her my pit bull." She did all the baking for this week's cakes. Alex showed them where the baking is done and where all the different supplies are kept. As she watched Taylor taking samples she said, "I know Cat didn't put anything poisonous into the cakes."

"That may well be, Ms. Applecake, but we must check out everything," Detective Baker stated calmly. "We will be talking to this Cat again, as we will be talking with each of your personnel."

Alex continued onto the cake cooling racks which were located not far from the ovens. She then showed them that next to the cooling racks, were the icing supplies and cardboard bases and such that are needed to base ice the cakes. Once iced they were put on the tables in the middle of the room. Once on these tables, the cakes were stacked or pillared, depending on their design, and allowed to set overnight. She explained that this allowed the cakes to "set" and any leaning or defects were than taken care of. There had been no noticeable problems with this week's cakes.

Alex does all the wedding cake constructions and decorations. On Friday, Alex decorates Saturday wedding cakes. She showed the detectives that she takes each cake to her decorating area, decorates the cake, then puts it back onto one of the center tables. Once all of her decorating is done, she puts any set-up equipment needed with the cakes. The only time this procedure differs is when the cakes are filled or have whipped cream icing. Neither of these two occasions occurred this week. She explained that she always gives the top tier, which is the anniversary tier, to the couple for free. When she delivers each cake, she always leaves a box for the anniversary tier with a list attached explaining what parts must be returned to her. She makes this box up sometime before delivery. The box and its list are put with the cake on the table also. This week she had everything needed with each cake as of Friday night.

Detective Taylor wanted something made crystal clear and asked, "So, with your way of doing things, anybody could figure out which cake goes to which bride. I mean, you label the cakes, therefore, if someone wanted to change a particular person's cake, they could easily figure out exactly which cake to alter. Correct?"

Alex looked at Taylor and then back and forth at the two tables and imagined cakes on them. "Sure. I guess so. I mean I set it up this way to try to prevent errors of any kind. I try to be organized. The last thing I want is to forget something I need for a cake. There is not always time to come back."

Detective Baker tried not to show his irritation at his partner's interference with Alex's recitation. He didn't want her to get confused or shut down on them. " Is there anything else you can add to your procedures or are you done?"

Alex thought a minute and tried to remember exactly what she had been saying when Detective Taylor interrupted her. "Ah, well, let me see," Alex pointed at the tables and continued, "the wedding cakes stay on these tables until delivery. The best I can recollect," she walked over to the table farthest from the outside door and pointed to the end that was right behind her decorating area," the Jordan wedding cake was right here until I…well we… that is ….Cat and I….delivered the cake. We just took each tier section out to the van and any necessary paraphernalia and went to the reception hall. We put everything together and left."

Detective Baker thanked Alex for her recitation. He asked if she would please take a seat while they finished looking around. This gave them time to think over everything that she said and see if there were any more questions for the present time. Alex watched as the detectives went through and searched every cabinet, shelf, counter, table, and finally the walk-in refrigerator. She chided herself as she found herself watching Detective Baker move and bend as he searched her place. She was incensed at her place being ripped apart and examined, but yet couldn't keep from admiring Baker's body. He had a great butt. That was one of her favorite body parts on a man. Presently, it was warm in the store and he took off his jacket. She noticed that not only was he well-toned, he was muscular without being overly muscular. She reminded herself to make sure her mouth was closed and that no drool was noticeable. Alex couldn't believe that she was actually checking out a man, especially one who could arrest her at any time. She had to chuckle at herself though, her timing, as usual, was really lousy. She hoped that in the not-too-distant-future, she and Cat would be able to laugh about this whole mess.

As the detectives were getting ready to go, Alex said, "I can assure you that nothing here caused the groom to die. I decorate all cakes with the same equipment. The baking ingredients are basically the same with all cakes that leave here. Unless you know otherwise, no one else has been affected." This last statement, also an unspoken question, was made with some trepidation that they were holding something back.

"We haven't heard of any other deaths from eating cake. And someone would have contacted us by now if there had been any." Detective Baker returned. "Ms. Applecake, we're sorry we've taken up so much of your time, however, we like to be thorough. You have a great bakery here. You keep it real nice. However, due to what happened tonight, we'll be back to talk to you at a later time." Detective Baker looked at Alex with deep regret, he really liked her and hated to have to tell her…but it was his job so he continued in a somber tone, "Ms. Applecake, I hate to have to say this but, you may have to close down your shop for a while. We'll know more in the morning after we get the autopsy report. I just wanted to let you know what might happen. This way you've been warned and can be kind of prepared."

Alex was stunned. "What do you mean? Close my shop? For how long? I didn't do anything!! I'm innocent!!"

Detective Taylor decided enough was enough, he was going to get some talking in. "Lady, please!! If you are innocent, then the autopsy will show that in the morning and your shop won't have to be closed. However, if you are guilty, and killed this man, than closing your shop won't be your *only* problem. It also won't be your biggest problem."

Alex replied harshly and with daggers of anger shooting out of her eyes. "So what you're telling me is that y'all came here for a preliminary check. You just wanted to see if I was stupid and left a big bucket of poison out on my table. So therefore, you could arrest me quick and solve the crime in record time. Well, I'm sorry to disappoint you two, but there is no poison and I did not kill anyone!!"

Detective Baker matter-of-factly stated, "I'm sorry for any inconvenience we've caused you Ms. Applecake, but the fact remains that Mr. Abrahms was inconvenienced much more than you have been. We are only doing our jobs. So far the facts have dictated that since he

27

apparently died from eating cake, your cake, we must follow up on it. The first forty eight hours after a death are crucial. If he died from natural causes, then everything tonight was done for naught and we'll apologize. However, if he was murdered as we suspect, than we are that far ahead by starting tonight. We should know by tomorrow morning and I will call and let you know the results. I'm sure you don't mind helping to find out what might have killed one of your clients." He paused for a moment and then finished up, "Thanks again. We'll be in touch." With that he closed the door behind Taylor and himself.

Alex heaved a deep sigh of apprehension and relief. She started to sit down at her desk and then almost immediately jumped out of her skin when the door quickly reopened. Detective Baker smiled sheepishly, "Sorry, I didn't mean to scare you. I just wanted to apologize for my partner. See ya!"

Alex thanked him but he didn't hear because he had already shut the door and left.

Chapter 3

After the cops left, Alex sat at her desk and started to worry. If her business closed down, she knew it wouldn't be long before the bills ate up her savings. She wallowed in self-pity for about thirty seconds before a severe beating on the door startled her back to reality. Almost instantly, the door flew open and all her employees, who she also considered her friends, came streaming in the door demanding to know what was going on. She told everyone to find a seat and she would clue them in. It took a couple of minutes for everyone to get seated, this gave Alex a few minutes to get her thoughts and emotions in order. She decided not to mention the name of the deceased at this time, she had to think about that for awhile first. She brought everyone up to snuff except for that one thing.

"There is one final item," Alex paused to make sure she had absolute attention, "as of tomorrow morning, we may be closed for awhile."

Pandemonium broke out as everyone started asking questions. A headache the size of Texas started immediately. Alex said, "Hold on a minute." There was no effect to the noise level, so she put two fingers in her mouth and whistled which didn't make her head feel any better, however peace was the result. Maggie raised her hand and Alex was reminded instantly of her gym teacher at school when she acknowledged her.

"Why would they close us down? Surely, they don't seriously believe that man's death is your fault."

"I don't know for sure, but I felt like one detective was convinced I did it, and the other one isn't or at least isn't sure. But, I won't know anything for sure until tomorrow morning. It's been a very long day, so let's call it a night." She continued when a loud rumble of disagreement started to swell, "and we can meet at my house tomorrow about four o'clock."

Everyone agreed and filed out of the bakery. Cat, Alex's closest friend and confidante, stopped and gave her a tight bear hug and said, "Alex try not to worry too much, since there is no way you can be involved in this, the cops will be able to exonerate you. You'll get a call from them in the morning alright, but it will be an apology." Then Cat raised her eyebrows up and down a few times and with a slight leer added, "or maybe a date." Before Alex could say anything, Cat ran out the door giggling. After making sure everything was either closed or turned off, Alex also left the bakery to go home.

Alex wished that she could be as optimistic as Cat. The events of the night and astonishment that accompanied them had kept her mind on overload. Now, however, with relatively little to preoccupy her mind, a memory slammed itself to the forefront. Alex stopped short, slapped her forehead with her hand, and swore loudly. She realized that if Cat would have known who had died, she would not have been as nonchalant about these events as she was. Cat would have made the connection faster than Alex. She decided to wait until the morning to give her friend the bad news. She knew *a* Matthew Abrahms, in fact they both did. She also knew that she could be in deep, deep trouble. Secrets always have a way of surfacing, especially in a small town where secrets are very rarely all that secret.

Chapter 4

Most Sunday mornings, Alex likes to sleep late or at least try to, because it's the only day she's not in the bakery by seven in the morning. After getting up late, she usually lounges away a few hours in a big comfortable sweatshirt reading the newspaper with her cat Micky curled up by her side. The rest of the day, she spends doing whatever she wants plus a few chores. All in all, Sunday is her day for relaxing. At night, she likes to go to church for the late service. However, this Sunday was not going to be normal for Alex in any way.

The shower is one of Alex's favorite places to think. After washing, she sits down on the floor of the tub and relaxes while hot hot water rains down on her. This Sunday as she listened to the water, her thoughts were on her bakery. It was a dream come true. It had been hard getting it started, but now she had a good clientele built up and things were going fine. She had some money in the bank for emergencies, but not as much as she would like to have. Alex knew that one of the big drawbacks of a little town was that rumors ran rampant, usually getting worse as time progressed. If people found out that someone died after eating one of her cakes, it could end up in the rumor mill as her intentionally trying to single-handedly wipe out the town. She knew that growing up in this town and not being an "outsider" would protect her somewhat, but that would not necessarily keep people from gossiping. One point against her was that she had left town for a number of years. To some people, it didn't matter that she had come back to stay and build her life here. She had left and while that didn't make her an outsider, to some she wasn't quite "one of them" anymore either. If she ended up closing the business, she would have to make sure it wasn't for long or she wouldn't have one to re-open. At that moment, Alex realized that if her business was going to succeed, she would have to take an active role in the so-called investigation. She not only had to make sure her business could open, she had to make sure her reputation was clear. If the guilty person wasn't found, suspicion would forever cloud her name and reputation. No one with any brains would order a cake from someone if they thought they could die from eating it, unless one sent it to an enemy or an ex-spouse. Although, in some parts of the world, that type of business would probably thrive. Alex realized that this thought wave was not exactly being productive, so she got off her duff, turned the shower off, and got dressed.

While Alex was feeding her cat and her bird, she decided she best get to her store and check on a few things. If they decided to close her down, they might decide not only can't any customers go inside, she might not be allowed inside either. She'd never been a part of a murder investigation before and therefore did not know what to expect. She knew she had paperwork that needed to be done. She also had to check her food and supplies to see if she needed to freeze anything or just wrap things tighter. She knew she had to get started shortly or she wouldn't have time to get much done. It was already eleven o'clock and she had to meet her employees here at four o'clock.

Chapter 5

Alex arrived at the bakery at about eleven fifteen. She took a quick look around and noticed that nothing really needed to be tended to, however, there was a lot of paperwork to get done. She sat down at her desk to get started. Somewhere around one o'clock the phone rang, she answered it and said hello but received no reply. She listened carefully and thought she heard breathing, but after asking hello again she hung up the phone. "You'd think people could at least apologize when they get the wrong number," she said aloud to the room. She started to do some of her payroll when the phone rang again. She let it ring a few times and then picked it up. "Hello?"

"Ms. Applecake?"

"Yes. Who is this?"

"Detective Baker, ma'am."

Alex sucked in her breath and asked, "Well, what's the verdict?"

"The autopsy has been completed. Mr. Abrahms died of anaphylactic shock."

When he made no sound to continue, Alex asked, "What's that?"

"It is a severe allergic reaction to something he ate or came in contact with."

"And this affects me how?" Alex queried.

"Well it may be a few days until all the tests result are in. Right now, we're not sure what to think. However, you're still not in the clear yet. His reaction was quite severe and fast acting. The doctor believes that whatever caused the shock had to have happened very shortly before his death. So while you can keep the bakery open for now, unfortunately, I can't guarantee how long the possibility of closing will exist. The samples we collected are being tested now and we'll know more tomorrow. If it's alright with you, I'd like to come over later and ask you a few more questions."

"It's okay with me, but I don't know how much more I can tell you."

"I just have some things to verify. How long do you plan on being there?"

Alex said she wasn't sure but agreed that she would meet him at the bakery in two hours. Alex called each of her employees and let them know either personally or by leaving a message on their answering machines, that the meeting was canceled for the day. She said that business would continue as normal the next day unless they were otherwise notified. She also said that she would answer all questions on Monday afternoon around two. Anybody who wasn't scheduled to work could come then and get clued in. Cat didn't want to wait until the next day for her info, so she told Alex she'd be over in an hour to get the scoop. Cat hung up before Alex could say another syllable.

Alex took a deep cleansing breath. Her store was not being closed, at least for the moment, so that took a small load off her back. Once she talked to Detective Baker, she could decide what her next move would be in finding the murderer. But for now, paperwork waited. She had just completed her payroll when she heard a familiar scratching from the basement. It never ceased to amaze her how well sound traveled in this old building when everything was quiet. It equally amazed her how hard it was to get rid of mice once they got into the basement. She had called her exterminator and all he had said was that he had put traps out and it was going to take time to catch the buggers. Since she was getting tired of doing paperwork, she decided to check the mousetraps.

The basement is comprised of three good sized rooms and one small room. The small room had the water heater and other paraphernalia necessary to keep a building warm and running. Wedding supplies fill one of the big rooms. Another room is filled with baking supplies. The last room has general supplies for the store in it. Each room is kept clean and everything is on shelves. Alex hated to clean that's why the mice were bugging her so much. She went through two of the rooms and checked the traps and they were clean. As she entered the general supply room, she noticed the one window that had had a small crack in it, now had a big hole in it. Shoot! If she didn't close that up, there would be lots of furry critters running around in her store. She ran upstairs and grabbed some cardboard and duct tape. Alex hustled back downstairs. Using the materials she had obtained, she patched the window the best she could. It should work well for a short time. She made a mental note to contact Cyrus on Monday to fix it. Cyrus Mendelhoffer was an older gentleman who was retired. He enjoyed puttering around and helping people fix things around their places. Alex checked the rest of the mousetraps and started back upstairs. Just as she closed the door to the basement, she felt a sharp pain on the back of her head and blackness engulfed her.

Chapter 6

As Cat turned into the driveway and parked beside the bakery's side door, she saw a two tone brown car disappear around the back of the building. She wondered briefly how many customers usually pass by on a Sunday to see if the shop is open or to just check for the regular hours. She entered the bakery in a hurry saying, "I'm sorry I'm late, but…" Cat stopped talking when she realized Alex wasn't around. Suddenly a chill went down her back, she realized something weird was going on. She was supposed to meet Alex and the lights were out. After she turned on the lights, she could tell Alex had been working at her desk. She looked around but there wasn't any notes from Alex telling her that she had left the store. Cat started to walk to the back window but stopped abruptly as she looked around and saw stuff on the floor. Items that had been on the counters and shelves were now on the floor. She hurried to the window and saw Alex's blue Volkswagon beetle in the back parking lot. She was scared. Her gut twisted into a knot as she looked around the bakery. She yelled, "Alex? Yo, where are you?" Her eyes came to rest on the walk-in refrigerator. She half ran to the door and ripped it open. Nothing. On the way to the front room, she started to pass the bathroom but stopped. She flung the door open. It was slightly messy, but no Alex. She ran to the front room and looked around. Each time she got real quiet, but each time only silence greeted her ears. A thought shot through her as she thought of the basement, maybe Alex fell and was hurt downstairs. She ran to the basement door and opened it. No lights were on but she starting yelling for Alex anyway. Cat was halfway down the stairs when she heard

36

someone knocking on the back door. She hesitated briefly, but decided to answer the door, maybe Alex was playing some stupid prank on her to get back for all the pranks Cat had played on Alex.

Cat reached the back door in record speed and threw it open with a bang. Detective Baker was real glad at that moment for his quick reflexes, for he had jumped backwards instinctively. If he wouldn't have jumped, he would be howling in pain. His temper rose quickly as he started to say, "What in the …..?"

Cat didn't give him a chance to get any farther. In a near panic, she shouted, "Detective! Why are…? How did you know…?"

Baker's senses went into hyper alert. "Whoa! Take a deep breath and tell me what's wrong," he commanded.

Cat tried to take that breath and managed to spit out, "I can't find Alex. I've looked around the store and bakery, but she's not here. The bakery's a mess. I was just going downstairs when I heard you at the door." Cat started to turn toward the basement again but Baker stopped her first.

"Wait a minute? Maybe she stepped out for a minute."

Cat was starting to get very impatient. "No! She knew I was coming, in fact I was a wee bit late. There's no note and she would have left one. Besides, as I said, this place is a mess. Things are all over the floor. I know something happened to Alex, I can feel it. I just can't find her," Cat fretted. She hurriedly turned toward the basement again and continued talking, "I've checked upstairs. I'm afraid maybe she fell or something downstairs. The stairs in this old place are narrow and steep. I hate them." Cat hurried to the basement, she was already down the stairs when Baker caught up to her. They checked all the rooms but there was no sign of Alex anywhere. Cat was nonplussed. Shaking her head from side to side and with a small shrug of her shoulders she said, "Maybe she did leave……. except her car is still here. Maybe a neighbor needed help with something and its taking some time to get done."

Detective Baker thought briefly. "Let's go back upstairs, I'll call in and see if she called or checked in at the station. We'll have another look around also. Maybe we'll find something you missed the first time through. Then we'll check with the neighbors." Detective Baker reached the top of the stairs and turned to Cat and quietly asked, "did you find any sign of struggle or maybe…" he hesitated slightly, "blood or anything?" He stopped asking when he realized Cat wasn't staring at him, but past him. He turned quickly in case it was some*one* and not some*place* she was looking at. He saw a door that probably belonged to a closet or maybe the attic. There was a bar lock on the door. The kind that required one to slide a bar across to latch and was locked only from the outside. "There's only one way she could be in there…" he said quietly. He quickly reached up, slid the bolt open, stepped back, and opened the door. At the same time he heard Cat inhale quickly, he gasped "Alex!" Alex lay crumpled up and unconscious on the floor of the closet with aprons half-covering her. Baker bent down and professionally checked her pulse and breathed a sigh of relief. She was alive and had a strong pulse. He quickly checked for any injuries. Detective Baker gently picked her up in his arms and carried her to the back room where there was plenty of light. "Is there somewhere soft I can put her?"

Cat replied instantly. "Yes! Give me a second and I'll set a cot out." As she got it ready, she explained that sometimes in the busy seasons, the crew worked so many hours, they would be dead tired. She said that Alex had gotten cots so people could sleep at the bakery, instead of risking falling asleep at the wheel driving home. Cat realized that she was babbling from nerves, so she snapped her mouth shut.

Baker couldn't believe his mixed feelings as he looked down at

Alex. He found it hard to comprehend how quickly he had grown attached to this woman. He barely knew her and yet he felt he'd been looking for her all his life. He had heard of such things but never believed them. He was mad as hell that she had been hurt. It was obvious to him that someone had attacked her. He was glad she was in his arms, except the circumstances were definitely not what he would have planned. Alex started to stir before he could put her down and unexpectedly she curled into his body. With embarrassment he felt his body start to physically arouse to her presence, so he bent down quickly to put her on the cot.

"Ms. Applecake, wake up." Detective Baker gently shook her. "Come on Alex." Cat brought over a cool wet rag and laid it across Alex's forehead. Within seconds, Alex started to come around.

"What the …?" Alex started to rise up and look around but stopped suddenly. "Ow! Ow! Ow! My head! The room is moving." She settled back down on the cot in order to get her bearings and gently touched the back of her head. "What's going on?"

"I'll get some ice." Cat jumped up and busied herself.

Alex looked up and was surprised to see Detective Baker sitting beside her. He asked how she was feeling and if she wanted to go to the hospital. She said she had a huge headache, but other than that she seemed to be okay. She didn't feel pain anywhere else. Cat came over and handed Alex aspirin and an ice pack. She suggested that Alex might have a concussion and that the hospital was probably a good idea. Alex told them both that she knew most of the signs of a possible concussion and if any appeared, she would go get a check-up. But for now, she wanted to know what was going on. They both started to talk at once, but shut up quickly when exasperation crossed Alex's face. Baker nodded his head to Cat and when she finished her story, he added a few remaining details.

Alex asked Cat if she was sure she saw a car leaving and would she recognize it again. Cat answered yes to the former and not sure to the latter. Everyone was silent for a few moments as they digested the recent events. Detective Baker asked Alex to look around and check if anything was missing. He told them not to touch anything or clean up, just look. Both Cat and Alex complied. Alex couldn't shake the feeling that he was paying too much attention to her and started to get paranoid. He couldn't actually believe she made the whole story up could he? Well, she didn't know everything but she knew she was innocent. Alex slowly and thoroughly examined her shop from top to bottom. She was highly irate at the mess on the floor. Cat and she conferred and agreed. The mess seemed weird, the items on the floor didn't look particularly busted up, just looked like they had been placed there. As she looked, she tried to come up with a reason for someone to not only be in her store, but to attack her, and mess the bakery up. She failed. And why did he or she decide to put her in the closet? Why not just leave her on the floor, or worse yet, push her down the stairs? Everyone followed her down to the basement to check the window that had had the hole. Alex couldn't remember if the window was tightly latched when she had fixed it. In fact, her memory was blank to sort of hazy when she tried to remember anything after starting to fix the window. Baker thought it was possible Alex's attacker had come through the window and had accidentally broke it. At this point, Alex didn't know what to think, but agreed it was possible. She told him that a few times she herself had used that window to gain entrance after accidentally locking herself out of the shop. In fact, the window had been cracked that last time she slipped through it and she forgot to fix it then.

"How many people know this is your extra way into the shop?" he asked her.

She thought it over and didn't like her answer, "Everyone who works here, I guess." She added slowly, "however, anyone who wanted to break in, could have checked and found it loose."

Cat also added, "A few others who used to work here or even some customers might have overheard one of us mention it."

"And with a town this small, who knows, maybe everyone knows by now." Alex added and then ruefully finished her thought with, "I guess it wasn't as secret as I thought."

Detective Baker looked at them with disbelief written all over his face. "Why even lock the place then? I cannot believe you two. You're a lot more trusting than you should be. This may be a small town, but it still has a lot of crime. Just because you may know someone, doesn't mean that person wouldn't take advantage of you. They could steal, vandalize, or even" and here he looked directly into Alex's eyes "hurt you!"

"OK, already. You made your point. It was stupid, but I don't deserve the predicament I'm in. I'll find another back-up for when I get locked out."

They made sure all the windows and the basement access door were locked and headed upstairs. They went around and made sure all window and doors were locked and met at Alex's office. Detective Baker suggested they get anything that they needed to take home with them and then leave the premises. He figured this way he would know what was removed if it became important at a later time. Cat didn't need anything, but Alex put some paperwork in a large carry bag. After making sure the door was shut properly, Detective Baker asked Alex if there was somewhere they could go for a short time because he still had a few questions to ask her. She said sure and suggested her place. He agreed and said he would follow her home. As he walked toward his car, Cat touched Alex's arm and snickered, "Good going girl!"

41

Alex looked questioningly at her friend and replied, "What are you talking about?"

"Man, you must've got whacked pretty hard to not know what I'm saying." She rolled her eyes and shook her head, "Detective Baker is one hot looking dude. Don't tell me you didn't notice, cause I know you did. I see how you look at him. I just think its cool that you asked him to your place."

Alex was shocked, but still blushed bright red. "Cat! You're nuts! I didn't ask him any such thing. I can just imagine what some of his questions might me and I do not want every gossipmonger listening in . He obviously wanted us out of the bakery, so where else is there?"

"Yeah right. I hear what you're saying." Cat answered with a twinkle in her eye.

They had just reached Alex's car and there was a small bouquet of flowers lying on the windshield. A mixed bouquet of flowers wrapped with a simple blue ribbon. Alex put her stuff in the car and then reached for the flowers.

Cat stared open-mouthed at the flowers for a second. "What are those and what do they mean?"

Alex looked at them, scrunched her forehead and had to think for a minute. There are two kinds here. I know the one is Begonias and the other one is......." She snapped her fingers. "Oleander. I had to think on that one."

"OK. Now what do they mean?" Cat inquired.

Alex rolled her eyes. "I am not an encyclopedia and I am not the internet. Give me a minute." Alex closed her eyes and pictured her Aunt Gertrude. Aunt Gertrude loved flowers and she believed that every flower had a meaning. It was like a secret code when people gave flowers and the receiver just had to figure out the message. Alex had spent a number of summers with her aunt when she was younger.

"Begonias mean 'beware' and I believe Oleander means 'caution.' I guess our mystery person is still looking after me."

Cat shivered quickly. "I don't like it! Not at all! 'Beware' and 'caution' do not sound good. For years, you've been getting flowers on your birthday, the anniversary of your parents' deaths, holidays, even on the day of your divorce. Now this! It gives me the creeps! Tell Detective Baker about this and see what he has to say."

"I'll think about it." Alex promised. "Now I have to get going. He's waiting for me to leave."

Alex got in her car and shut the door. She wound down the window and had a funny look on her face. "Cat..?"

Cat bent down and looked with concern at her friend. "What's wrong Alex? You look a bit weird. Do you want me to come along? Is it the flowers? Does Detective Baker scare you? I'm sure you're right about him just wanting to ask you questions."

Alex swat at the air with her hand, "No, nothing like that. You're too man intensive. Neither the flowers nor the detective is the problem." Alex opened her mouth to say something and shut it.

"Then what?" An irked and worried Cat fired back. "What's up?"

Alex leaned closer to Cat and quietly asked. "Do you know who got killed yesterday?"

"No. You never told us. Every time I started to ask you some questions about it, something popped up to change the subject or else you put me off until later. So who was he? Do I know him?"

Alex looked directly into Cat's eyes and said very quietly but loud enough for her to hear. Alex did not want to repeat herself. "I'm not sure, maybe, maybe not." Alex hesitated for a moment, "It was *a* Matthew Abrahms."

Cat inhaled quickly, her eyes got real wide, and she asked, "Not *the* Matthew Abrahms?"

"I don't know. That's what I'm going to try to find out tonight." Alex looked over toward Detective Baker's car. Earlier he had been busy in his car and talking on his cell phone, now he seemed ready to go. She looked back at her friend, "Wish me luck."

"Luck!" Cat whispered earnestly back to Alex. As she got into her own car, Cat hit the steering wheel with her hand and cursed. "We could be 'up the creek without a paddle' in a very short time."

Chapter 7

As Alex opened the door to her house, she said, "Hi guys! It's just me and a guest" to the room in general. She motioned Detective Baker into her living room and suggested he take a seat wherever comfortable. "Detective Baker, would you like a drink? Water, soda, or iced tea perhaps?"

"If the tea is sweet, I'll take it, otherwise, soda will be fine. Thank-you." He answered and started to look around her place a bit. "Who were you speaking to when you entered the house?"

Alex laughed and replied, "To my animals. Micky's my cat. He's a beautiful red-point Himalayan. Micky's on the shy side and doesn't usually get close to strangers." Alex pointed toward the kitchen dinette, "Against the wall in the other room, there are a bunch of fish in the aquarium. Who knows? Maybe one day you'll get to learn all their names." Alex nodded to a small parrot in the corner of the room and added, "That over there is Georgy. He'll speak to you once he gets used to you."

"What kind of bird is he?" Detective Baker asked as he squinted at Georgy.

"He's a sun conure. Isn't his coloring beautiful?"

"Are all sun conures marked like this one?" Detective Baker asked as he took in the bird's coloring. Georgy's basic plumage was yellow with orange on the forehead, sides of the head, lower abdomen, rump, and the lower back. His wings were yellow and green with blue tinges on the edges. His tail was olive gray and blue. Each eye had a black ring around it.

"Basically, yes."

While Alex got them drinks, Detective Baker continued taking in his surroundings. Alex's house was on the small side. It consisted of a living room, bathroom, kitchen dinette, and two bedrooms (one of which was a combined den and guest bedroom). Her living room was done in a kind of country effect. When one entered the living room from the door, on the immediate right a hallway led to the bedrooms and bath. The rest of the wall on the right had a big stone fireplace in it. A couch that was blue with white swirls throughout it faced the fireplace. If one sat on the couch, a recliner was to the left and a papasan chair and matching ottoman was to the right. One end table between the recliner and couch provided room for a lamp whose base was in the shape of a lion. A brass lamp curved over the papasan chair and provided light for that area. A brass bird cage was on its own stand a couple feet from the side of the fireplace. The couch helped to separate the living room from the dinette. Blues, browns, creams, and wild rose made up most of the coloring in the living room. Alex's interests in cats and wolves was well shown in the knickknacks and paintings that decorated the place.

Detective Baker sat in the papasan chair and was surprised by its comfort. He looked toward the kitchen and dinette, he liked how Alex had decorated that area with an apple theme. The colors seemed to blend right in with the living room. A huge aquarium was located against the one side of the dining room. Tom didn't know much about aquariums except to notice whether they were nicely kept or disgustingly dirty. This aquarium was clean looking. There didn't seem to be an overabundance of fish though. This place had a wonderful homey atmosphere that seemed to envelop its occupants.

He noticed that while the place looked neat and clean, he could tell she was not a total neat freak. He liked how she did not apologize when

46

they first came inside about the place not being clean. Clean freaks irritated him. He had to laugh at himself. Here he was investigating a murder, and he's checking out his compatibility with one possible suspect, in fact the prime suspect. He realized just how long it had been since he had been interested in a woman. Just his luck that the first one to catch his eye might be a murderess. He barely knew this woman, but his gut feeling was that she was innocent.

Alex came into the room with the drinks. She was a bit surprised that the detective had chosen the papasan, it wasn't usually the chair of choice. Depending on the person, it could be a bit hard to get into or out of. Alex handed him a drink and sat on the end of the couch closest to the papasan. "Detective Baker, you said you had a few questions?" she inquired.

"Yes, I do." Baker reached for his tablet, flipped it open, and continued, "I was wondering if you could give me a list of anyone you can think of that could have come into contact with the Jordan wedding cake."

Alex thought carefully as she rattled off a possible list. "All of my employees, including myself of course, and anyone at the reception hall after the cake was delivered."

"How long have you known your employees?"

Alex could feel her temper rising, but she kept telling herself that he was only going over all the possibilities. "I must say that I'm not happy at what you are thinking. I truly don't believe any of my employees are responsible for this murder. I've known all my employees most of my life. Of course, before I hired some of them, it was only to say hi or talk about the weather and such generalities. Cat, Maggie, and I are real close friends. Cat and I are a little closer than Maggie and I, mainly because Maggie's married and has kids and we're not and don't."

"Can you give me a quick rundown on each of your employees?"

"Sure. Cat's my best friend. Her real name is Caitlin Farrell. We grew up only a few houses away from each other. She helped me start my bakery. She's the main baker but on occasion does help with the decorating or works in the shop. She's my age, twenty-nine. She's never been married. She's currently dating a gentleman by the name of Mike Porter. He drives truck for a living."

"Next is Maggie Marchetti. She has worked at the bakery for about three years, almost from day one. She's one year older than Cat and I. She's married to a great guy by the name of Jake. Mags has three children. She decorates novelty cakes and when needed works in the shop."

"Then there's Didi Gambini. She's worked for me for approximately two years. She graduated school with me. She's my front person, which means she takes the novelty cake orders and handles the customers. She's married to Carlos Gambini. She knew my other employee Joyce before I hired her."

"Last is Joyce Hentzel. We call her Jo-Jo. She's been with me for only about one year. She's thirty-eight and married to Rick. She mainly does the clean-up, however, she will fill in wherever she can if necessary."

When Baker realized she was done, he asked if that was everyone.

She was shaking her head yes when she stopped and said not quite. "Well, there's also Cassie. Her full name is Cassandra Victorio. She's a real good friend of mine who owns a pet store. She's thirty years old. I kid her all the time about being older than me, however, its only by about ten months. She helps me out in times of crisis and I do likewise for her. But Cassie hasn't helped me out for at least two months now. I've talked to her on the phone and stopped by her store to talk, but she hasn't been to the bakery for a while. And that's everyone."

"Did you receive any deliveries since Wednesday?"

"One or two, however deliveries are made to my office, the delivery people do not enter my bakery." Alex answered emphatically. She continued when Baker gave her a quizzical look. "Sorry, that subject still has the tendency to raise my dander. I noticed a few things amiss in the bakery a year or two back and traced it to the delivery person. I decided to make sure that wouldn't happen again."

"Anyone help with maintenance or lawn care that might enter your building?" Baker inquired.

"Oh, yeah," Alex said sheepishly. "I kind of forgot. That would be Cyrus Mendelhoffer. I'm not sure how old he is. He seems pretty old. I figure when God created the Garden of Eden, Cyrus was there to prune the bushes. He is retired, from where, I don't honestly remember. He likes to keep busy by helping out anyone who needs help. He handles my lawn care and any handyman kind of fix-ups that are needed. I like him. No matter what happens, he seems to have experienced something like it and always professes to have some words of wisdom. Most of the time, he is spot on."

"I have one more question and then....."

Alex looked up from her drink to see why he had stopped mid-sentence and noticed him staring up and to her left. She turned around and screamed, "Micky! No!" Alex watched as her cat walked, no stalked was more accurate, across the curtain rod at the top of her living room picture window. He was about to attack the bird cage. She thought he would have learned by now that it was a futile maneuver. He'd never been able to get to the bird. The last time he tried, all he did was knock the cage over and make a huge mess. "Don't..." She leaped toward Micky flailing her arms but he had tuned her out a long time ago. Just as she reached him, he jumped, so she tried to tackle him mid-air, but missed. Her fingertips just grazed his tail. As she did a belly flop onto the floor behind the recliner, she heard her cat scream, her bird screech, the cage crash, and herself groan, but later she wouldn't be able to recall in what order. Then she heard laughter, not just a simple chuckle mind you, but wholehearted full blown laughter. She pushed herself off the floor and looked over the arm of the chair. There sat Detective Baker, laughing so hard he was holding his stomach and tears were running down his face. He managed to croak out one question. "Are?...Are you?...Are you okay?"

She just squinted her eyes at him and answered, "Yes, but just what exactly do you find so funny?" She barely got the question out when a single green feather floated down in front of her. Baker just ended up laughing even harder. There were feathers everywhere. As she looked around the mess, she noticed Micky was not to be found. After she made sure her bird was alright, she started to laugh also. After a few moments, they wiped their eyes dry. Georgy was screeching his head off, he was not amused. He hated that cat.

"Ms. Applecake, where's your vacuum cleaner?"

"In the closet by the front door, but you don't have to clean up anything." She answered without too much enthusiasm.

"I know, but I want to." He smiled and she could have sworn his eyes twinkled some. "However, you'll owe me."

"Oh, yeah?" She was suddenly wary. "Like what?"

"Dinner? Tonight?"

"Well," she hesitated and couldn't fathom why. "We'll see." Her stomach did flip flops as she watched Detective Baker try to hide his disappointment but fail. Without thinking about the results, she added, "Maybe we'll be too tired after cleaning this mess up to go out. Maybe we could order in instead?"

A smile lit up Baker's face. "Sure. That'd be great."

"Only one thing" Alex added solemnly.

"What is that?" Baker was instantly concerned.

50

Alex smiled, "You have to call me Alex. I don't like being referred to as Ms. Applecake."

"Okay, Alex." Detective Baker returned, "Please call me Tom."

She took Georgy out of his cage and placed him on his jungle gym by the window. "Sorry, boy!" She tried to pet him and calm him down. Instead, he promptly turned his back to her and shook his butt at her as if saying "up yours." "Well, be that way." She chuckled. Tom helped her right the bird cage. While Alex fetched clean water and food, Tom vacuumed the floor and anywhere else he could find feathers. A few minutes later, everything was put back into place and one couldn't tell anything ever happened. Micky walked through the room and looked at Georgy, Alex, and Tom and just smirked as he headed toward the den.

"That cat's got quite an attitude." Tom commented.

Alex just grinned. "Yep. I just love cats, don't you?"

Tom ignored her question. He thought cats were opinionated pain-in-the-butts. He preferred dogs much better. "How about going out to eat? Fresh air would be perfect, don't you think?"

Alex agreed. Since it was June, there was no need for jackets. Alex double-checked that the place was properly locked up and out the door they went.

They decided to go to an Italian restaurant that was located on the other side of the lake from Alex's house. The sun was just starting to set and a warm gentle breeze was blowing. It only took them about fifteen minutes to cross the park and reach their destination, but it was a nice peaceful walk. They came to a mutual and silent agreement to just enjoy the walk, without the nuisance of talk.

It didn't take long to get a table and place their order. Once done, Tom looked at Alex and said, "You've told me about all your employees, but you didn't tell me anything about yourself. Do you care to elaborate?" He finished with a warm smile.

"Sure, but turn about is fair play. I give, you better give too. Deal?" Alex asked returning his warm smile. She told herself to be careful. He was still a cop and she was still somewhat of a suspect.

"Compared to you my life probably seems rather ordinary……that is until recently." Alex had stopped, but continued when Tom didn't say anything. My full name is Alexandra Jean Applecake. I don't much care to be called Alexandra. It's too formal for my taste, I'm twenty-nine. I was born and raised in this town. I left for a few years to go to college near Lancaster, Pa. When my aunt died, she left me her old house in her will. I've always been on the creative side and I enjoy baking and making people happy. After decorating cakes for a hobby for some time, I decided to try my hand at a bakery. I remodeled Aunt Gertrude's house into a bakery and called it the Slice of Life Bakery and Supply Shop. My business is about three years old now. In between college and opening the bakery, I drove truck for a few years. I also had gotten married, but it didn't last long. My divorce was final somewhere around four years ago." Alex shrugged her shoulders slightly. She raised her eyebrows briefly, tilted her head a tad, and said "and that's about it."

During her summary, the meal had been delivered and they had started eating. Silence prevailed for a few moments while Tom digested what all he had just heard. While formulating his next question, he finished eating his garlic bread, took a sip of water, and slowly wiped his mouth with his napkin. He waited until her mouth was empty, looked directly into Alex's eyes, and asked, "Are you dating anyone serious right now?"

Alex dropped her eyes to her food. She played a little with her manicotti before answering him, "No. No, I'm not." She took a small sip of her drink and looking up at Tom she continued, "In fact, I haven't exactly been looking for anyone. I've been too busy with the shop and everything else. Cat tries her best to set me up, but so far no one's caught my interest." She sliced the air horizontally with her one hand and pointed a finger at Tom, "but enough about me, it's your turn to spill your guts."

Tom smiled and started. "Here comes the life and times of Thomas Andrew Baker. Tom to my friends, *not* Tommy. I was born thirty-two years ago and raised in New Cumberland, Pa. It's a town about three hours drive from here. Since I was little, I've always wanted to be a police officer. I went into the academy right out of school. I worked in my hometown for around seven years. One day I decided I needed a change of pace. When I heard about a job opening up here, I came to check it out. The town seemed just like what I was looking for and so I decided to stay. I moved here about one and a half years ago. People seem to think that a cop's life is full of the kind of excitement that TV shows portray, but it's far from that. I've never shot anyone. In fact, I've only drawn my gun a few times. I enjoy my job immensely but it is very time consuming. It doesn't leave much time for a social life. There's been a few girlfriends in the past but nothing took. No one's caught my eye either for at least a year." He cleared his throat lightly and made sure that he had her attention, "until now, that is."

Alex's face blushed violently when she realized exactly what he was saying. "Uh... that's nice." She stumbled out.

Just then the waiter showed up and asked if they wanted dessert. They both declined and he went for their bill. Tom smiled and spoke under his breath, "Saved by the waiter." Alex heard him and turned even redder.

By the time they left the restaurant, the full moon was out and gave them plenty of light to walk by. As they started through the park, Tom reached over with his right hand and took Alex's left hand. He had moved hesitantly and more than just a tad nervously, he didn't know for sure how Alex would react. But he shouldn't have worried, Alex instantly opened her fingers and interlaced hers with his. As they passed a big tree not far from the lake, Alex slowed and so did he. She lead them back to the tree and stopped. Alex looked up at Tom and then glanced at the lake. "I love it here at night, especially with a full moon. Everything takes on a glow of serene peacefulness. Do you mind if we just stand and absorb it for awhile? Or does that sound weird?"

"No problem." After a few minutes, Tom whispered, "You're right, this is really nice." Tom watched Alex as she surveyed the area. He watched the moonlight reflect beautifully off her face. He was still watching her when she turned to face him.

"What are you looking at?" She asked curiously.

"You." He answered simply but honestly.

She slowly scanned his face. "What?"

"You're beautiful." He returned. As he spoke, he gently touched her face with his right hand. Looking into her eyes, he placed his thumb just under her chin. He leaned down towards her as he gently lifted her face up to him. Slowly and with extreme tenderness, he bent down and kissed her softly on the lips. Alex couldn't believe how gentle he was. This had to be a dream. The moonlight showed all the contours of his face as he got closer and closer to her. They both felt electricity surge through their bodies as they kissed. Instead of separating, Tom kissed her a little harder. She responded in kind. He gently pushed her backwards until she felt the tree against her back. As they stood holding each other and kissing, Tom started to slowly slide his one hand up her side. He followed the curves of her body until he stopped with his hand caressing her ribs. She tingled as she felt him move up her body. All of a sudden she froze. He felt her react and quickly withdrew his face from hers. "What's wrong?"

54

"We're outside. That's what's wrong. Every gossipmonger in this town is probably looking out their window or is on the phone, as we speak, spreading what we're doing." Alex explained. She noticed he didn't move his hand. She also noticed how good it felt.

Tom scanned the park area and smiled. "Well, since we're already news. Let's give them some more." And with that said, he quickly kissed her again. Then they turned and walked toward her house laughing. He also took note that she hadn't removed his hand earlier nor drew away from it. Tom had to admit to himself one more thing. He had wanted her so bad, that he had forgotten their surroundings. He had tuned out everything but Alex and himself. Professionally, this was definitely not a good thing.

Chapter 8

When they reached Alex's house, she unlocked the door. She turned to Tom and thanked him for a wonderful dinner. He kissed her lightly, and said that he would call her tomorrow. As she started to push the door open, he turned to start down her walkway. Alex took one look at her living room and howled. Instantly Tom was by her side, his senses on full alert.

Alex's living room was ransacked. Pillows from the couch and chairs were on the floor. Books and knickknacks were lying everywhere. "Who…?" Alex started to ask a question when she stopped quickly. Tom watched as Alex rushed toward Georgy's cage. That poor bird. He was sure getting the wrong kind of attention this evening. It was turned over again. Vaguely, he wondered why the bird wasn't screaming like he was earlier. He reached for his cell phone to alert the police station and to have the crime scene unit sent to the house. He was in the middle of his phone call, when he heard Alex cry out in anguish "Noooooooo!" She had started loudly and ended muffled in tears. He immediately turned and watched her slowly slide down behind the recliner. Tom hurried over to Alex while finishing his request for aid. He found her clutching a pillow and crying while staring into the bird cage. He gave her a quick look over for injuries before turning his attention toward the cage. For some reason, tearing the place apart wasn't enough for the earlier intruder, he found it necessary to kill Georgy. Georgy lay mashed against the side of his cage, his head laying at a weird angle. Suddenly Tom realized he was screwing up. He forgot to check the rest of the house and got to it immediately.

As far as Alex was concerned, the house being destroyed was the "straw that broke the camel's back." That was until she saw Georgy. Emotions already on overdrive, turned to overload, and she slid down the chair back and hugged her pillow and starting crying. Her shoulders shook and tears flowed freely as she looked at Georgy. What in the world was going on around here? She didn't deserve the trouble she found herself in and Georgy definitely didn't deserve what he got. Finally a sound made it through her thoughts and anguish. Her mind cleared and she looked to her right. There was Micky. He was bumping gently into her arm and meowing quietly. It took only a microsecond to realize what he wanted. She threw the pillow to the side and he jumped into her lap. Cats are wonderful creatures. Even though at times, they can be spiteful and nasty, they can also be compassionate and very caring. Anytime Alex felt low and in need of some loving, Micky was always there.

Tom came back into the room and over to Alex. He found her with arms wrapped around Micky and her face buried in his side. "Alex. Alex?"

"Yeah. What?" came her muffled response.

"I checked your place out. Every room has some kind of damage or another. The crime lab guys are on their way. They'll check for fingerprints and other evidence to try to catch whoever did this." He bent down and touched her lightly on the shoulder and softly said, "I need you to walk with me for a while and see if anything is missing. The sooner we get started the better."

Alex hugged Mick for another minute and took a deep breath. "Thanks Micky. I needed that. Love you too." She put Mick down and took Tom's hand to stand up. She wiped her eyes and said, "Let's get on with it."

Alex let streams of tears run freely down her face as she viewed the damage to her house. It seemed a tad strange to her that while a lot of her stuff was on the floor, it didn't look particularly damaged. However, there were a few things missing. Her TV, VCR/DVD, and stereo were gone. Alex double-checked the fish tank for damage. She was relieved that it was not cracked and all the fish were safely swimming around.

They had just finished looking the house over when the doorbell rang. Alex sat on the couch in a daze while Tom answered the door. He left the officers in and supplied them with the list of missing goods and gave them a rundown of what happened. As they got started, Detective Taylor stepped through the door. He headed toward Tom highly irate. "What in the world is wrong with you?" He pointed a finger at Alex and continued on, "She is a murder suspect and you're getting involved with her. I didn't want to be teamed up with you in the first place. But, they said you were one of the best on the force, so I agreed. But, I think they were lying. I don't think anyone else wanted you and so I got stuck with you."

Now it was Tom's turn to be angry. "Cliff, this is neither the time nor the place to discuss this. We can talk later at the office." Tom was ticked but his voice was quiet and controlled. "Now you can stop with the accusations and get on with the investigation."

"Are you trying to tell me you are not involved with this woman? How is it you just happen to be here?"

"I'm not saying anything of the sort." Tom didn't need the entire force hearing about this. "I had a few questions to ask, that's all."

"Oh, I sincerely doubt that!" Cliff spit out. "We're working on this murder together. You never told me you had more questions for her.

She's our prime suspect, for Pete's sake, and you're having dinner with her. You're even kissing her in the park!" He threw his hands up in the air in exasperation.

Tom was blown away by Cliff's verbal assault. Technically Cliff was right. Tom had a gut feeling of Alex's innocence, but no proof. Yet! He had gotten his butt in a sling and he would have to get it back out, or his job could be history. He realized everyone was watching their confrontation. "Everyone back to work. Cliff, we'll deal with this later." He turned to Alex, "Do you have somewhere you can go for awhile? I don't know how long this is going to take."

Earlier he would have suggested his place, but that was impossible now.

"Yes, I do. Cat should be here shortly."

Tom was more than a bit taken back at her comment. He looked questioningly at Alex, but Cliff asked the question first. "Just how in the world does she know you need a place to stay? Did you call her or was this part of the plan?"

"What are you implying? What plan? No, I didn't call her. I did not need to. She only lives up the street. The whole neighborhood is probably outside now. Cop cars in the area tend to do that, you know."

As on cue, Cat hurried into the house. Cliff turned quickly. "How did you get past the guard?"

Cat looked at him as she would a dog turd. "He *did* try to stop me. But I rather insisted, and here I am. Where's Alex, what's…?" She stopped mid-sentence as she looked at the destruction. Then she swore up a blue storm.

"I'm right here." Alex piped up.

"Thank God you're okay! I was worried when I saw all the cop cars." She looked around slowly as she asked a question. "By the way, whose two-tone brown car is outside?"

Cliff spoke up irritated, "It's mine. Why?"

"Just curious," Cat answered reservedly while looking him up and down.

Alex was impatient and wanted to get out of the house instantly. The tension was high all around. Now, Tom was in almost as much trouble as she. Alex froze a second as she looked at Cat appraising Cliff, because she realized the ramifications of Cat's question and Cliff's response. She asked if she was needed any longer. Tom said no and asked for Cat's address and phone number. Then Alex picked up Micky and left with her friend, while Cliff tried to get in Tom's face again.

Chapter 9

Cat allowed Alex to walk in total quiet until they reached her house. Alex took that time to make a few decisions. She had to find out who had it out for her. Anger replaced her self pity. She knew she had to collect her thoughts and focus on solving this murder. But as soon as they entered Cat's house, she was thrown for a loop when Cat asked, "Well, was he any good?"

"What are you talking about?" Alex asked while carefully dropping Micky onto the floor.

"Sometimes you're so slow. I'm talking about you and that cop kissing, you doufus." Cat rolled her eyes as she spoke and bumped her shoulder lightly into Alex's.

Alex blushed quickly. So much had happened since the kiss with Tom that it felt like it happened a long time ago. "That's neither here nor there. You'd think by now, the speed by which gossip spreads in this town would cease to amaze me." Alex took a seat in front of Cat's fireplace and encouraged Cat to find a seat also. She rubbed her hands down her face and said, "Cat, we have to figure out what's going on and by whom."

"Nice change of subject Alex." Cat chuckled. "Okay, where do we start?"

Alex thought for a few moments. She'd never been involved in a murder before, but one of her favorite hobbies was reading murder mystery books. She suggested they get a few tablets and pens and start writing stuff down and see if anything connects.

Cat agreed but suggested they get something to drink and a few munchies first. "You know, to *fuel* our thoughts."

Alex laughed, "leave it to you to think of food at a time like this. But it's cool with me."

When they finally sat down to figure out what they knew, they realized it was actually very little. They knew the victim's name, but not anything about him. They were hoping that there was more than one Matthew Abrahms. Alex had hoped to discuss just that over dinner with Tom, but events occurred that blocked that intention from her mind. They knew when he died but not the actual cause. So Alex looked at their first column called victim and only had the name. She'd have to ask Tom for more info tomorrow.

Cat suggested they review what they knew about the attack. Alex felt like the attack on herself happened eons ago. So much had happened today that she found it hard to remember everything. Who knew Alex was at the bakery this afternoon? Alex only knew of two people: Cat and Tom. Who knew Alex would be out of the house tonight: Tom. She sat back and looked at what was written so far and paled. This was crazy. No way could Tom be responsible for what's been happening to her. There had to be another explanation. Somebody they didn't know about.

"Alex. Why make it hard? Why can't it be Tom? You remember that old saying, 'Acts like a duck. Talks like a duck. Then it's a duck?' Well, that prick is just using you. Or...?" Cat jumped up and rapidly paced back and forth. "...Wait a minute. I saw a two-tone brown car leave the bakery as I arrived. Detective Taylor just happens to drive such a car. The cops could be in it together." Cat spun around and faced Alex, excitement exuding from her.

"You're nuts! Why would they do it? What's their motive?" Alex spoke quickly. "I didn't even know them before Abrahms was killed. As far as I know, they didn't know me either. There has to be another explanation." Alex raised both hands up, palms upward, shrugged slightly and said, "It might only have been a coincidence."

Cat gave her a look of disgust and shook her head. "Yeah right, and I'm Aunt Jemima. Think about it for a minute, Alex. Just give my scenario a chance. One or both of them want Abrahms dead. They figured out how to kill him. They're cops, so they can fix it right. Either they planned to frame you, or you just ended up being convenient. Either way they're in a position to make it work.. Taylor whacked you at the bakery for some reason we don't know yet. Tom shows up and makes sure that you are found safe. It wouldn't do for you to be found dead in a locked closet. He's keeping you off balance by getting your emotions involved."

"But why? Tom called earlier and we agreed to talk. I mean he might have told Detective Taylor about our meeting. But his showing up at the bakery was a planned thing, not an accident. And why put me in the closet?"

"Who knows? If this is our Matthew Abrahms," Cat hesitated and her eyes watered a little as she looked Alex in the eyes, "maybe he killed one of their family members just like he did yours."

Alex felt her own eyes fill with water also. She turned and looked into the fire to help control her emotions. "Who knows? I guess it's possible. But I just can't shake the feeling that we don't know enough yet. Why did my attacker take time to put me in the closet? Why did the intruder take the time to kill Georgy? In both cases, valuable time was spent in which someone could have come in and caught the person. The person or persons must have had a valid reason for spending the time. I'll make you a deal. You keep an open view on the possibility of someone else being involved in the attacks (we'll call the person Mr. X, for lack of a better term), and I'll keep your scenario in mind until we know some more."

Cat thought about it for all of one second and agreed. But she warned Alex to be careful with Tom for now or else her feelings could get burnt bad. Alex was getting extremely tired and decided to call it a night. Cat's house was a duplicate set-up to Alex's, so Alex slept in the guest room. As she fell asleep, memories of her sister played in her mind.

Chapter 10

Nine o'clock Monday morning, the phone rang at Cat's house. The call was for Alex. It was Tom. She picked up the phone with apprehension. He said that they had gotten done at her house late last night, so she could return whenever she wanted. He had felt the hour was too late to call her at that time. The back door had been jimmied opened. There was some minimal damage, however, she should put a new lock on the door. Then he took a pause, he knew this next bit of news would not be welcomed one bit. "Alex."

"Yes." She could feel his discomfort.

"We're going to have to close your shop down for the time being. I'm sorry."

"What? Why?" Then she sucked in air quickly and asked, "Did you find something in the samples y'all took?"

"No, not yet. But we obtained another search warrant."

"I don't understand."

"Mr. Abrahms died of an acute reaction to the cake. That's all I can tell you at this moment. I'm really very sorry." Tom gently hung up the phone.

Alex slowly put the phone down and sank into the closest chair. Cat took one look and could tell that the news was really bad. Despair overtook Alex momentarily while she filled Cat in on the news. Anger quickly replaced the despair, as the friends came up with a battle plan. First they would finish getting ready, then they would go to Alex's and clean up the place. Hopefully the cops would be done at the bakery by the time the last pillow was put into place. Alex would call Tom and find out some information. Then, they would solve the crime and get back to a normal life.

"Simple." Cat said with a shrug of the shoulders.

"Yeah, right." Alex replied sarcastically. "Wishful thinking is more like it!"

"Now look who's being the pessimist?" Cat laughed.

Chapter 11

Alex and Cat put their "battle plan" into action. They buried Georgy in the backyard by Alex's favorite "Peace" rosebush. By the time they had Alex's place in order there came a knock on the door. Alex opened the door and allowed the two detectives to enter the house. Behind the two detectives were two uniformed police. Cliff gave Alex a search warrant for her house.

"My house?" Alex was confused and showed it. "Why? We just got done putting it back right. Couldn't you all have easily searched last night?"

"Sorry, no we couldn't." Tom came to the point quickly. "Do you have any penicillin anywhere in your house Alex?"

Alex was bewildered by the change of subject. "I might. I really don't know. Why?"

Tom was all business. "Would you please show us where any might be?"

Alex was about to move when Cat spoke up, "Don't move Alex. Why should she show you anything? Isn't it your job to find whatever you're looking for?"

Tom gazed down at Cat. "Yes, it is. But, as Alex just mentioned, you two just got done cleaning up. Do you really want us to tear the place apart?"

Alex's temper was rising fast. "Cool it, guys. I have nothing to hide. If I have any penicillin, it would be in my medicine cabinet."

She turned and led the men to her bathroom. Cliff stopped her before she could enter the room. "Wait a minute please. We'll get it."

He entered the room and opened the cabinet. Sitting at the back of the top shelf, behind other stuff, was a prescription bottle. He reached up and pulled it down. It was penicillin. He turned around and shook it in the air for Tom to see. "Here it is!"

Tom looked at Alex. She couldn't read the expression on his face. It was what she would soon recognize as his "cop look" but with a little sorrow thrown in. "Ms. Applecake, we need you to come down with us to the station house."

Alex was surprised to say the least. "What's going on ? What's with the penicillin?"

"We'll talk down at the station. Let's go." He added briskly. He turned to Cat and suggested calmly, "You might want to contact a lawyer, if she has one."

"You bet I will. This is outrageous." Cat spit back. "Go on Alex. We'll be there shortly." While everyone walked out the door, Cat called Ben Gifford, Alex's attorney, and filled him in.

Once at the station house, Tom and Cliff led Alex into an interrogation room. They advised her of her rights. Tom asked if she wanted to wait for her attorney. Against her better judgment, Alex agreed they could start. She knew that she had nothing to hide. Alex turned down their offer of something to drink. She wanted to get back home as soon as she could. She figured it wouldn't take long for Ben to show up. Alex hoped that he could clear everything up quickly. She knew she was clutching at straws, but she still hoped. She was right on the former, but not on the latter. Ben showed up at the point where Alex had just agreed that they could start questioning.

Ben Gifford is a well-liked home-grown lawyer. He is a tall man who is on the husky side. Ben has a way of making anything he wears look sharp and custom-made, even sweatpants. He has an excellent reputation as being a fair but extremely tough officer of the court.

68

Prosecutors take care not to underestimate him, no matter how *strong* their case, or how weak *his* case appears. He shook the detectives' hands as he entered the room. Ben asked why Alex had been brought in. They informed him that they were only questioning her. "She's a suspect in the murder of a Mr. Matthew Abrahms," Detective Baker said. Ben asked for a few minutes with Alex alone. The two detectives got up and left the room.

Ben asked Alex to briefly tell him what was going on. She was shaking a little while she quickly recounted her problems. "You should have contacted me yesterday, Alex." He reached over and patted her hand. "But don't worry, we'll get this cleared up. I know that you're innocent. However, depending on the outcome of this discussion, we may have to prove it. Let's try to find out what they have." He explained that she should answer any questions asked of her until he tells her otherwise. Ben emphasized that Alex should keep her answers as simple as possible. Do not give any more information than what they ask for."

After he was done giving instructions to Alex, Ben looked up and nodded to the two-sided mirror on the wall. At her questioning glance, Ben explained that in all likelihood, the cops had been watching for their cue to come back in. They can see through the mirror, but not hear, while client lawyer confidential talk was going on. Tom entered the room and was taking his place when Cliff bustled in looking very smug. As he entered, he hurriedly placed a paper in his pocket. Cliff led off the questioning. He asked Alex to review some of the information that she already had given them. She ran them through the decorating routine once more.

"Run through the application and use of the edible glitter one more time please."

"Okay. Edible glitter comes in a container in small flakes. They're not small enough for me. I pour some flakes into a plastic baggy and close it. Then I take a rolling pin and roll over the baggy a few times. This breaks the flakes into real small "salt-like" pieces. I then empty the baggy into a clean salt shaker. Then whenever I need glitter, I just pick up the salt shaker and shake it wherever I want. This way I have better control of where the glitter goes and how heavy it's applied. It also helps to keep my hands clean. If I handle the glitter directly and my hands are too warm or moist for whatever reason, the glitter ends up sticking to my fingers."

"So, the only thing in the shaker is edible glitter?" Cliff sternly asked.

"Yes." Alex replied simply. She opened her mouth to continue, but closed it without speaking. She had a bad feeling, but kept quiet.

"Nothing else?"

"No. Nothing else. Why?" Alex's temper was starting to rise. Her attorney quietly placed his hand on her arm and Alex visibly worked at calming down.

"Why did you have the penicillin?" Cliff asked quickly.

"I honestly don't remember having any. But it's been quite some time since I cleaned out my medicine cabinet, so who knows. May I see the container?"

Cliff reached into his side pocket and removed a small prescription bottle wrapped in a plastic bag. It had the typical pharmaceutical information on the side. The patient name was Alexandra Applecake. The medicine was listed as penicillin. The name of the doctor was Dr. Bridgewater. Alex looked at the bottle perplexed. She thought back a few minutes. "Dr. Bridgewater?…Oh, yeah. He's the orthodontist who pulled my tooth about eight months back. There was swelling and such. The penicillin was prescribed to fight off any infections." She looked up really confused now and slowly said. "I thought I'd finished off that prescription. That bottle should be empty!"

"Nice acting Ms. Applecake," Detective Taylor sneered. "You actually looked upset."

"I'm not acting," Alex pleaded.

"Oh, I believe you." Cliff sarcastically replied.

"Are you accusing my client of something?" Ben Gifford calmly inquired.

"Yes, of murder. I know she killed Mr. Abrahms." Cliff retorted.

"You know it for a fact, or is it just your opinion? What's your reasoning? Where's your proof?" Ben continued unrattled. Alex was glad someone wasn't rattled. She was sure glad she had her shaking hands under the table on her lap and out of their view.

"I know it!" Cliff held up his right hand. He raised one finger per component he listed. "She had the means, opportunity, and the motive." He had started answering by looking at the lawyer, but ended with his gaze first on Alex and then on Tom. Tom turned a blank face toward Cliff, but Alex thought she momentarily recognized some surprise in his eyes. Tom also seemed to be leaning in closer to her and Cliff than he was originally. "The victim died of anaphylactic shock. It was the result of an acute reaction to penicillin. The lab found penicillin all over the cake. The cake that you made."

Alex jumped out of her chair and her chair flew back and hit the wall. Slamming her hands on the table she shouted, "No freaking way mister! That is totally impossible. I did not put any penicillin on the cake! Why would I? No one puts penicillin on a cake."

Cliff had pulled back at the force of Alex's verbal attack. Ben rose quickly beside her and told her to calm down until they heard everything. "You best control yourself Ms. Applecake," Tom quietly chimed in. He hated to be kept in the dark on a case. He couldn't help wondering why Cliff was so sure of himself. At their last talk, they had no motive for Alex. Everything was circumstantial.

71

"That was the means. You had plenty of opportunity. You yourself explained how you put glitter on a cake. The cake order called for glitter, not only on the flowers, but on the cake itself."

"Some glitter, yes." Alex hesitantly replied.

"We took a team of guys into your bakery yesterday. The search turned up four salt shakers."

"So what?"

"Does the count seem correct to you?"

"I don't know. We don't count them. We started off with only one, but we would misplace it or two people needed it at the same time, or whatever. I trust my decorating people. They are excellent people and I don't stifle their creativity. Nor do I question every time they need to run up front and bring back more coloring paste or other supplies. I try to keep what we need in the back but that's not always possible." She looked at Detective Taylor and finished with, "I don't count individual tips or bags either. Some are used, some are destroyed, so what? That's business."

"So you couldn't tell me where the shakers are located in your bakery."

"No, I couldn't. I can tell you where they might be, but sometimes we have to look for one when we need it. That's probably why there were four."

"Do you mark which shakers are for glitter?"

"No, we don't need to mark them. Just what are you getting at here detective?"

"I'm just trying to point out your opportunity, Ms. Applecake." Cliff innocently said. Then his eyes narrowed in on Alex's, "You see, one of the bottles we found had penicillin mixed in with the glitter."

Alex abruptly paled. She was speechless. How could that be? She was confused and upset. This meant that someone at the bakery killed this man. That also meant that she was going to be the scapegoat. No way, she told herself. She had to get out of here and find the bastard who was framing her. Her inner strength rebuilt once again, she straightened her shoulders and looked Detective Taylor right in the face and replied, "I'm being framed."

He chuckled at her comment. "How original. I don't think so lady. Earlier, maybe I'd have believed you, but not now."

"Why not now?"

"You see the computers have been down since Saturday morning. The department has been severely hampered by this problem, let me tell ya. But right before we came in here, I was informed that everything is back in working condition. And guess what? I found you have a real strong motive for killing Mr. Abrahms."

Tom had never seen anyone as pale as Alex and still be in the vertical position. He was worried for her, but his professional side was intrigued. He turned his full attention toward Cliff. Cliff just drilled his stare into Alex. He was relishing this moment. He didn't like his partner nor his partner's apparent interest in this lady. He didn't know this woman, so it didn't really matter to him what happened to her. But maybe, just maybe, he could get a promotion out of this case. Then he would make sure everyone knew how wonder-boy Tom screwed up.

Cliff's thoughts kept him from hearing Ben's question. "What?"

Ben mentally rolled his eyes but only showed his irritation through lifting his one eyebrow. What an incompetent arse he thought, but didn't say for obvious reasons. "What's her supposed motive, detective?"

Alex's fears were confirmed when Cliff zeroed in on her once more and scowled. "You killed him, because....." he hesitated to elongate her pain and his pleasure, "he killed your sister."

Silence enveloped the room and hung in the air for what felt to Alex

73

like an eternity. She had dropped her eyes to the table on hearing his statement. Her rebuilt bravado crumbled instantly as her strength fled. She felt as if the room was going to tilt. She felt tears well up in her eyes. They ran unchecked down her cheeks and onto her clothes. Now what? She didn't know to whom to look. She felt the hand of her lawyer and old friend on her shoulder. She glanced at Tom and saw amazement, sorrow, and utter disbelief on his face. "I did not kill him." She said quietly but with conviction while staring at Tom.

Ben raised his right hand slightly off the table, "This interview is now over." He turned to face Alex. " I need to go check on bail. I'll be by to talk to you later. Do not answer any more questions without me being present." She mutely nodded okay. Ben got up and quietly left the room. Tom looked at Cliff and told him to leave. He wanted to talk to Alex alone for a few minutes. He would take her back to her cell when they were done. Cliff opened his mouth to rebuff, but one look at Tom ended that thought and he left. Tom looked at Alex and wasn't sure how to start. He was thoroughly disgruntled and it came through in his voice. Even though Tom spoke very quietly, Alex didn't have to lean forward to hear him. "So you knew Mr. Abrahms this whole time?"

Alex heard the weariness and disbelief in his voice. She hesitated for a minute, Ben had just told her not to answer any more questions. But she wanted Tom to know why she had done what she did. "Not for *sure*, I didn't. I knew *a* Mr. Abrahms, but I wasn't sure it was *the* Mr. Abrahms. I planned on asking you for some more info last night, but we sort of got sidetracked. I also planned on asking you today, but I got arrested instead."

"Would you have told me about your sister if you found out that this was the correct Mr. Abrahms, or the incorrect one depending on how you look at things?"

74

"To be honest, I don't know. I knew y'all would think I was guilty for sure, if you found out about Natalie. I, or I should say we….uh…that is Cat and I, thought maybe we could find out who killed him first. Then we'd tell you about Natalie." At least she had the courtesy to have a sheepish look on her face as she spoke her piece.

Tom thought it over and shook his head back and forth slowly. "So you think amateurs can be more effective than professionals? Didn't you think we'd find out the connection between you and the victim without you saying something?"

"He died Saturday and you just now found out about the connection. I thought you'd have found the connection earlier if he was the same guy. I didn't know about the computers crashing. Look, I'm sorry. I should have told you sooner, but I didn't want to muddy the waters if I didn't have to. It's entirely possible that more than one Mr. Abrahms lives in this area. In fact, sometimes the grooms don't live in this town. They come here to marry because the bride's family is here. It doesn't mean that they live here or will live here. So this Mr. Abrahms could have been just about anyone. I can tell you one thing. If my business ever gets going again, the groom's name will now be included on the cake order form. And I can promise you one thing. If I would have known whom the groom was, we would not have done this cake for any amount of money or reason. I know the bride from way back, but we are not what I would call close. I cannot understand how she hooked up with this bastard."

Tom sighed, "Okay. Apology accepted,….for now. I understand your thinking, or I should say, your hoping. It could have worked out a number of different ways, but it didn't. Now you're in this up to your armpits." He handed Alex a tissue for her tears. Tom almost reached up to wipe them away with his hand, but figured that Cliff was watching, if not listening in, and he didn't need to fan the flames licking at his career.

Alex saw hope shining on the horizon. "You mean…you think I'm innocent?"

"Innocent? No. But I do think you're not guilty of this crime."

Alex grinned. "Humor! That's a nice switch." Then she frowned, "What about your partner?"

"He still thinks you're guilty as sin. He has an entire scenario built up to show your guilt. He's pretty convincing. To be honest, he just about had me convinced."

"What changed your mind?"

"We'll discuss that later. First I have to take you back to a cell. Then I have to make sure Ben Gifford gets you bailed out. We'll get together afterwards and figure out a game plan."

"Sounds great! Except the part about my cell." Alex scrunched her face as she spoke.

Chapter 12

Monday evening found Alex and Tom at her place in front of the fireplace, talking and waiting for Cat to show up. Alex was out on bail. Her bakery was still closed pending the outcome of the investigation. Tom was in hot water over his possible involvement with a murder suspect. Rumors aren't facts, so therefore there was no grounds to suspend or penalize him, so Detective Baker had stated and his boss agreed, for the present. Cliff was mad but so what. He was still partnered with Baker and that was that, for now.

Tom took a sip of his drink and looked at Alex. "I'd like to ask a question if you don't mind. I'd also like to get an honest answer."

"Sure. Go for it." She smiled.

"Did you only agree to dinner the other night to get information?" Tom asked. He hesitated briefly to check his voice. "Was everything just an act to get me on your side?"

"That's two questions." Alex tilted her head for a second and then got up from her end of the couch and walked over to his. She bent over and stared deep into his brown eyes. She pressed her one hand against the back of the couch to the left of his head, she cupped the side of his face with her other hand. She leaned down and kissed him sensuously on the lips for quite a long time. When she finished, she stood up, and returned to her end of the couch. As she regained her breath she plopped down with one leg resting on the couch cushions and asked, "What do you think?"

"That was wonderful. Now, I don't want to hurt your feelings, but I really need to hear you answer my questions vocally. I don't want any misunderstandings." He replied with an intense look on his face. He leaned toward her as he continued. "Alex, I don't believe in playing games with matters close to the heart."

She relaxed at his statement. "Good. I don't believe in playing games in that area either. I honestly wanted to go to dinner with you. I was quite serious in what happened afterwards. I'd be lying if I didn't admit to feeling some qualms on the way back to my place though. As I said at dinner, it's been some time since I've been with a man. Dating was never my forte. And now with AIDs and such around, I'm almost petrified about getting involved." She blushed as she continued, "but, I feel a definite possibility exists with you. This thing with us has popped up in turbo speed. I did plan on asking you some questions about Mr. Abrahms, but that was far from being the main reason I went out with you."

Tom smiled sincerely at Alex as he grabbed for her sock foot. He gently massaged it. "Yes, I believe a definite possibility exists for you and me and yes, I agree about the speed of this thing. I've heard of ….'love' at first sight, but did not believe it." A serious tone entered his voice as he continued. "However, we must clear you first. I almost forgot to tell you something. On the way over here, I took a drive past your store. I noticed your van was missing. Did you know about that?"

"Yes, I know it's gone. Cat has it. She's helping her brother move some furniture or something. Is that a problem?" Alex asked with worry and apprehension apparent on her face and in her voice. "No one said we couldn't use the van."

Tom raised his hands in a calming fashion. "It's okay. I was just curious, that's all."

"Speaking of Cat, I wonder where she is. She was supposed to be here over an hour ago. She always calls when she's running late."

"Maybe, she's tied up or forgot. Or maybe, she can't find her phone. Who knows?"

"No, this isn't like her. Half hour late is the max. If she doesn't have her cell phone for some reason, there is one in the van. I'll try her phone first and then I'll see if I have her brother's number in my phone or elsewhere. I know she wanted to be here tonight. She was excited about her scenario and wanted to be here to see your reaction to it. I'll just try her number quick." Alex reached for her phone. "Maybe she got a flat tire or something and didn't realize the time."

Just as Alex started dialing Cat's number, her house phone rang. "Speak of the devil, that's probably her." She picked up the phone and said a hearty hello and waited for Cat to speak, but it wasn't her. "Oh, hi Toni." She spoke with Toni for a few minutes and agreed that she could help her out in two weeks. No sooner did she hang up and the phone rang again. Alex answered this time a little more cautiously, "Hello?" Then, "Hello? Hello? Anybody there?" She noticed Tom's posture stiffen up as she contemplated hanging up.

"Wait! Wait!......," a voice floated from a distance. The sound of the phone banging around came over the phone. "Sorry, I dropped you on the floor." A voice spoke closer to the phone. "Alex, is this you?"

"Yeah?"

"You're okay?"

"Yes. Why wouldn't I be? Is this Jo-Jo?" Alex sensed a wave of concern, surprise, excitement, and relief charge though the phone with Jo-Jo's voice.

"Yes, it is. Man, you really had me worried there for a minute Alex." Jo-Jo exhaled noisily.

Confused, Alex tried to make sense of Jo-Jo. "What are you talking about?"

"Rick just ran in here a minute ago and told me he saw your van out by Sullivan Road."

"Yeah. So what?"

"Oh, man! Didn't anyone call you yet?"

"About what for Pete's sake?"

"Your van, Alex. It's been totaled!"

"What?! Are you sure?" Alex turned pale and grabbed the kitchen counter for support. Tom jumped up and was at her side instantly. He cocked his ear close to hers so he could listen in.

"Well, not one hundred percent." Jo-Jo responded. "Rick ran in a minute ago and told me that he thought he saw your van being pulled back onto the road. It looked like it had run off the road and over the embankment on that corner out near the creek. Know where I mean?"

Alex felt her legs start to fail her. Tom reached for the phone and pulled out a chair for Alex to sit in. "Mrs. Hentzel?"

"Yes. Who's this?"

"Detective Baker. Could I please speak to your husband?"

Tom heard the phone change hands. He asked Rick for all the details he could remember. He also asked Rick if he saw the driver of the van. Rick explained that he had been heading back into town from a business trip. As he approached town, he saw all kinds of emergency lights flashing up ahead. He slowed as he approached what looked like an accident. An officer motioned him to slow down and proceed onward. As he passed, he saw a tow truck pulling a van up onto Sullivan Road. He was pretty sure the van belonged to Alex's bakery. It looked like it had gone over the embankment. It was all smashed up. He thought about stopping and checking to see if he could help, but it looked like the emergency crew was just finishing up. Rick stated that he saw no driver. He also hadn't seen an ambulance. Rick was an experienced fireman. He told Tom that he just had a feeling that from the attitude of the guys working that no one had died, but that wasn't fact, it was supposition, and for his ears only.

Tom thanked Rick for the information. He hung up the phone and called the local hospital. A nurse in charge of admittance answered the phone. Tom identified himself and asked if the ambulance had shown up with a patient. After receiving an affirmative response, he asked the nurse for the patient's name. It was Cat alright. "Can you tell me if she was seriously hurt?"

Nurse Wilson hesitated, "It's not normal policy to give out information on a patient."

"I don't need any in-depth details. Can you just tell me if she's in reasonable good condition or if things are really serious." He sensed a continued reluctance on the nurse's part, so he added, "I won't tell anyone where I got my information." He looked at Alex as she anxiously examined his face for an answer. "A close friend of hers wants to come to the hospital. I want to know if I should use the siren or if I can travel at a safe speed. It wouldn't do any good to risk a possible accident, if it's not necessary."

Nurse Wilson thought it over briefly and with a shrug of her shoulders answered his request. "As far as I can tell, she'll be okay. She bawled out one of the ambulance attendants for accidentally running the stretcher into the corner of the wall as they navigated the hallway. She said she was banged up enough already and wasn't interested in any more damage. That girl's got a real temper and quite an unique vocabulary." The nurse chuckled good-humorously as she finished.

Alex felt the tension ease out of her body as she observed Tom on the phone. Apparently her friend had been injured but not near death. She got up quickly and prepared to leave. She was just locking up when Tom hung up the phone. Before she had a chance to question him, he relayed the pertinent information to her. A smile crossed her face as relief filled her body when he described Cat's actions with the attendant. "If she's hollering, than she must be alright."

As they got into Tom's Honda, Alex added, "I bet the attendant's name was Alvin Cahill."

Tom was intrigued. "Why's that?"

"Because Cat thinks he's the biggest klutz around. She can't believe he's actually allowed near injured people. He's also the only one I can think of that Cat would ream out in public." Alex's eyes took on a faraway look momentarily as she recalled an incident and chuckled.

Tom decided that he best get to the hospital as fast as legally possible, just in case something went wrong with Cat. He didn't think Alex could take another catastrophe. However, he realized that she was stronger than what he originally gave her credit for. He looked toward Alex, "Out with it. What's so funny?"

"Oh, it's something that Alvin did to Cat in high school. She's never forgiven him for it. The poor soul."

"Yeah? So what happened?"

"Well, he asked her to go to a dance with him. Against her better judgment, she accepted. They went out for a dance. Unfortunately, he had the proverbial two left feet. He crashed her into just about every couple around their area. Before she could get away, he had knocked her into the punch bowl. The table went over with them and covered them in punch. As she was getting up, he had the bright idea of trying to help her. He wasn't off the floor at the time and ended up pulling her back down. She fell on top of him in a most unflattering manner. The whole party was in an uproar. Everybody was laughing. She, of course, was humiliated. She ended up reaming poor Alvin up and down right there in front of everybody. Then she turned around, and stalked, er…, sloshed out of the room. I, being her best friend of course, ran after her. I found her in the bathroom trying to clean up. She asked me how I found her. I tried not to laugh as I informed her I just followed the trail of juice. There were little puddles of punch on the floor leading from the gym room to the bathroom. She was steamed. I couldn't stop laughing. She was completely covered in punch from top to bottom. It was even dripping from her hair. She was in the middle of yelling at me, with me still laughing of course, when she started to laugh also. Before I knew it, she was thanking me for being such a good friend with a quick hug. I screeched as the punch sunk into my outfit. I smacked her on the shoulder and called her a swine. We left the bathroom laughing."

"I found my date and we left the party. We left Alvin in the gym room dripping in punch. I'm glad we didn't live far from the school, because my date refused to let Cat into his car. He didn't want any punch to get all over his *precious* car seats and have anything get sticky. So I told him he could shove his car seats where the sun don't shine. I can't stand a man who puts a car, or its parts, above a person in need. We left old what's-his-name beside his car and set off for home. Cat was the butt of jokes for weeks afterwards."

"But that was how many years ago? Hasn't she forgiven him yet?"

"Yeah, right!" Alex rolled her eyes to the heavens. "We're talking major embarrassment. Cat's got a long memory when it comes to that department. She was super steamed at him. I don't think she talked to him the rest of the year."

"Incredible. I don't think I'll ever figure out the way a woman's mind works."

"Well, if you ask me. I think Cat was attracted to him at the time, and maybe she still is." Alex quickly turned her head toward the window as she felt a tear run down her face.

Alex thought she had turned before Tom saw the tear, but she hadn't. Tom was about to say something that would have sounded inane or clichéd, but his arrival at the hospital stopped him from doing so. He had barely stopped the car, when Alex flew out the door. He watched her wipe her face with her hands as she reached the door. He had only been a few steps behind her, but she was already at the admittance window asking about Cat. The nurse checked her computer and informed Alex that Cat was in room 305. Alex half ran to the elevators and punched the appropriate floor button. The doors were just about closed when Tom flew sideways between them. "Geesh, Alex! Give me a break. I'm concerned too!"

"Sorry." A red-faced Alex replied. "Sometimes my mind gets on a 'one thought' train track and shoves all others to the side."

"That could get you in trouble if you're not careful."

"I know. I know. It already has in the past to one degree or another." Alex answered back as the doors to the elevator opened.

Tom followed Alex as she shot down the hallway to room 305. He caught up to her as she stopped before the door to compose herself. Alex slowly opened the door and peered into the room. "Alex! Get your butt in here!" Cat roared to her friend.

"Cat! Are you okay?"

"Yeah! Relatively speaking. I'm okay. Just a tad sore." She said as she scrooched up a little higher on the mound of pillows behind her.

Alex rushed to help her friend get comfortable. Cat took one look at her friend's face. She could tell Alex had been crying. She took Alex's arm and gently squeezed it. Looking directly into Alex's eyes, she solemnly reassured her. "Really, Alex, I'm okay." Tom stuck his head in to ask if he was allowed to enter. Cat said sure and waved him into the room with her right hand. Alex stepped back to assess her friend's injuries. Cat was in a hospital gown. She was laying on the bed with the covers off to her side. A big bandage, with a gauze pad under it, was wrapped around Cat's forehead. The gauze pad was above her right eye. Cat's left hand was bandaged as well as her upper right leg. Her lower right leg was in a cast. She could see bruises over much of Cat's exposed body. Alex gave a sidelong glance toward Tom and covered Cat's lower body with a sheet. In response, Cat cocked her head and raised one eyebrow. With a grin on her face and a twinkle in her eye, she grabbed the sheet and pulled it up a little higher.

"You sure you're just a *tad* sore?"

"Oh, I'm positive." She said with a real mellow smile. "This place has some wonderful drugs. You'd be amazed at how well some of them work. Although, when the drugs wear off, I'm going to be one hurtin' puppy."

"What the heck happened, Cat?" Alex asked with a sudden fury. Her friend was hurt and she was furious.

"I don't know if I can remember everything. Some things are a little hazy." She hesitated as she noticed Tom reach for his pen and pad.

"Do you mind?" Tom asked with a show of his hands and items.

"Go for it, detective."

"Why don't you start with you getting the van from the bakery." Tom suggested.

Cat took a minute to compile her thoughts. "The weather was nice, so I decided to forego my car and walk over to the bakery. I started the van and drove over to my brother's place. He had bought some new furniture earlier this week and he needed the van to help bring it home. Before we could pick it up, we needed to get rid of the old stuff. It was simple work, but very time consuming. When we were done, I realized I'd have to hurry to get to Alex's place. I knew I'd be about five minutes late, as per usual."

"I had a weird feeling when I turned onto Sullivan Road that I was being followed. I noticed a brown car right behind me. I pulled off to buy a soda at McPherson's to see what the car did. It went by and I realized it was a two-toned brown car. It reminded me of the car that was at the bakery when you were attacked. I thought I was just being paranoid. There must be lots of two-toned brown cars around. The car seemed to pass by without hesitation, so I shook off my paranoia. I got back into the van and headed toward your place." She nodded to Alex. "After about a mile, I noticed the car off to the side of the road. It was at a mailbox and the person was leaning toward the box. I assumed the person was just getting their mail. I remember laughing at myself and thinking I must be watching too much television. Then the car pulled back onto the road and came up behind me again. Within minutes, it started ramming the van. I tried to get away, but couldn't. Soon, it was alongside of me." Alex heard the frustration in her friend's voice.

"Anyway, it wasn't long before the car shoved me over the embankment." She hesitated briefly. "Now here, I'm a little fuzzy. I remember getting knocked around quite a bit. I didn't quite lose consciousness, however, I don't believe I was totally there either. If you know what I mean, it felt kind of like in a twilight zone. I could feel the blood running down my face, but I couldn't get the energy up to remove it right away. I was kind of taking a mental check of my injuries. I'm not sure, mind you, but I believe I remember someone coming down the embankment and looking toward me. I'm sure it was a man and he seemed to be smiling."

"Smiling? Are you sure?" Alex gasped.

"No. I'm not sure, but almost. I remember being surprised at this guy's reaction. I was incredulous. This ass just ran me off the road and he seemed happy. Then I believe he said, 'Gotcha bitch.'" Cat threw her hands up in disgust and ire.

"Gotcha bitch? What is going on here?" Alex spit out in irate confusion as she looked from Cat to Tom. "You mean this person just walked over to make sure you were hurt?"

"Or dead." Tom interjected seriously. He looked at the two astonished faces turned his way. "Think about it for a minute. Cat was your hair over your face?"

"Yes."

"I may be wrong, Cat, but I believe your attack may have been an accident."

"Accident?!" both Cat and Alex huffed.

Cat answered back emphatically, "If you ask me, it was done on purpose. Weren't you listening to what I just said?"

Alex paled as his comment sunk in. She tapped Cat on the shoulder lightly a few times. "Wait a minute Cat. I think I know where he's heading. It *was* an accident but done on purpose."

Cat screwed up her face as she looked at Alex, but winced and stopped. "I'm the one that got bumped on the head, but I think you're the one that's suffering the effects."

"Just listen for a sec. The 'accident' was that you were hurt and not me. You and I look a lot alike. Lots of people think that we're twins. This person thought you were me, and attacked you. For some reason, someone wants me out of the way. Unfortunately, you were hurt instead. I'm really sorry."

"Knock it off, Alex. You're not responsible for this jerk. I'm okay and that's what matters. Maybe you can use your 'untimely death' to your advantage. Everybody thinks you're dead."

"No, they don't." Alex said and related everything about Jo-Jo's and Rick's earlier call.

"It would have been a perfect plan, except too many people know the truth already. The hospital and ambulance crew probably have talked to others by now also. This whole town has probably heard by now."

"You're probably right. Now what?" Alex asked looking at Tom.

He glanced down at his tablet and then up at Cat. "You said the car that hit you was a two-toned brown car. Now that you had some time to

87

think about this car, do you recognize it from anywhere?"

"I'm not sure. But, as I said, it looked like the car that was at the bakery when Alex was attacked. It also looked like…." She mumbled something low and then squinted suspiciously toward Tom and shut up.

Tom was surprised to put it lightly. "What's wrong? Why are you looking at me like that?"

Cat remained quiet until Alex spoke up. "What Cat? What did it look like?"

"Have you told him my scenario for your problems?" She asked Alex.

"No. It's your scenario. I knew that you wanted to see Tom's face when you told him because…." She also turned to Tom and shut up.

With irritation oozing out of him, Tom exasperatingly growled, "Out with it! I don't care who does it, but one of you better start."

Alex inclined her head to Cat. Cat shrugged her shoulders briefly and winced again. She opened her mouth to start but shut it quickly. She decided to ask Tom a question first. "How long have you been partnered with Detective Taylor?"

Somewhat confused by the seeming change-of-subject, Tom responded "just a couple of days. Why?"

Alex looked at him in surprise. "I wondered about you two. There didn't seem to be any working chemistry between you. Why so recent?"

"My regular partner, John Whitamyer, had an attack of appendicitis. He'll be out of commission for about two weeks, depending on how he heals. When the call came in about Mr. Abrahms, Cliff and I were both available and were partnered up for this case."

"Why was he on his own?"

Tom quietly looked at Cat for a short time. "Before I answer any more questions, why don't you tell me your scenario Cat."

"Sure." She bobbed her head up and down slightly while looking at Tom through squinted eyes. As she weighed her opinion about him silently, Tom was starting to feel funny under her look. Cat gave a final nod of her head and winced once more, "At first, I thought that you two were in it together, but now I'll accept that he's on his own. At least for now."

Tom was baffled. He thought maybe Cat conked her head harder than anyone thought. "You've lost me. In on what together?"

Cat looked directly into his eyes and stated flatly. "I think Detective Taylor is behind everything."

"What?" Tom was nonplussed.

"You wanted to know what I thought and I'm telling you. Now just shut up for a minute." Cat reacted defensively. Alex raised her eyebrows in surprise but remained quiet. "Alex and I were talking about the murder and her attacks. We realized that you were the only one who knew where she'd be at each time of attack. Alex felt you were innocent. She reasoned that you could have told your partner the same information. We also weren't sure if the dead guy was the same person who killed Alex's sister. Here again, we reasoned that maybe one of you two, or *for now*, only Taylor, wanted Abrahms dead. We know that *our* Abrahms killed more than just Alex's sister. Maybe he killed someone y'all loved too. You guys are in the position to frame Alex. We didn't know if she was the planned target or just one of convenience. We know that *she* is innocent, so the real killer is still loose somewhere."

"That's it? How in the world did you come up with this idea?" He quickly breathed out.

"There's one other thing. I saw a two-toned brown car leave the bakery when I arrived. I was also attacked by a two-toned brown car. Your partner, Detective Taylor, drives such a car." She answered smugly.

"So what? As you yourself has admitted, there must be lots of two-toned brown cars around."

"See, I told you Alex! He's not going to believe us! They protect their own, no matter how slimy they are." She waved her arms in the air and gestured with her hands as she shouted to Alex until the pain registered through her anger and commanded her to stop.

"Just hold on a minute Cat. I'm not slam-dunking anything. I just want to be sure of what you're saying. Accusing an officer of murder is a very serious offense. I believe that you are jumping to conclusions. No evidence supports your theory. Let me assure you though, if Taylor is guilty, he will be brought to justice. Let me state for the record though, that I have had no part in *this*, or any other murder. I also don't believe Cliff's played any part either. I might have given Cliff Alex's expected locations for when she was attacked, but I'm not sure. I sure didn't do it so that he could harm her." Tom slapped his hand down on his leg and glared at Cat.

Alex noticed that tempers were flaring pretty high. "Whoa, anybody notice how warm it's getting in here? Why don't we all take a deep breath and chill for a moment?"

Tom agreed. He had a lot of pent up emotions and yelling at these women wasn't the way to clear his head. He got up and announced he was going to get something to drink. He asked if either of them wanted a drink, only Alex said yes. After Tom left the room, Cat turned to Alex, "I hope you're right about Tom's innocence. We just showed him our hand."

Alex glared at her friend. "Yes. I'm sure. We need some professional help and Tom's it." She increased the intensity of her stare and asked, "Agreed?"

Cat refused to drop her eyes and stared right back. "Agreed."

Tom returned with the drinks. When everyone was settled once again, they decided to get down to making a game plan. Tom agreed to check out his partner's car and whereabouts at the necessary times and to try to keep an open mind. Alex asked Tom what other names were on the computer readout that Cliff had gotten on Matthew Abrahms. He looked at her dumbfounded. He didn't realize until now how much he had let his emotions disrupt his professionalism. He was starting to feel like a "Keystone Cop." He was irritated as he admitted to them that circumstances prevailed such that he did not get a look at the readout. He stated that he would swing by the office tonight, review the case, and see in which direction the case is going or should be going. Cat was expected to stay in the hospital for at least one more day, but perhaps two. Her job for now was to heal and keep her ears open. Tom would contact Alex tomorrow and they would decide where to go from there. Alex and Tom said their good-byes to Cat and left the hospital.

Once they arrived at Alex's house, Tom insisted on checking out her house before he left for the police station. Once he ascertained that no one was in her house, he asked her to make sure she locked up tightly after he left. He made her promise to call him if anything out of the ordinary happened. "Even if you find out that only a tree branch is rubbing your window, you call me."

"I will." She assured him. "What number do you want me to use first?"

Tom clarified his numbers. "I always have my cell phone with me, but if you have trouble reaching me or it's an emergency, just call 9-1-1." He kissed her a quick good-bye and left.

Chapter 13

When Tom arrived at the police station, he looked for Cliff's car. Tom wanted to fulfill his promise of checking out Cliff's car, but he didn't honestly believe that he'd find anything. Tom found the car parked in the corner of the parking lot, facing a wall. He casually walked over to see if the car had any kind of damage. A green van was parked beside Cliff's car, blocking Tom's view of it. As he passed the van, Tom's senses snapped to attention. The front left side of the car was crumpled up. There were scratches all along the driver's side of the car. Tom was shocked. His anger fueled him as he hustled into the station. He threw the door open with such force that it slammed into the wall behind it. The few people in the room turned in his direction with first alertness for danger and then irritation before returning to work. Tom looked around futilely for Cliff first, and then spun around to look for the officer in charge. He zoned in on Officer Bernelli and asked about Detective Taylor's location. The officer informed him that Cliff had gone for dinner. Tom picked up a phone and dialed quickly.

"Crime lab. Brian here."

"Hey, Brian. I'm glad to hear your voice. Can you escape the lab for a short time?"

Brian scanned his desk briefly. "Sure. Nothing doing this moment that can't wait. What's up?" Tom sketched in some background on the case to Brian before explaining about finding Cliff's car damaged.

"Can you go up, take pictures, go over the car in general, and collect any evidence? You know, just do your thing?"

"I heard rumors that there's some bad blood between you two guys, Tom. Do you really think Detective Taylor is guilty of the attack on this woman?"

"I don't know what to think anymore. What I do know is that his car is damaged. Cliff's out, so I can't ask him about it. He could be anywhere for dinner and I'm not chasing his butt around town. There looks to be some paint on the car that appears close to the color of Ms. Applecake's van. There could be another explanation, but for now I would like the car examined and we'll go from there. You're an impartial person and therefore the perfect one to do it." Brian agreed and hung up the phone to get started.

Tom then headed for his desk to look at the case file. He looked through the file once and then twice. He couldn't find any computer readout pertaining to Mr. Abrahms or his alleged victims. He looked over the rest of his desk and then turned to Cliff's. He was perplexed and was fast on his way to irritation. He booted up the computer and requested the background check for a Mr. Matthew Abrahms. While he waited for the slow running computer to answer his request, he started to review the case file again. He tried to keep an open mind so as to be as unbiased as possible. He knew that he'd arrest anyone who ended up being the guilty one or ones. He might not enjoy the end result but so be it. Tom had just reviewed a few pages when the computer showed him Abrahm's background. He scanned over the the usual personal information. As he reviewed the man's criminal past, he quickly stopped and swore. This man was a real piece of work. He had a history of drunk driving and drunk crashing. The DUIs started back at least seventeen years ago. There were five victims listed under the DUIs: Applecake, Duncan, Engle, Martin, and Wolf. Three of the victims died in the same crash: Applecake, Engle, and Martin. The other two were killed in another crash. Each time Abrahms had gotten off on a technicality.

Abrahms also had a history of date rape offenses. The date rapes took place around ten years ago. There were three arrests, but no convictions. Each time something had popped up that caused the case to be dropped. The three names listed were as follows: Lerew, Maloy, and Taylor. There was nothing new on the record for the past eight years. That alone was strange, someone with his history would not stop his crimes. So what happened? Tom stared at the last victim's name again. He wondered if his temporary partner could be related. Depending on the answer, Cat's scenario had some definite possibilities. Tom puffed his cheeks and slowly blew the air out, he did not like where this case was headed. However, he did know one thing for sure. He had to find Cliff and ask him some questions.

Tom was just reaching Officer Bernelli's desk again when Cliff came walking through the doors. "Where have you been Cliff?" Tom quietly asked.

"At the Laredo, having dinner. Why?"

"I was reviewing the Abrahms case and I have a few questions to ask you."

"Sure." Cliff responded and headed towards their desks. Tom followed. Since the station was almost totally empty, Tom didn't suggest going anywhere private like an interrogation room.

"First, I'd like to know what your feel for this case is."

"I already told you. I think Alex Applecake killed Abrahms. I think she had help or conspired with another or others to kill the man."

"How do you figure?"

"I didn't get a chance to tell you that I checked into the will of the deceased. I found out that the bride and groom each had a will leaving all their possessions to the other in the case of his or her death. There was also a life insurance policy, but only one. The policy is in the name of one Matthew Alonzo Abrahms. There is only one beneficiary: Bevirly Jordan. This policy is for the amount of five hundred thousand dollars. Bevirly Jordan is an old friend of Caitlin Farrell. She in turn is an old friend of Alex Applecake. I believe we should look to prove a case of conspiracy between these three people. I believe Ms. Jordan informed Ms. Farrell of Mr. Abrahms allergy to penicillin. I don't know who came up with the actual murder plan, but that's not important right now. I believe that Ms. Farrell teamed up with Ms. Applecake to make the murder weapon. Ms. Jordan probably promised to share the life insurance money with them. Your friend, Ms. Applecake, probably had no problem going along with the plan. The man did kill her sister, after all. I also believe that the attacks on herself and on her house are just her cohorts trying to throw attention off of her. Did you notice that other than a few pieces missing, most of her stuff wasn't damaged, it looked as if it was just placed on the floor? They must think that we are dumb or can easily be persuaded to change our thinking. Didn't you ever wonder why she got involved with you? It lets her know what we are thinking and in what direction we are heading. If we find out anything possibly damaging, they will have the time to come up with a viable explanation. That's what I believe happened and that's what I'm going to prove. You best leave that lady alone."

Tom looked at Cliff for some time before supplying a response. "That's interesting. However, what…" The ringing of the telephone

95

interrupted his next question. It was Brian saying that he was done with Cliff's car. Tom thanked Brian and told him he would be down later for a report. Tom turned to Cliff and asked, "When was the last time you were in your car?"

Cliff was visibly confused at the quick change of subjects. "My car? This morning. I drove it into work and parked it in the lot. Why?"

"You haven't been near it all day?"

"No! Why?" Cliff narrowed his eyes with suspicion.

"Where have you been since your interrogation of Ms. Applecake? What have you been doing?"

"I've been working on this case and a couple others that are open yet. This isn't our only case you know. I'm sure the families involved in the two burglary cases we're working would like some progress done. Since you don't seem to be working on anything but courting our number one murder suspect, I thought I'd better get working on what needs to be done. I noticed you helped make sure she made bail. I won't ask where you went after she left the station house, because I believe I already know. You went to her house. To be honest, I'm surprised you're here. Didn't she invite you to stay over tonight? What's wrong, did she get all the information that she could out of you and throw you out for the night?" Cliff scoffed at Tom.

"Enough, Clifford! Just shut up! You have no idea what's going on." Tom spit in Cliff's face. He realized he better back away or else he was going to deck this jerk. His job was too important to him to throw it away on such a Neanderthal. Tom also realized that he missed his regular partner John more than he thought. His old partner and him made a great pair. If one ever lost his temper, the other was able to stabilize the situation, and thankfully neither lost their temper very often. This partnership started off on the wrong foot and was just getting worse. It would be risky to try to get Cliff off this case, if not impossible. Cliff would make sure the captain heard about him and Alex. The captain would, in all probability, take Tom off the case and pair Cliff with someone else. Cliff and his new partner would make sure that Alex got arrested and possibly indicted for the murder. Tom could not risk that. He had to stay on this case to exonerate Alex. Tom took one look at Cliff and decided that he was just playing into his hands. Cliff was really enjoying this and it was high time to turn the tables.

Tom lightened his voice as he asked Cliff, "So Cliff, you're telling me you don't know about your car being in a wreck?"

Well, that did it. Cliff's eyes got big and round as he exploded, "What?" In the space of a heartbeat, Cliff was out of his seat and heading for the door.

Tom followed closely. He wanted to see Cliff's face when he surveyed the damage. To Tom's surprise, once they reached the lot, Cliff stopped short. "What's going on here Tom?"

"What do you mean?"

"Where's my car? If this is a joke, you're not funny and I'm not laughing." Cliff continued to survey the lot as he spoke. "Oh! There it is. Why did you move it?" He asked as he turned and walked toward the car.

"Move it? I didn't move it."

"Well, someone did! I parked near the entrance this morning." As he rounded the van, he shouted "MY CAR!! What happened?"

Tom knew that Cliff was innocent of any wrong doing in the murder case as he watched Cliff jump up and down in anger. Cliff hadn't known of the damage, Tom was sure of it. He knew that Cliff couldn't act worth a darn. The man was never given any undercover work, because he couldn't act himself out of the proverbial paper bag. Cliff turned on Tom with a barely contained rage. "What's going on here

97

Baker? If you know anything, now's the time to give."

"I'm not really sure. I figure that this car was used in an attack on Alex's bakery van. It chased the van and then pushed it over the embankment on Sullivan Road."

Cliff just stared at him for a moment. "How do you know this?" Almost as an afterthought, he added, "Was anyone hurt?"

Tom suggested that they head on down to Brian's lab and check on the report. By the time they reached the lab, Tom had filled Cliff in on the accident. Brian gave them the nutshell version of his findings. Cliff's car had been used in the attack on the van. Since it's an older car, it was easy for the perpetrator to unlock the car and by-pass the ignition system. Cliff's fingerprints were in the car, of course, as were a few others that are unidentified. Brian thought the unidentified ones probably belonged to some of Cliff's friends or family because of their locations. The steering wheel, door handle, gear shift, and anywhere else someone would touch to drive were either wiped clean or else the person wore gloves or both. They picked up a copy of the report and headed back upstairs.

"Why did you look at my car, Tom?" Cliff quietly inquired.

"Because a witness reported seeing a car like yours at the scene of the accident and asked that I check into it. And I did. You know the rest, Cliff."

"Yes and no. Who was the witness?"

"Let me hold on that a minute. I need to ask you where you were on the Sunday morning when Alex was attacked."

"What are you implying here?" Cliff inquired heatedly.

"Nothing, as of yet. I just would like an answer to my question, please."

"Not until you explain why."

"Okay. A car fitting your description was seen leaving the bakery at the time of Alex's attack. I'd like to know where you were. You can either answer my question here or we can talk to the chief in the morning."

"You actually believe that I'm behind the attacks? That's ludicrous." Cliff shouted, a vein bulged on the side of his forehead. "That cake lady must really have you wrapped around her little finger."

"I'll hold my response to that until after I hear your answer."

"I don't believe this," he huffed.

Tom continued to stare at Cliff and remain silent. He was beginning to think "the man doth protest too much."

Cliff exhaled noisily. "I was at church. There are plenty of people who can vouch for me, I can assure you. The service ran late. There was a youth spaghetti dinner afterwards. I helped in the clean-up when the dinner was over. I didn't leave until around three o'clock."

"Did you notice anything different about your car or its location?"

"Not really. I had accidentally left it unlocked, but it was roughly where I remembered parking it." He was quiet and thoughtful. "Do you really think it was used both times?"

"Yes, I do believe it's possible. Anything is possible."

"Not necessarily anything. I didn't kill the man. Why do you suppose my car was used?"

"My guess would be to set you up." Tom responded.

"I believe we're back to my conspiracy theory. Only amateurs would believe that using my car would screw up the investigation."

"Why wouldn't it? At the least, it throws a wrench into the investigation. It ties you into the attacks on Alex. Your job gives you the knowledge to kill anyone you want and in any way you want. So there's your means and opportunity. You also can adjust any and all evidence that's found or at least try. Your car was used twice, and you didn't even know it. Most people wouldn't remember exactly who was

99

at church and who wasn't. You could have left for a while, done the deed, and returned to the church. Unless there's someone who knows exactly where you were every moment of the times in question, your alibis are sketchy at best." Tom hesitated to make sure that he had Cliff's attention and then continued slowly. "And you also have one heck of a motive."

"What possible motive could I have?" Cliff sputtered.

Tom watched Cliff turn pale as he answered him. "I couldn't find the report that you mentioned earlier in the case file, the one with Abrahms' criminal past. So I ran a new one." Tom stared hard at Cliff. "Abrahms raped a woman named Taylor and got away with it. I did some checking and believe the woman was your sister. That's an excellent motive for anyone."

"Yes, you're absolutely correct on that one." Cliff hissed.

"You see, Cliff, you caused me to doubt you when you didn't come clean with me. You have the same motive as Ms. Applecake, the victim hurt one of your family. You seem hell bent on her being the murderer, even to the point of closing your mind to any other person. Someone else might even think that you are acting the way you are because you did, in fact, kill Abrahms. You need a scapegoat and Alex is it. With your car involved, you're more of a suspect than she is. But that's exactly why I don't think you're involved. You're not skilled enough to use your own car and pass it off as if someone stole it." Cliff sputtered and fumed as Tom continued. "You should have told the chief and excused yourself from this case. At the very least, you should have told me about the connection between you and Abrahms."

"You're right, I should have said something. But I knew if I did, I wouldn't be on this case. I wanted on this case Tom. Now we're kind of even. Both of us are a problem if we screw up, because neither of us should be on this case. I think my scenario still works though. Maybe the players aren't all correct, but I think something is there to work on."

"Then work on it. If you can prove your case, then I'll support you. Fair warning though, I'm going to check up on a few things to cover my butt. I'm either going to clear you or convict you."

"That's fair enough." Cliff stated with a shake of his head. "Don't waste too much time though, because I didn't do it."

"Then let's get this case sorted out and find out who did." Tom stated with resolve.

Chapter 14

Alex was wondering when Tom was going to call. She had the cat and fish fed and was antsy to get started on the day. She thought about calling him at the station, but didn't want to get him into any more trouble than he already was in. She decided to visit Cat at the hospital. If Tom called, he could talk to her answering machine or try her cell.

On the way to the hospital, Alex decided to stop at the reception hall and see if anyone could remember anyone near the cake before the guests arrived. She pulled up to "Jacob's Hope" and went to the office. She knew the manager of this hall from years of supplying cakes for many of the weddings that took place here. As soon as she entered the door, Veronica Waters saw her and waved her into the manager's personal office. Veronica was a delightful person to her friends but a slave driver to her employees. She made up for her lack of height, she being only five foot tall, with attitude. Veronica was in her mid-to-late fifties, however, one would guess her to be no older than in her mid-forties. She always seemed to be of sound mind and dress. Running the type of business that she did, she was a woman of order. However, it was rumored that her pickiness and demand for order caused her first two husbands to go nuts. Speculation was rampant that her third man was going the way of her first two.

"Sorry to hear of your troubles, Alex. I know that you had nothing to do with the....ah...'occurrence'."

"Thanks Veronica," Alex sat in one of the chairs facing the desk, "I was wondering if you could help me. My shop is closed for the time being and I want to get it open. So I'm trying to help the cops solve the 'occurrence' as you called it."

"How can I help you?"

"I was wondering if you could tell me who all was here to help get the hall ready for the wedding."

"Sure. Except one thing Alex, the hall was decorated the night before the wedding by the wedding party. Minimum crew was here until the caterer showed up. In fact, that morning only old Mrs. Johnson was here. She opened up and turned the power on. I called in to make sure that there were no problems. Mrs. Johnson assured me all was well. The catering people had just showed up and were doing their thing. I was running late that morning. I didn't arrive until about one half hour before the people were to show up. The wedding cake was already here."

"Can you tell me who the caterer was?"

"Sure. It was Connie's Catering."

"Thanks. Do you remember seeing anyone that seemed out of the ordinary here when you arrived? Any strange cars?"

"No, nothing I can recall. Nobody was leaving when I showed up. As for strange cars, who can really tell with all the out-of-towners and such who come to weddings. The caterer was already here, as I already told you. I can't even tell you how many of the cars in the lot belonged to her people." She threw her right hand into the air and swirled it in a circle in the air. "I'm sorry I'm not much help."

"That's alright. Can you tell me how I can reach Mrs. Johnson?"

"Now, there I can help. She's out front doing a little extra cleaning. Feel free to ask her whatever you want. That is, if she wants to answer. I, of course, can't speak for her."

"Of course, I understand what you're saying. Thanks Veronica!" She started to leave when she stopped and turned to ask one more thing, "Oh, yeah, one more thing?"

"Go for it!"

"Did you see the cake?"

"Yeah, I just told you it was here when I got here."

"I know. What I mean is, did you take a close look at it? I know you usually check out the cake and see what all the bride picked out."

Veronica seemed to hesitate briefly before answering. In a reserved tone, she looked at her desk as she stated, "Yeah, I took a look."

"And? What did you think?"

"Well,….I don't mean to be rude…..but I thought it wasn't your best work."

"Come on, Veronica. I've known you for quite some time now and I've never known you to mince words. Neither one of us could be described as tactful. In fact, I believe you derive a sort of twisted pleasure from being rude. Now, please be blunt."

"Okay, you asked for it. It was really nice, the basic decorating was beautiful, except there seemed to be an awful lot of glitter on the cake. I was going to ask you if you were trying a new person out or what. But I know you usually do all the wedding cakes yourself. I've seen your work and it's usually gorgeous, unless the bride picks out a weird or gaudy design. In those cases, it's not your fault if the cake looks odd, it's the bride's. I've seen some of your past glitter cakes. Your touch is usually light and delicate. This cake almost looked like you dumped the glitter on it. I thought it was gross. But, I just figured the bride must have really liked the stuff and let it go at that."

"Really?! It was that thick?"

A look of surprise crossed Veronica's face. "Well, maybe I'm exaggerating a wee bit. But the glitter was kind of thick. I know glitter's supposed to be for effect only. I would guess that the glitter was about one-sixteenth of an inch thickness over the entire cake." Veronica raised her one hand into the air. She separated her thumb and forefinger about one-sixteenth inch to show Alex roughly the thickness of the glitter. "I would think that that would taste a bit weird, almost like a mouth of short dog hair or something." She made a nasty face as she finished speaking.

Alex's mouth dropped open and her eyes widened. "But, that can't be. I'm the one who put the glitter on the cake. You're right, I only used a little. It was all over the cake, but only very lightly."

"I saw what I saw, Alex." Veronica stated sternly forthwith.

"I know. I don't doubt you. Now, I just have to figure out who put the extra glitter on the cake. I think I'd better get started on that immediately. You've been a big help Veronica. I owe you one….no at least two." Alex gave a quick hurried wave of her hand and shut the door.

Alex headed to the reception room to look for Mrs. Johnson. As soon as she opened the door, Alex caught sight of the older woman in the back corner ot the room. People guessed Mrs. Johnson's age to be in the mid-seventies. She would neither confirm nor deny any guess. The lady was not known to be particularly kind to people outside her family. To her family though, she was extremely generous and loving. Originally, she had stood somewhere around five foot five inches tall, however osteoporosis had caused her to stoop over and robbed her of about five inches. She had wrinkles all over that caused some to guess her to be approaching ninety. Mrs. Johnson was a hard worker, maybe not the fastest anymore, but was truly dedicated. As long as people could remember, she always seem to wear basically the same clothes. People joked that she must had gotten a good deal years ago and bought about a hundred of the same outfit. This way her color-blindness would not cause her to clash her colors. Each article of clothing was the same color. She never changed her style of outfit except on Sunday for church. And there again, it was always the same, plus or minus a jacket depending on the weather. Alex observed the old lady counting plates or something as she approached her. She made some noise as she crossed the room so she wouldn't scare her when she spoke. "Mrs. Johnson?"

The old lady held one finger up in the air to motion to Alex to wait one minute. After said time, she raised her face toward Alex, "Yes."

"If it's alright with you, I'd like to ask you some questions."

She looked toward the direction from which Alex had come with weariness and replied simply, "Yes."

Alex smiled, "I cleared it with Veronica. She said as long as you agreed, we could talk."

Mrs. Johnson gave a small smile, pulled out a chair, and motioned for Alex to do likewise. "What would you like to ask?"

"Do you remember the day that Mr. Abrahms died?"

"Remember?" She huffed. "Who can forget?" Her eyes narrowed as she looked Alex up and down, "They say that you killed that man. Did you?"

"No ma'am. I definitely did not. But, I'm trying to find out who did. I was wondering if you can remember if anything out of the ordinary happened that day? Or maybe something that just piqued your interest?"

"No. I can't really say anything was different than usual, at least that is, until the man died. That was pretty unique. I haven't lived here all my life, but I do know that the dead man was no good. I've heard stories on that one, I have. I just thank the Lord that I never got the chance to meet him. I know Bevirly slightly, and I must say that she can do a lot better than him"

Alex was getting disheartened, this was harder than she thought it would be. Her one good lead had fizzled out. She thanked Mrs. Johnson and got up to leave.

"Didn't you notice anything when you returned that Saturday?" the old lady queried.

Alex stopped short. Puzzled, she turned to look at the woman. "What do you mean? When I returned? Returned when?"

"That same day. You came back to add something to the cake."

Alex felt an arctic chill course through her body. "I didn't come back Mrs. Johnson."

"Yes, you did. I saw you." She adamantly replied.

"I think we'd better sit back down. Would you please run through your day with me? Start at the time when we first met that morning."

The lady looked Alex up and down, not sure what to think of this young whippersnapper who didn't remember things that she did. "Okay, but this is going to take some time. Let's go to the employee lounge. The chairs there are a lot more comfortable than these."

Alex agreed and let her lead the way. Once they were settled with coffee for Mrs. Johnson and Pepsi for Alex, the old woman started her tale. She said that after she had indicated to Alex where the cake was to go, she had watched from afar. She saw Alex and Cat set the cake up, arrange the flowers, take the pictures, and leave. She said that she returned to her usual duties after they had gone.

A short time later, she heard a door open. She could tell it was the door to the hall that opened directly to the parking lot. It has a weird squeak when it opens. She remembers turning around to see who came in the door. She was in the corner farthest from the cake. She couldn't remember exactly what odd thing she was doing at the time. It was the catering people. They had showed up at the back and the door they needed to use was locked. They asked if she would open it for them. She went to the back and unlocked the door and then returned to her corner. She heard the door squeak open again. This time when she looked up, she saw "Alex" come in and go directly to the cake. She

107

observed this person taking something from her pocket and acting like she was shaking salt all over the cake. Mrs. Johnson knew it couldn't be salt, but she didn't know what it was. That was just the best way to describe the action the person was doing.

"I hollered, 'What are you doing? And you answered that you forgot to add some additional glitter earlier. You said the bride wanted lots of glitter. And no matter what, the customer is always right, no matter how wrong they might be. And then you said good-by and left. Shortly thereafter, Ms. Waters showed up. Do you want me to go on?"

"No. You can stop now."

"Don't you remember coming back? What did you do? Hit your head or something?"

Alex almost told her that's exactly what did happen, except someone else did the hitting. "I didn't come back after the original cake delivery. Are you sure it was me? Did you get a clear look?"

The lady's eyes squinted dangerously. "Are you accusing me of lying? My vision is still twenty-twenty."

Alex backpedaled a bit. "No, I'm not accusing you of anything. I'm just trying to figure out what exactly happened. I didn't mean to offend you. It's just that, maybe the lighting was off or something, and you just assumed it was me. I mean, who else would be going to the cake and adding glitter to it. Do you kind of understand where I'm going here?" Before the lady could say anything, Alex continued. "I mean if the lady didn't know you were here, she was probably startled when you spoke. She realized that you thought she was me and just played along. Did you see her clearly or maybe she was in shadow? Could it be she turned slightly from you so you couldn't see her face clearly? There are quite a few people who are roughly my build and shape." Alex took a breath, "Is any of this possible or isn't it?" She felt her body tense as she waited for an answer.

108

Mrs. Johnson's eyes took on a far-away look. Alex decided that silence was the best policy at the moment. Patience wasn't one of Alex's virtues. Just as she was about to say something, the old woman's head started to slowly bob up and down. "You might have something there, young lady. Now that I think back on it, you're right. Whoever came in that time did turn slightly away. I was trying to get everything done before the people showed up for the reception, so I didn't really pay much attention to you...err...whoever when she came in. The lighting wasn't the best because the lights were on dim. I know the place real well. I don't like to see electricity wasted, so I don't turn the lights up high until I have to." Once again the older woman became quiet and introspective. After a few moments she continued, "The voice was also a wee bit muffled. I didn't give it another thought because it just wasn't any of my business. I guess I did assume it was you because there was no reason to think otherwise. The person acted like they knew exactly what they were doing. Who would have thought someone would kill the groom?"

"Nobody I know of, that's for sure. If you don't mind, let's see if we can pin down some details about the person. Are you positive it was a woman? Not a small man or man in drag?"

"It was a woman. I'm sure of it. I don't know of a man anywhere in these parts that could sound as close to you as this person did. The person who came in knew exactly where to go, they didn't hesitate like a stranger would. I believe you're looking for a woman of your basic body build. Her voice shouldn't be raspy or have any clear aberrations either."

Alex looked shrewdly at Mrs. Johnson. "You just *act* like a crotchety old woman who might be on the verge of losing it, but in reality you're very sharp. Why the act?"

With a chuckle she replied, "Because that's what people expect when they see me. I just give them what they already believe they know. This way nobody bugs me. I can do just about anything I want and nobody cares. People now days overlook the elderly. Just because my age is rising, my body is wearing, doesn't mean my mind is going."

Alex nodded up and down. "You're absolutely right. My grandmother says the same thing. I try not to stereotype older people, but sometimes I'm in such a hurry it happens anyway. Can you tell me anything else that might help. Like how the person was dressed?"

"Sorry. Similar to what you and your friend was wearing earlier that day. Similar to what a lot of you young people wear today. It wasn't outlandish or I'd of noticed."

"Okay. How about the vehicle? Did you get a look at how the person got here or left?"

"Again, I'm afraid that I can't help you. Since I thought it was you, I had no reason to look in the lot to see your vehicle. I don't usually check the lot anyway, because again its none of my business what people drive. I just returned to the job that was on hand and got ready for the horde of people to show."

"Can you pinpoint the exact time the person was here?"

She sighed quickly and raised her eyebrows. Once again an unfocused haze crossed Mrs. Johnson's eyes as she thought back to that particular day. "When did you leave?"

"Four o'clock."

"That's about what I had figured, so I can't be far off here with my calculations. The caterers came shortly after you, I'd say about five minutes later. That's four oh five. I went to unlock the door and then returned to my corner, say another five minutes in total. That's four ten. The person must have come through the door approximately three to five minutes later. Somewhere around four thirteen to four fourteen." She grinned at Alex while slightly nodding her head up and down.

"That's great, Mrs. Johnson. Veronica said she showed up about an half hour before the people. About four thirty. Does that sound accurate to you?"

"Yes, she's right." Mrs. Johnson said knowingly.

"You sound absolutely sure on that. Is there any particular reason you remember the time so well?"

"I'll say there is." She sniffed with indignation. "Just the week before, she bawled me out for being ten minutes late. That was the first time I have ever been late to work here. That Saturday, Mrs. Waters was real late. Normally, she's here at least two hours before the reception is to start, but that day she showed up only thirty minutes early. She came in here huffing and puffing all over the place. As soon as she arrived, I checked my watch. The next time she goes to yell at me for lateness, I plan on throwing that day in her face."

Alex chuckled. This lady was one interesting character. The one thing about Veronica that irritated Alex was that she sometimes treated her employees like peons. She would very much enjoy seeing Veronica's face when one of her employees had the audacity to return her fire. "Well, if you get fired after doing that, give me a call." Alex winked and thanked the older woman. After saying good-by, she headed on her way.

As Alex headed toward the hospital, she smiled. Now she knew a little of what happened. She felt good that she knew the scenario of "what" and "when" the crime happened. Now, all she had to do was figure out the "who" and if possible, the "why."

Chapter 15

As Alex approached Cat's hospital room, she started shaking her head and smiling. She could hear Cat arguing with someone in her room. Alex entered the room and was immediately drawn into the "conversation." Cat threw her hand toward the man standing beside her and screamed at her friend, "Can you believe this guy, Alex?"

"I don't know, Cat." Alex placatingly said. "Why don't you explain it to me?"

Cat glared at her friend and then hissed, "Don't you dare use that tone with me girl." She nodded to the doctor and then complained, "He wants to keep me in this place for another twenty-four hours."

Alex slowly faced the man and introduced herself. He reciprocated with a twinkle in his eye and a slight grin. He could tell that Alex was enjoying Cat's irritation and was goading her even more with her casual greeting of him. "Dr. Eric Chadsworth, do you think she truly needs to stay another day?"

"I believe her injuries warrant another day. She hit her head pretty hard. She was not wearing her seatbelt after all." He reprimanded gently. "I just want to make sure that there are no aftereffects of a concussion or further internal bleeding. It's merely for precautionary reasons."

"That settles it Cat! You're staying."

"Alex! I'm not a child." Cat hollered. "I'm okay. I want out of here."

"Then stop whining like one. People wait on you hand and foot here. So, just sit back and relax."

Cat took one look at the serious no-bull facial expression and sighed. Alex looked at the doctor and grinned. "Anything else doc?"

"Don't push it Alex." Cat snarled.

The doctor laughed and replied, "No, that's everything. I'll be in first thing tomorrow, Cat. If everything checks out, you can too." Seeing his patient's grudgingly given affirmative nod, he left the room.

Cat had been observing her friend carefully. Even though Alex seemed calm, Cat could tell that her friend was excited and couldn't wait to tell her something. "Out with it, girl. What's up?"

Alex excitedly pulled a chair to the bed. She sat down and started to tell Cat everything she found out at the reception hall. She bounced up and down out of the chair a few times to emphasize the points of her story.

"Alex, that's fantastic. So now all we need to know is where everyone was from roughly four fifteen to four thirty. That ought to make things go a little easier and faster."

"I hope so. But Veronica didn't see anyone leaving when she arrived, so I think we're looking at narrowing the time even more to between four ten and four twenty-five. I'm going to check with Connie after I leave here and see if she can help us."

"Alex, I'm bored and restless. I wish I could help you somehow. This place is driving me nuts."

"Oh, really? I couldn't tell." Alex sarcastically laughed. "There is one thing you can do." Alex laughed again as her friend's face lit up instantly. "Actually, there's two."

"What?" Cat excitedly asked.

"Chill, Cat. Maggie will be visiting later. Find out where she was from four ten to four twenty five on Saturday."

Cat's eyes bulged and she sputtered, "Alex, you can't seriously believe that she had anything to do with..."

"Of course not!" Alex interrupted. "But we need to prove not only my innocence, but that of our employees. For that, I want to be able to show Tom that we were thorough. That we didn't assume anyone's alibi or innocence. On our tablets, we wrote our own alibis down or at least the locations where we were. Since we were alone, we really don't have solid alibis. Think about it Cat."

Cat bounced her head slightly as she thought it over. "You're right. But, you said two things. Maggie's only one."

"Find out about Jake too."

Cat opened her mouth to say something, but closed her jaws with an audible snap. "Swell, can tick off two friends for the price of one." Before Alex could reply, Cat raised her hand to keep her quiet and replied, "But, you're right. I'll do it. I'll do it."

"Great. And don't worry, they'll understand." Alex visited her friend for a few more minutes. After assuring Cat that she would be careful, she departed for Connie's.

Chapter 16

Alex was heading toward Connie's when she looked at her watch. It was eleven forty-five and she hated to visit people at lunchtime without prior notice. She didn't want anyone to feel compelled to feed her. Alex's stomach started to growl when she saw the sign to "Eats Galore!" She decided that she'd better eat before going to a catering place. Alex was trying to lose a few pounds. Connie always had such tasty treats piled around her shop within easy reach of her customers. If Alex didn't eat first, she'd walk out of Connie's ten pounds heavier than when she went in.

As soon as she entered the restaurant, she smiled at her incredible luck. Connie was seated at a booth toward the back. She looked to be by herself and the table was empty of any lunch plates. Connie was only a few years older than Alex. She was as wide as she was tall, which was about five foot. Connie strongly believed that she should taste everything she made for her clients. It didn't matter to her if the recipe was a new one, or if it was one that she'd been using for ten years. Alex enjoyed the few times she had worked with this woman in the past. It never ceased to amaze her how emotional and open this woman could be. One time she could be screaming at a supplier, and with a turn of the head, be sweetly talking to an employee. Alex walked back to Connie's table and said hello. After a few amenities, Connie asked Alex to join her for lunch. "If you're sure I'm not bugging you or anything."

"I'm sure. Now, sit down. I haven't seen you for some time." She lightly slapped the table top across from her with her left hand. "I heard a few rumors about your shop and I hope they're not true." She said with sincerity.

"I don't know what all you heard, but I have been closed down pending an investigation. In fact, that's why I'm here." Alex said as she scooted into the booth. "I know it's the police who are supposed to solve the crimes, but they have a lot of crimes to solve and I don't. Besides, they get paid whether they solve the crimes or not. If this crime is not solved, they get paid, but I don't, I get unemployment but without money. I was wondering if you would mind if I asked you a few questions?"

"I don't mind Alex. If at all possible, I really do want to help. I know you wouldn't kill anyone, especially not with one of your creations. People who earn their living making food would not endanger their own livelihood to kill someone…unless they're stupid or mentally unbalanced, and you're neither."

"Thanks." Alex was about to continue when the waitress came over to get her order. She quickly asked for a bowl of potato soup and a grilled cheese sandwich. As soon as the waitress left them alone, Alex asked, "Connie, can you run down the happenings of that Saturday for me? I heard that you showed up at a little after four. Don't you usually show up much earlier?"

Alex almost laughed as she watched numerous emotions cross over Connie's face in just a matter of seconds. Helpfulness was replaced by thoughtfulness, then by concentration with a squint of the eyes, then a roll of the eyes with exasperation, replaced by anger and splotches of red in her cheeks. Connie huffed, "Boy, what a day! I don't have to try to remember anything, Alex. I just wanted to put things into some semblance of order. It will be a cold day in you-know-where before I forget that Saturday. It started bad and only got worse." Alex was surprised as a quick snicker escaped Connie's lips. She looked curiously at the lady sitting across the table from her. "Sorry about that. I was just thinking that if I can handle the groom dying at a reception, I can handle any disaster. Never had that happen before," Connie reached over and patted Alex's arm, "and now I can tell you that I definitely hope to never have it happen again. You see, as you stated, I usually arrive at the reception hall much earlier than I did on that day. But, I'm 'putting the cart before the horse,' let me start from the beginning." Connie took a sip of water as the waitress deposited their meals in front of them and took off again.

"This couple wanted things a little different from the way I usually work. They didn't want me to make the dinner at the reception hall, I had to make it at my place. In order to make sure everything would be hot for the dinner, I had to prepare the meal close to the start of the reception and then transport it to the hall. I almost refused to do the dinner. When serving a sit-down meal, I like to cook at the hall. There's less problems that way. The food is easier to keep warm. It's also easier to cover up when running late and such other problems. But to make a long story short, I did all the cooking at my place. I had a couple of my employees help to prep, cook, and load the food into the vans. We were running a tad late and I tried to hurry my people along.

One of my people tried to quicken things up and ended up dropping three trays of hors d'oeuvres on the ground. I just about killed him. Of course, they had to be the ones the groom especially ordered, the hardest to make, and the most expensive." Connie dramatically shook her hands in the air to emphasize the situation. She didn't realize that she was splattering salad dressing in all directions from the fork in her one hand. Since it didn't damage anything in particular, Alex didn't point it out. "After screaming at the kid, I ordered him to clean up the mess and headed inside to start a new batch. I instructed Rachel on how to finish the recipe and directed her to bring them over to the hall when they were done. Then I headed out to the vans and got the food started for the hall. I'm afraid I tend to get single-minded or single-tracked when pushed to hurry. Something like tunnel vision if you can understand what I mean. I focus on what I'm doing and block out everything else. The space shuttle could have landed right beside me as I drove to the hall and I wouldn't have noticed. We were much later than I planned. It didn't help that the back door to the hall was locked when we arrived. I sent Ronda around to the front to see if she could find anyone to unlock the back, which she did. We hurriedly unloaded and got to work. Everything from that point on went like usual except a little faster. Like usual, that is, until the groom keeled over and died. Do you want me to go any further?"

Alex shook her head no and pondered the tale she had just heard. "Do you remember when exactly you got to 'Jacob's Hope'?"

"Since we were late, I remember exactly. It was four oh five."

"I just missed you then. I left at four. Since we come from different directions, that would explain why I didn't see you. Did you happen to look out into the front at any time? Maybe see someone by the cake?"

Connie shook her head no and then decided to elucidate. "No. I mean I didn't see anyone by the cake until the reception started. Since we were running behind, I didn't look at the cake area. I knew you were doing the cake and would place the server where you usually do. With your work, I don't need to go anywhere near the cake and double-check things. I only go near the cake when its time to cut it up and serve it to the guests. This time we didn't get that far. I did watch the bride and groom cut the cake. As soon as they fed each other their respective pieces, the groom started choking and gasping. At first I just thought the cake went down the wrong pipe or up the nose. You know how messy the cake feeding can go. I didn't approach the couple because a group was already gathering around them. The first I realized anything was wrong was when I heard Bevirly scream. Someone yelled that they had called 9-1-1, so I just sat back and waited for help to arrive."

"To you knowledge, did any of your people look out into the front room?"

"Not that I know of. But to be perfectly honest, I can't be sure. Things were pretty hectic when we first arrived. I guess Ronda might have checked out the front room when she went to have the door unlocked. If she did, she couldn't have seen much, because she returned to me pretty fast."

"Don't you need to set up anything on the table when you arrive? Like plates or cups?"

"Not at 'Jacob's Hope' we don't. Veronica has her people put out the plates and any needed accoutrements. She's afraid we might break stuff. Even though she lets us do all the clean-up. Figure that one out why don't you. If we could break things setting them out, don't you think we could break things cleaning them up and putting them away?" Connie shook her head and threw her hands into the air once again. "The bride and groom decorated the hall the night before. I believe Veronica had her people set the place settings out at the same time.

That way any favors or name cards that the couple wanted to sit out could be done without any mix-ups. It takes us about a half hour to set up the hors d'oeuvres table and drink station and get ready for the people. We had just finished when the first guests started to show."

"Could you give me a list of your employees that helped you that day?" Alex asked as she finished her meal. "Do you mind if I call them and ask if they remember seeing anyone near the cake?"

"No problem. Why don't you follow me over to my place after we're done here. I can get you the list and respective numbers. I'd offer to do it for you, but I suspect the kids will be more forthright talking to you. For some reason, nobody wants to tell the boss that they were doing something other than what they were assigned to do." She chuckled as she said the last item.

"Sounds like a plan." Alex agreed. They asked for the check and left a short time later. She followed Connie to her shop and after about fifteen minutes, was on her way again wiping her mouth as she went. Connie had insisted she try the new dessert that she had just created that morning. As usual, it was scrumptious. Alex decided to go home and start making phone calls.

Chapter 17

Alex had just finished calling each of Connie's employees who had worked on the Saturday of the murder and was disheartened. No one had seen anybody around the wedding cake. No one had seen anyone leave the reception hall. Everyone said that they were too busy to do anything except the job at hand. She sighed deeply and went to the kitchen to grab a soda. She decided she needed a change of scenery and plunked down in front of the aquarium to clear her mind. Micky jumped into Alex's lap and curled up to sleep. Alex let her hand sink into his deep fur and started to absentmindedly pet him as she watched the fish swim. Slowly her mind calmed and she let the facts of the murder float through her head. She was just starting to form a plan of action when the phone rang and startled her back to reality. Her hand knocked the soda to the floor. She jumped up and swore at the mess. Micky crashed to the floor quickly. With a nasty look at Alex, he growled a quick "Yat" and left the room.

Alex reached for her portable phone as she grabbed for some towels. "Hello?"

"Alex. Thank gosh you're there! I don't know what to do! Maggie just ran out of the room. I wanted to follow but I couldn't. I got all tangled up in the contraption that my leg is in and ended up hanging upside down from the bed...dang it! She just ran out." Alex could feel the frustration and despair in her friend's voice. She couldn't figure out what all the noise in the background was. Her ears tuned in quick when she heard a crash of glass.

"Cat! Cat, what's going on? Are you okay?"

"Yeah. I'm here." Cat frustratingly spit out.

Even though Cat couldn't see it, Alex put her hand out to calm her friend. "Take a deep breath and tell me what's going on. First, what's that crashing noise? Second, what's this about Mags?

"The noise is nothing. I just threw my water pitcher at the wall and managed to break the mirror. I fear the nurses may arrive shortly."

"Yeah, I'm sure you're just quaking in your backless hospital gown." She answered with more than just a touch of sarcasm. "If I may ask, why'd you throw the pitcher?"

"Because I'm mad, that's why. Mags ran out all upset and I couldn't help or even follow."

"Okay. That's worth a mirror. Now, what did you do to Mags?"

"Nothing that you didn't ask me to do, girl." Cat growled back to Alex.

"Whoa! Back up a minute. Take me through everything---step by step."

"Mags showed up with flowers. We talked awhile. I tried to explain why I needed to ask her a question. Then I asked her for her whereabouts and/or alibi for the necessary time. Her eyes flashed and she screamed at me. She shouted, 'After all our years of friendship, how dare you and Alex accuse me of murder?' I tried to explain, but she got all huffy, even teary, and ran out."

"She was actually crying?"

"It looked like it took all her strength to keep from crying. I hurt her, Alex. I'm not sure exactly why or how, but I did."

"Don't worry. She must have misunderstood you somehow."

"Alex, I was straight forward. I don't see how she could have misunderstood anything. It's as if…" Cat faded to quiet.

"As if what Cat?"

"I don't know, Alex. It's as if she's hiding something. She acted almost like she was guilty or something. You don't think that she actually had anything to do with that jerk's death, do you?"

"No, I don't." Alex just wished she felt as sure as she sounded.

"You're right. As soon as I said it, I knew it was a foolish idea. I just wish I knew what happened."

"Well, I'll leave immediately to go find her. I'll try to find out what's going on. Now don't worry, I'll call as soon as I can."

"Uh, oh!"

"What? What?" Alex cried out with worry coming into her voice once more.

"The nurses are here. They don't look too happy. Talk to you later." With that, Cat hung up the phone.

Chapter 18

Alex pulled into Maggie's driveway. She knocked loudly on the door for a few moments. When there was no response, she started to ring the doorbell. "Mags? Are you in there?" No response. "I bet I know where she is." Alex mumbled under her breath. She ran around to the back of the house. Maggie had a big backyard. In the one corner, she had planted a beautiful garden. In the middle of the garden, beside the gazebo, there was a gorgeous water fountain made of mountain stones. A huge wooden swing sits in the middle of the gazebo. Whenever she needed some peace and quiet, Mags would escape to her swing and listen to the waterfall. Maggie was an expert on plants. Beside the herbs she cooked with, there were flowers that attracted hummingbirds and butterflies. Alex always figured that when she could afford it, she'd ask Maggie to make a similar oasis for her.

Just as she figured, Alex found Maggie swinging back and forth with a faraway look in her swollen red eyes. Alex saw a mass of balled up tissues in Maggie's lap and on the ground under the swing. She approached slowly to give herself time to think of an approach. She was worried. Her friend looked frazzled and deeply distraught. The thought that her friend might be involved in the murder came unbidden into her mind. She pushed it away. That was impossible. She knew Maggie most of her life and couldn't fathom an explanation for the present situation.

"Maggie? Can I speak to you?" Since there was no negative reply, Alex approached even closer. "Mags? You okay?"

Mags raised her eyes to Alex. As she slowly focused on her, Alex saw deep and personal sadness. She knew that look. A long time ago, she saw it in her own eyes. She could still see it, whenever she let herself think of her sister for too long. She tried to remember anything that happened to Maggie in the past that could account for her present expression. She drew a complete blank. "Mags?"

Maggie's reply was gruff. Her throat was sore from crying for hours. "Yeah."

"Is it okay if I sit in the seat by the falls?"

"Sure." She answered solemnly.

Alex sat down. She looked at her friend. "Cat didn't mean anything at the hospital. She's sorry if she said or did something wrong. Neither one of us is accusing you of anything, least of all, murder. We're just trying to figure out what happened. By clearing each of us, we can get my shop open again and clear my reputation at the same time."

"I know." She sighed.

"You know? Then what's going on? Cat just about killed herself trying to get out of bed?"

"Why did she do that?"

"Why do you think? She was concerned. Now she's in trouble with the nurses."

"Huh?" Maggie was totally confused now.

Alex just shrugged her shoulders. She waved a hand in the air as if to push the idea aside. "It's nothing. You know Cat. What I'd like to know is, what's wrong with you? Will you please tell me?"

As tears welled in her eyes, Mags looked at Alex. "For me to tell you, you must promise not to tell anyone."

"May I tell Cat?"

After some thought, Mags said, "Okay, but no one else. Not even the cops. And Cat must also agree before you tell her."

Now Alex took some time to contemplate the possible ramifications

125

of her answer. "Okay. I agree. I may come to you and ask you to tell the cops, if it becomes necessary, but I won't tell them myself."

"Agreed." Maggie became quiet for a few moments. Tears started to flow freely down her cheeks as she started her story. She led out with one heck of a bombshell. "Nine years ago, I was raped by Matthew Abrahms." Alex's mouth dropped open immediately, but she didn't make a move. She didn't want to interrupt her friend. As she listened to Mag's story, she too started to cry. "As you know, I have been married to Jake for ten years. We had a smaller house than we do now. We decided we wanted a family and needed a bigger house. Abrahms was our realtor. Actually, it was supposed to be Mrs. Acres, but she had become sick and sent him instead. He had a clipboard with a list of things to check out about the house. After a few basic questions, he asked for a tour of the house. He either checked things off the list or filled in the blanks as we went along. Everything seemed legit and probably was. I didn't think it was unusual when he asked the whereabouts of my husband. I naively told him the truth. Jake had an emergency meeting at work and wouldn't be home for a few hours. After twenty minutes, his list was completed. He asked me if I had any questions about selling the house. I said no, not at the present time. He made a move as if to leave the house. Instead, he locked the door and turned back to face me. I asked him what he thought he was doing. Instead of answering, he hit me across the face and forced me to the floor. And then…," she took a deep breath, "he raped me. I won't go into all the details. But to make a long story short, I was quite bruised and shaken and freaked by the time Jake got home. We never reported the rape to the police. I did go to my doctor and to a psychiatrist. The upshot of everything was that I ended up pregnant. We don't know, even to this day, who's the real father of that particular child. We don't think we could handle it if Jake ended up not being the biological

126

father. The only people other than Jake and I that know about the rape are the two doctors and, of course, Abrahms. Jake and I didn't tell anyone. The two doctors haven't said anything and won't because of patient doctor confidentiality. That left Abrahms."

"Abrahms recently came to us. He said that he had put two and two together and figured out that maybe he was the father of my eldest child. He figured that we wouldn't want Carol to know about the mystery over her biological father. He was right. We didn't want to risk screwing her up. Even if we did a DNA test and proved Jake was the biological father, the town would not forget. The publicity and gossip would be unbearable for a while. It would have brought all the horror back again. He said that if we gave him money, he would leave us alone. He said something about moving out of town. Jake and I knew that that would only be the beginning, that he would keep coming back for more money in the future. We had decided that paying him money was an impossibility. We were still trying to figure out another possibility when Abrahms died." Maggie looked up into Alex's eyes, "You see, Alex, we had a perfect motive to kill the bastard. But I swear to you, neither Jake nor I killed the man. If we had, there's no way that we would have implicated you or the bakery. I hope you realize that."

Alex was overwhelmed with emotions from hearing her friend's story. "Of course, I believe you. We never truly thought that you had anything to do with the murder. We just wanted to know where you were at the time. But dang it Mags, I find it hard to believe what you told me." She quickly raised her hand to keep Mags from screaming at her. "I mean I don't doubt you. It's just....I thought we were pretty close friends and I never even picked up on anything......that far out of the ordinary. I mean....." Alex was totally bowled over.

"It's okay Alex." Mags broke into Alex's stammering. She wanted to give her friend a break. "You didn't know, because we didn't want

127

you to know. And let me tell you, it was hard, real hard. Your friendship means a lot to me, to us. I was afraid that if you knew, and maybe Cat also, you two might have tried to exact some kind of revenge on Abrahms. And I was right, wasn't I?"

Alex looked at the slight smile on her friend's lips and returned one of her own. "Yeah, you're right. At least, we probably would have tried something."

"Probably? Who are you trying to kid? Definitely." Maggie's posture and voice took on deeply serious tones. She looked directly at Alex and continued. "I know what he did to your sister, Alex. I also know that shortly after her death, Abrahms was involved in some kind of 'accident' that almost killed him. I didn't ask any questions at the time or since, because I don't believe that I want to know the real truth. I think you two had something to do with that accident. But that's only my opinion."

"Really?" Alex quietly asked. "Why's that?"

"Rumors, mostly. Someone said that they thought they remembered two girls walking in the general area of the accident about the time the doctor thinks it took place. Remember, I'm your friend. A good one. Maybe I think I know you better than you think I do."

"Maybe you do." A grin passed over Alex's face quickly. Just as quickly, the grin turned serious, very serious, "Then again, maybe not?"

"Well, now you know why I didn't tell you earlier. For the record though, Jake and I did not kill Abrahms, and we know that you didn't either. We had absolutely nothing to do with the murder. However, we only have each other for our alibis. We took the kids to a movie at two. Afterwards, we dropped the kids off at Jake's parents. Then we went home to have some fun."

"Any witnesses?"

"Good grief, I certainly hope not." Maggie's face turned bright red as she observed Alex's quizzical expression. "You see, we're trying to have one more child. And that's what we were trying to do during the time before the party. We were late for the party for the same reason."

Now it was time for Alex's face to turn bright red. "Oh! I'm sorry to intrude." Her face lit up as she asked, "Another child? How many do you two want?"

"Just one more."

"Well, good luck. However, I do have one more question."

"Shoot."

"When did Abrahms want the money from you two?"

Maggie cast her eyes to the ground again and then raised them to her friend. "When he got back from his honeymoon."

Alex whistled and took a minute to let that piece of information sink in. "Whoa. I don't doubt your alibi, but your timing was beautiful. If asked, I'll tell the cops that you did have a motive but that you also have an alibi. As promised, though, I won't tell them what the motive was."

Maggie smiled and gave her friend a warm hug. "Thank-you. If you need any help, let me know."

"Sure thing." Alex got up to go, but hesitated, pointing a finger up in the air. "Oh, I almost forgot. Do you have any penicillin?"

Mags shook her head. "I don't believe so, Alex. Is something wrong with you? I have some aspirin or Tylenol if that will work."

"Ahhhhh, no. I'm okay. I'm just asking everyone about it. Abrahms apparently died from a reaction to some penicillin that was on the cake."

"Penicillin? How'd that get on the cake?"

"I'm not totally sure. I believe someone added it to the cake after Cat and I delivered it to the reception hall. But I'll find out sooner or later. If you would though, please call Cat and let her know that you're okay and don't hate her."

"Sure thing." Maggie smiled again.

Chapter 19

Alex looked at her watch. It was getting kind of late to be popping in on people to question them. She wanted to talk to her remaining employees without their husbands sitting beside them. It was five thirty. Dinner time at most houses. She had turned her car in the direction of home when she remembered Cassie. Cassie helped out at the bakery in times of need. Theoretically, that made her a potential suspect also. Cassie always stayed open until nine during the week, so Cat headed for the pet store.

Pet Haven was located three miles from the bakery. It was located at the end of a strip mall. Alex pulled in beside her friend's car and parked. As she got out of her car, she noticed that Cassie's front end was crunched. On seeing the damage to the car, Alex quickened her steps into the store. "Cassie?"

"Yo."

"Where are you?" Alex anxiously looked around as she half-shouted the question.

"Over here. By the fish tanks," Cassie shouted back.

Alex quickly walked over and visually checked her friend up and down for injuries. "Are you okay?"

Cassie looked up perplexed. "Of course. Why wouldn't I...." Comprehension dawned on her and she started laughing. "Oh, you mean the car."

"Yes. I mean the car." Alex answered back with irritation edging her words. "What happened?"

"Jerry. That's what happened." She rolled her eyes at her friend.

"You didn't actually let him drive your car did you?" Alex asked incredulously.

"Yeah, I did."

"I thought you wouldn't even let your own brother drive that car."

"Weeeeelll. This was an emergency. I'm afraid that I let the crisis go to my head. Looking back, it was nothing. But at the time......" Cassie shook her head to shake the frustration from her mind. "To make a long story short, I let Jerry take the car. He completed the tasks I needed done in record time. On the way back, he was showing off to

131

some young girls and promptly ran into the back of a truck. The jerk!"

"When did this happen?"

"Yesterday. Why?" Cassie inquired.

"There's no question as to his negligence in the accident then?"

"No. Again Alex, I ask why?"

Alex waved her hand toward the front area. "Do you want to sit down?"

"Yeah, I could use a break. A huge order came in today and I've been trying to get it priced and put out on the shelves."

The pet store was on the small to average size when compared to most pet stores today. At the front of the store, near the door, is the cash register and counter area. Cassie and her employees sit behind the counter when eating or when they have some free time on their hands. Shelves full of fish products are located across from the counter. The back corner of the store is filled with aquariums full of fish and live plants. The corner closest to the counter has shelves full of pet food. The walls around the store are covered with pegboards. The pegboards themselves were heavily covered with products related to pets in their respective areas. Cassie's style of management is kind of laissez faire. Her temper has a long fuse. As long as the work gets done, with a minimum of horseplay, she's happy. She doesn't care if the employees take their time to get things done, as long as the customers are properly taken care of and the work does get done. The one thing that raises her ire is cell phones. She does not permit their use in front of customers for any reason. Her business has a huge base of loyal customers that has been built up through the years. She bought the business from her uncle and aunt, who in turn had bought it from that aunt's uncle. Pet Haven has an informal but caring atmosphere about it. Customers love it. Cassie also has the reputation that if she doesn't have a product, she'll get it, and within only a few days. She loves talking to the customers and making them feel like one of her old friends. Cassie also loves to introduce people to the wonderful world of animals. The only thing that really gets her goat is when people are thoughtless, disrespectful, or cruel to animals. Then watch out. She has even taken some people to court over their treatment of animals.

Alex and Cassie sat down in two seats in the front area. Cassie took two sodas from the little refrigerator for them to drink. Alex reached for the ever present bowl of M&Ms from the counter behind her and placed it on the table with the sodas in front of them. Just as they were getting comfortable, a customer came in and Cassie got up to wait on her. Alex leaned back and started to figure out what all she wanted to ask her friend. Immediately, the phone jangled by her ear and made her jump. She yelled out to Cassie that she would answer the phone and not to worry about it. A few minutes later, Cassie returned with the customer and a couple bags of fish. She noticed a weird smirk on Alex's face and with a grin of her own rang up the customer's bill.

Seated again, Cassie looked at her friend and said, "Okay, out with it!"

With a huge Cheshire grin and innocent eyes, Alex asked, "Out with what?"

"Alex, come on. I know it had something to do with the phone. Now what happened?"

Alex started to laugh. "If I hadn't helped out here in the past and still do whenever you are in need of my services, I would truly wonder about people now days. My customers can sometimes be a little slow in the mental department, but yours beat mine out every time."

Cassie started chuckling even before Alex started relating her tale. Cassie had a few customer tales of her own that never failed to elicit a smile whenever she thought of them. "The customer said that he had a bird. I said, yeah? He said that it wasn't moving and wanted me to tell him why." She started laughing. "I wasn't sure what to say next, so I asked him if he knew for sure that it was alive or not."

"Alex! You didn't?" She laughed, "I'm sure he would've known that."

"Hey. I'm not so sure of that. Remember the guy who thought his guinea pig was just sleeping and brought him here for us to take a look at. I mean, get real, the thing had slept for four straight days. I would've thought that his animal being cold and stiff would have given him a clue. The smell wasn't the best either, if you remember."

"Yeah, you're right. But also remember, he had a bad cold and couldn't smell anything. So what about the bird?"

"Well, he said he was sure it was alive. I said that without seeing the bird, I wouldn't be able to help him. I said that depending on the problem, it may need some medical help or advice. Since we can't legally do either, I referred him to his veterinarian."

"Good, glad to hear it. I don't want some lunatic claiming we gave him bad advice and suing me." Cassie quickly rubbed her hands together as if to brush off dirt. "Okay, enough of all that. What brings you to my little corner of the world?"

"Oh. Well. You know of my problems, right?"

"Yes, I course. If you find yourself in need of some cash, you can help out here until you're cleared and the shop is open again."

"Thanks." Alex smiled. She felt water pool in her eyes and blinked quickly to clear it. She knew that she was lucky to have such a good friend. "But that's not it. I'm trying to figure out who did the murder myself."

"Cool. Are you sure you haven't been reading too many murder mystery books?"

Alex rolled her eyes and put her soda down on the table. "Thanks for all your support." She responded sarcastically.

"Sorry. What can I do to help?"

"That's more like it." Cassie stuck her tongue out at Alex after she spoke. Alex straightened up in her chair and reached for her pad and pen while pretending to ignore her friend's response. After explaining the whys and wherefores behind her questioning, and after getting repeated assurances from Cassie that she understood and everything was okay, Alex started asking her friend various questions. "Where were you on Saturday between four ten and four twenty-five?"

"Wow! You really have the time narrowed down don't you?"

She smile back mischievously at her friend. "We aim to please!"

"Let's see." Cassie thought back to that Saturday and said, "Oh yeah! I was here." She held up her hand to keep Alex quiet and continued on. "I have witnesses. One of my employees was here working and we had some customers here at the same time. On Friday, the supply truck arrived extremely late with a huge order. We worked all day Saturday putting out the order. Normally, on Saturday, we close at six. But on that particular day, we didn't leave until seven thirty. I can give you their names if you want."

Alex motioned for Cassie to slow down. "No, you don't have to give me all the names. If the cops want to know names, they'll ask." She hesitated and grinned. "However, since you offered, what's the name of the employee that was here at that exact time frame? Do you mind?"

Cassie laughed. "Heck, no. His name is Jason Goodheart."

"Goodheart? I bet he gets a wee bit of ribbing at school." Alex chuckled.

"Oh, just a *wee* bit." She laughed back. "He's talking about changing his name. I keep telling him that teasing builds character. Besides, the ladies will love it in the future."

"You betcha! Though I bet he'll have a ton of character by the time he graduates." She finished writing and looked up at her friend. "Just to let you know, for the record, I'll be asking him about that day. I want to show the cops that I was thorough."

"Go for it girl. I have nothing to hide. Is that everything? Any other questions, Ms. Sherlock Holmes?"

"Just one. Do you have any penicillin?"

"Penicillin? For what?" Cassie was thrown. "Aren't you feeling well? Do you have some kind of infection?"

Now it was Alex's turn to be confused. "Huh? Oh, oh, ohhhhhh. No Cassie, that's not it. Didn't you hear? Penicillin was the murder weapon." She quickly filled Cassie in on the necessary information. "Do you have any?"

"Some. Here. In the back room. There's probably only a few there. Remember I had that tooth pulled last month?"

"Yes, I do. Cool. I figured most of us would have penicillin around for one reason or another. I thought it would be easy enough for someone to get penicillin, but I didn't realize just how easy. It's nice to know that I'm not the only one who doesn't always finish their prescriptions....." she trailed off and quieted.

Cassie waved her hand in front of Alex's face. "Hello? What's up?" After a small pause, she continued. "Earth to Alex?" She gently knocked Alex on the forehead. "Anyone home?"

Alex shook her head and rolled her eyes at her friend. "Yes, I'm here. Or at least I'm back. I was just thinking back a few years. I got bawled out a while back when I didn't finish my one prescription. My temperature came back and I went back to the doctor. He asked me if I finished the medication he had prescribed for me. I said no and he exploded. I told him that my legs had felt weird and started to shake for some reason, so I stopped taking the pills. He said that I should have called him, however that was no reason to decide on my own to stop medicating. I got reamed out pretty bad, but I learned my lesson. That's why the fact that the cops found that penicillin in my medicine cabinet is so confusing. I thought I had finished it, and now I'm sure of it. So how did it get there?"

"Don't know. Good luck in finding out. Any other questions?"

"Not really. Unless you know who would have wanted Abrahms dead."

Cassie just stared at her friend for a long period of time. With a deeply serious tone, she said, "You're kidding, right? Alex, many people wanted him dead. That, my friend, is where you can end up in trouble. You have one of the strongest reasons for wanting that man dead. He not only hurt quite a few people, you know, but he killed a few. But I don't need to tell *you* that, now do I? Whoever set you up, knew what he or she was doing." She watched as her friend's eyes started to water. She knew Alex was desperately trying not to cry. So to help Alex out, Cassie lightened her tone, "Enough of that. If I hear of anyone in particular, I'll let you know. Now…" She wiggled her eyebrows at Alex.

Questioningly, Alex examined her friend. She noticed a twinkle in Cassie's eyes as she warily asked, "Now what?"

"What's this I hear about you kissing a certain cop in the park?" Cassie smiled and immensely enjoyed herself as she watched Alex's face turn different shades of red.

"It was nothing." She responded quietly and started to intently examine her soda can.

Cassie sat up straight in order to hone in on her friend. "Spill your guts here girl." Cassie lightly hit Alex on the leg. "You know, that can design is not new, nor is it about to mutate into something new."

Alex smiled as she looked at her old friend. "What have you heard?"

"Just that you two were about to procreate by the lake in plain sight of everyone." Cassie's chuckling turned to full blown laughter. "You know, Alex, I didn't think a person could turn such a deep shade of red. I'm not sure what that shade would be called. You're excellent with color shades, want a mirror? This is amazing!"

Alex smacked her friend's shoulder. "Oh, shut up. And we did not even get close to procreating."

"Not what I heard."

"Well, you heard wrong. It was just a kiss." Alex's eyes roved over the store as she talked to Cassie. As she looked at Cassie, she wilted under her intense glare. "Okay. Okay. It was a little more than just a kiss, but nothing like procreation. Believe me, it's been awhile, but I can still remember what it's like."

"Good. Glad to hear it. I was starting to get worried about you. You know, too much work is detrimental to one's sex life."

"No kidding, really?" They both started laughing. "Speaking of Tom, I better get going. It's starting to get late and I'd like to compare notes on this case."

"Is that what they call it now days? Comparing notes?"

"Stop it already. I think you've been working too many hours alone yourself."

"I think you may be right. Take care. Anything I can do, just let me know." She moved to pick up the phone.

"Sure thing. Who are you calling?"

"Donovan." She answered casually. Then with a slight leer continued, "I believe it's time to 'compare notes.'" Alex laughed and waved good-bye as Cassie's call was being answered.

Chapter 20

Alex pulled into her driveway and looked at the door. Perplexed, she got out of the car and cautiously approached her front door. There was a note on the door with a big smiley face on it. She reached for the note hoping it would be as friendly as the face indicated. She slowly opened the note and read it. A big smile spread across her face as she read the contents:

Hey beautiful!

Want to compare notes? Hungry? Come around back and see what I've got. One never knows what's around the corner, until one looks.

Tom

With curiosity filling every cell of her body, she quietly walked around to the back of her house. She felt strangely exhilarated as her eyes roamed over the scene set up in her backyard. It had been a long time since anyone, especially a man, took the time to set up something special for her. There was a full moon in the sky, so Alex could see everything pretty clear. Tom had spread out a blanket picnic-style. On the one corner sat a closed insulated cooler. Tom was laying on the blanket with what appeared to be a pillow under his head. She was surprised that Tom didn't get up or say anything as she approached, until she heard a slight snore emanating from his still form. She tip-toed toward Tom and quietly observed him for a few minutes. Even though he was sleeping, he looked weary. She wondered how long he had been sleeping, and wasn't sure she wanted to wake him. The sky looked clear and she was sure it wasn't going to rain, but it wouldn't be prudent to let him sleep outside all night. Besides, she was curious what all he had planned out for the night and what all he had found out on the case.

Alex looked around her yard. She smiled when she saw Micky sitting on his window bench looking out at them. Alex waved at her cat as she reached down and picked up a feathery weed from the ground. As she slowly sank onto the blanket beside Tom, folding her legs under her, she realized his "pillow" was a jacket bundled up to resemble one. She slowly traced Tom's face with the weed barely touching his skin. She chuckled softly as he raised his hand to brush away the nuisance. She had just brushed the end of his nose when he shook his head and his eyes opened up. It took him a few seconds to get his bearings. "Hi, Beautiful," rumbled low out of his throat.

"Hi, yourself," she smiled. She looked around and waved her hand to indicate the blanket, the cooler and himself, "What's all this?"

Tom checked his watch briefly as he stretched and got up. Alex

140

heard a few soft groans as he got up and moved. "Did you forget how hard the ground can be?"

"Well, it just goes to show that I'm not a young pup anymore. It didn't use to bug me at all."

"Do I detect a hint of past camping experience?"

"Indeed, you do, and I still camp." Tom took the lid off the cooler. "I hope you like fried chicken."

Alex's face shone with delight as he removed a small tub of chicken from the cooler. "I love it."

With a flourish, Tom went about setting out the food and place settings. Along with the chicken, there was potato salad, macaroni and cheese, rolls, and a couple of sodas. As he was getting resituated on the ground, Alex looked around with curiosity. "You put both cold and hot stuff together in one cooler and it works?"

"If one does it right, sure."

"Never thought of it. I always use two separate ones."

"I like to ride my motorcycle on long trips. The bike doesn't have a lot of space for that kind of luxury. Eat up and then we can discuss the day's events."

Alex and Tom talked small talk and ate. Each enjoying the company and the surroundings for about forty-five minutes. Alex realized it had been quite some time since she felt such inner peace and quietness. She communicated her feelings to Tom and then suggested they clean up and go inside to talk business. It was great outside but there were way too many ears around. He agreed and they got into action.

Once inside, Alex placed the blanket on the table. "Thanks for the picnic Tom, I really appreciated it. It's been a long since anyone spent so much time and energy on me."

"You're quite welcome." Tom placed the cooler with the blanket. He reached out for Alex and enveloped her into his arms and body.

Tom tilted his head to her and kissed Alex hard. She returned it equally hard. He pulled away from Alex and fought with his emotions. Business won out. He suggested that they best talk and compare notes before they got carried away and ran out of time. She looked at the kitchen clock and offered him her guest room for the night. "Thanks for the offer. I'll think it over while we talk."

Alex and Tom each grabbed their notes and they settled onto the couch for their discussion. "I tried to catch you at work this morning, but whoever answered would only say that you were out. I didn't want to be a nuisance, so I left word for you to call me. Did you get my message?"

"Yes, right before I came here. Sorry, I didn't get it earlier. There was a terrible accident up on Route Eighty this morning and police from all the nearby towns were called in to help. Ten tractor trailers and forty cars had been involved in one of the worst accidents in the area. It had taken most of the day to clean up the mess. Unfortunately, that also means that I only got to spend a few minutes on your case. Sorry about that."

"That's okay. I realize that me and my shop are not the only things in this world and that you have a lot of other things and cases to cover."

Tom appraised her for a moment and smiled. "Thanks for understanding." He wiggled down into the cushions a bit and asked, "So what did you do today?"

Alex briefed him on her day. She asked if anyone had interviewed Mrs. Johnson. After flipping through his notes, he shook his head. "No, I don't see her name anywhere, but I'll double-check the file in the morning. Is she certain it wasn't you?"

"What do you mean, is she certain? I wasn't there Thomas, so she has to be sure."

"Don't be getting all upset, Alex. I know you weren't there, but someone was. This lady says that someone looking like you was there. Cliff and the prosecution will say that you distracted her and purposely interfered with the investigation. They'll say that you were indeed the person she saw and soon she'll be convinced also. Do you see where I'm going here Alex?"

"Yeah, I see. I don't like it, but I see." She took a big sip of her soda and then put it down and looked at Tom. "Do you have that list of people victimized by Abrahms?"

"Yes. It's out in the car. I'll get it in a minute. I didn't want to have it in the backyard, in case I fell asleep." His face turned a tad red to silently admit that that had actually happened.

"Good thinking." She smiled knowingly back at him. Her smile quickly faded when she noticed his face sober up. In fact, she couldn't read his true expression. Her puzzlement ended as he spoke.

"Alexandra."

"Oh-oh!" She murmured under her breath. Her stomach sunk as she intuitively guessed what he was thinking about. She hoped that she was wrong.

"Cliff uncovered some interesting tidbits while going through some of Abrahms old records. He made a few calls to verify and clarify some of the information. He knew that I was coming over here to talk to you. He clued me in and asked me to double-check the info with you. We would like to hear any contributions that you might have. Okay?"

"Sure. If I can help, I will."

"Shortly after your sister was killed in the accident, Abrahms had a near fatal accident."

Alex's eyes left Tom's face and wondered around the room. "Yeah, so?"

"Do you know what I'm referring to?"

Her eyes briefly rested on his face as she said, "I'm not one hundred percent sure. Fill me in and I'll tell you, if I can."

Tom was starting to fill uneasy himself. Earlier, he would have sworn that Alex was incapable of hurting someone else, now he wasn't so sure. "About two weeks after your sister's death, Abrahms was released from jail. He would not be tried for his part in her death. A technicality kept the police from being able to charge him with anything at all."

"Uh-huh. I remember." Alex answered quietly. Her eyes filled with water, but she refused to let the tears run down her face. She wasn't sure how long she could hold out.

"That night, he went out to a bar to celebrate. He got plastered. When he returned home, he managed to fall down a steep set of cement stairs. He was injured pretty bad, but not killed."

"Isn't it strange how drunks seem to be able to do that?" She looked at Tom briefly and continued. "They can hurt and kill people in accidents, but they barely get scratched. Likewise, in other kinds of accidents. I heard once that it was because they don't stiffen up, they stay loose like rag dolls." Alex was speaking, but to the room in general, not to anyone in particular. Her eyes were locked onto the floor."

"Yeah, that's what I've heard too." Tom replied as he observed Alex. "Cliff found some witnesses' statements that indicated that two girls were seen leaving the general accident area about the time the doctor figured the accident to occur."

"Really?"

"Yes, really," Tom inhaled and stared at Alex. "Alexandra, the witnesses say that the two girls were you and Cat."

"Not true." Alex looked up. "The witnesses only *thought* that the two *could* have been us. Our build and walk were about right, but so were a lot of other girls'. It was late at night, and there was very little light. They couldn't be positive. Besides, we *did* have an alibi."

"Yes. You did have an alibi." Tom concurred. "But honestly, not a very strong one. Cassie said that you were with her during the suspected time. You were having a sleep-over at her place."

"That's right. We were there all night."

"Someone else had indicated seeing Cassie at a store picking up a few munchies during the time of the 'incident.' So she couldn't have been at the house at that exact time."

"That person also recanted his testimony. He said that he had made a mistake. He wasn't positive on the time factor. So our alibi stood. If it was not an accident, which it could have very well been, there were many many people who hated his guts. There still are."

"Yes, your alibi stood. But I know that you read mystery books, so I also know that you know that alibis can be faked or coerced."

"Is that what *you* think happened?"

Tom was getting exasperated. This was not going as he had planned. He thought, or perhaps hoped, she would clarify everything, and prove that she was nowhere near the accident site. "Stop dancing around the issue. Tell me what happened, Alex. Please?"

"Okay, but first…." She hesitated as Tom sighed with impatience. "What did Mister Abrahms say happened? I'm sure that's in the report."

"It is. He didn't know what exactly happened. He said that he was drunk and didn't remember everything. He thought he had managed to get up to the top of the stairway. He also remembers losing his balance, but he didn't remember how that might have occurred." Tom observed Alex as he spoke. "He said he didn't remember seeing anyone around at the time. That's all there is to his story. Now, tell me yours."

Alex was quiet for a few minutes. "Let me get this straight, you want me, to tell you, a cop, that I took part in an earlier attempted murder, on a man that I'm now suspected in killing. I may look dumb at times, but I don't think I look that dumb. And Ben would not be happy at all either."

Tom ran his fingers through his hair in irritation and blew air out through clenched teeth. Dinner was definitely not settling right in his gut right now. "Alex, I just want to know the truth."

"I can't tell you the truth Thomas." Alex rubbed her hands over her face and continued before he could respond. "I can tell you that a guardian angel was looking after both me and Abrahms that night. You see, since that night, I have a renewed faith in God. I had gotten mad at God when my sister died and her murderer had gotten away with it. But God makes the final judgement on our souls. To be forgiven, one must repent his/hers sins onto the Lord. I could not have done that. I would not have been sorry to see Abrahms dead. I have no intention of spending eternity being roasted, so therefore I'm glad that he did not die that night. I also realize now that life and energy is too precious to spend on negative thinking and negative ways. I try not to hold onto grudges or irritations too long, though I admit, I'm still working on this aspect." She leaned toward him and looked into his eyes. "Does that answer your question?"

Tom was very troubled by what he had just heard. "Yes, I believe it does." He got up and reached for his stuff.

"Where are you going?" Alex inquired.

Tom didn't even risk a glance toward Alex, his emotions were all mixed up. He quietly responded, "I have a lot to think about Alex. I believe I'll turn down your offer of the guest room tonight. Thanks anyway. I'll talk to you tomorrow." He headed for her front door.

"Thomas?" Alex asked as she followed him. "Please talk to me."

He stopped without turning around, with a steely calm that belied his inner turmoil he replied, "Not now, Alexandra." He hung his head and

146

whispered, "tomorrow." The door closed gently behind him.

Chapter 21

Alex tossed and turned all night. She was upset with how things were going with Tom. She was frustrated about her shop being closed. Every time she started to get into some serious sleep, some other worry woke her up. When she looked at the clock and realized it was five in the morning, she decided she best get up and get moving. Staying in bed wouldn't solve any problems. As she was getting out of the shower, she heard someone knocking on her door. Alex quickly wrapped a towel around her head and grabbed her robe. Chills ran up and down her spine as she tightened her robe and approached the front door. "Who in the world would be at my door at this ungodly hour?" Alex asked Micky, who was following hot on her heels. She checked the peephole in the door, rubbed her eyes to clear water from them, and rechecked it.

"Good morning, Alex." Tom quietly spoke as she opened the door. "May I come in?"

Alex waved her hand toward the inside of the house as a silent yes to his question. She saw that once again Tom had his cooler with him. "Did you forget to leave that thing at home?"

He looked up at her and realized that she was talking about the cooler. "You mean this? No, I didn't forget. I need to talk to you some more before I go to work. This is breakfast."

"You must be very hungry. How did you know I'd be up?"

"This is breakfast for us both. And I didn't know. I couldn't sleep much last night, so I got up and made some food. I wanted to catch you before you left this morning, so I waited until you turned on some lights. Do you mind?"

"No, I don't mind. How long were you out there? Normally, I don't get up for a few more hours."

"I wasn't out there long. Maybe half an hour or so. But I only would've waited about another half an hour or so before knocking and waking you up."

At his suggestion, Alex got dressed while he set up breakfast. Alex put on a pair of comfortable jeans and a blue t-shirt. She was walking into the kitchen area as she put her hair up in a blue tye-dye scrunchee. She took one look at the food and then did a quick double-take. The table was covered in a multitude of pasta dishes with different sauces. Salad and garlic bread finished out the selection. Then Alex looked at Tom questioningly. "Italian food? For breakfast?"

He started laughing. It was good to see him laugh. "I thought you said that you like Italian food. I love it. I can eat it anytime. Besides, it's all I really know how to cook."

"No other type is needed." Alex sat down and started nibbling at the food. "This is wonderful, Tom. I mean it, it's fantastic."

"Thanks." He smiled. "Do you mind if we talk while we eat?"

"Not at all. Anything in particular?"

"I thought about what you said last night for quite a long time. I'm still not exactly sure how I feel about what you did, but I understand your feelings. I may want to talk a little bit more about it at a later time, but not now."

"Okay. Anytime you want to talk, just let me know." She dug into some more food. Alex was glad that Tom knew her secret and would probably, in time, be able to accept it. At least, he was here with her and talking. "Do you really think I would have waited until now to get revenge on the man?"

Tom ignored the question. "Something else came up while Cliff was asking around. Your friends reluctantly told him that you have a saying 'you don't get mad, you get even, just not right away. It may take two days, it might take two months, but it will happen.'"

"Cripes! Lots of people say that, except for the time thing at the end. Besides, that's with pranks and such. Not murder." She hesitated briefly as something flitted on the edge of her brain and then disappeared. "I'm a little slow with comebacks, sometimes it takes me a while to come up with a good one. Besides, people expect get-backs to happen immediately. I prefer to give them time to forget about their incidents before I strike back. That way they let their guard down. But I emphasize again, it's with pranks NOT murder."

He nodded his head up and down a few times. "Sounds reasonable. What do you plan on doing today?"

"I have two more employees to question today and then my people are all clear."

"You sound awful certain."

"I am. Then I can start on that list of victims. That is, if you ever get it to me."

"Here it is. I realized once I left last night that I had forgotten to give it to you." He handed Alex the list. "But, I don't want you to work on the victim list, just to think it over and see if any names stick out. Investigating the list and people on it is the job of the police, me, my job." Tom said while tapping himself on the chest. "Okay? You understand?"

"Yeah, yeah, yeah." Alex waved her hand in the air. Just as she was starting to review it, Micky started howling.

"Alright, already. Let me see what you'd like."

"You're not going to feed him any of this food are you?"

"Of course I am. He loves Italian food as much as I do. I just make sure that I lick off most of the sauce first. Too much sauce irritates his gut."

She picked out a piece of lasagna, licked off most of the sauce, and dropped it on the floor in front of Mick. Mick didn't see it land. He started sniffing around, but gave up and looked at her like she played some kind of nasty trick on him. Alex chuckled and leaned over to point it out to him. All at once he saw it and pounced. While he was eating, she fed him some more. Tom started laughing, "I thought cats were supposed to have good sniffers."

"They do. It's just that I think Mick's is wearing out or something. Lately, his sniffer has been pretty weak. I think it has something to do with him being ten years old."

"It's a good thing he's a house cat. He'd starve otherwise."

"I'm glad he is too. Otherwise, he'd probably be dead. Outside cats don't seem to live this long."

"Alex, can you think of anyone in particular that's mad at you?"

"No, not really," she replied while shaking her head and eating.

"You told me you were married before correct?"

"Correct." Alex scrunched her forehead trying to figure out where

150

Tom's questions were heading.

"How about your ex? Does he have an axe to grind with you?"

"David? Not that I know of?"

"Your divorce amicable?"

Alex stopped eating and pushed her plate away. "Not particularly. But we didn't bring out the claws either. He was a tad upset that I asked for the divorce, but he made it through it. I don't believe I'm at the top of his 'A' list if you know what I mean, but I don't think he really wished me any ill will. Why are you asking me about him?"

"Usually the spouse, or ex-spouse is a prime suspect in cases similar to this one."

"He's not even in town."

"Yes, as a matter of fact, he is, or at least was."

"Really? Here? How do you know?"

"One, David Darr, was ticketed for speeding on the night of Abrahms murder?"

"You actually checked?"

"Or course, I try to be thorough. I requested any and all information possible on him before coming over last night. It should be on my desk when I get to work. Why were you so certain he wasn't in town?"

"Because he moved here when we got married. He has no family in this town. He did have some friends here while we were married, but whether they're still here or not, I wouldn't know. When we divorced, he moved back to his hometown. I haven't heard from him since."

"I'll check into why he was here." Tom took a few minutes to brief Alex on the damage to Cliff's car and Cliff's reaction. "I really don't believe Cliff had any knowledge of his car's misadventures. Please inform Cat of what I just told you. Tell her that I'll keep my eye on Cliff until he's proven to be in the clear, but I believe that her scenario is kaput. I admit that at first it didn't sound possible, but it has turned

151

out to be more probable than I originally thought. I'd ask you to apologize for me, however, I think Cat would probably prefer to hear it from me directly. Who knows? Maybe she'll even approve of me in terms of you, me, and us."

"I think she already approves of you..and me...and us. But you're right, Cat would just love to hear your apology straight from your mouth. She loves it when people have to admit that she's right. It happens so seldom." Alex laughed.

Tom chuckled. "Well, I'm glad that's settled. One more thing."

"What?" Alex asked.

"Before we got alerted to Cat's accident, you got a phone call from a Tony. Do you remember?"

"Yes, I remember."

"Who is he? Someone that could figure in on this case?"

Alex looked unsure for a moment. "He?"

"Yeah. You said Tony." Tom repeated.

Alex smiled slightly and replied, "Oh, I see where the problem is. Um…Toni is a woman, not a he, but a she. Toni is short for Antoinette. She and her husband, who also is named Tony, but spelled differently, own the local ice cream shop, Ice Cream Delights. She called to see if I could help out, because they will be having a bit of an employee shortage for a couple of days in a few weeks. When necessary, either I or one of my people will go over and help decorate cakes there."

"Should we be looking into them as possible suspects? They are not on any of my lists, I believe that you forgot to mention them earlier."

"You're right, I did forget. But where I have a key to their place, they do not have one to mine." Alex held up her hand to stop him from talking as she took a breath and continued, "And they were in Sacramento, California. Toni and Tony were visiting her favorite aunt when this all went down. They just got back to town. So they have very strong alibis."

Tom looked at his watch and stood up. "Alright, that's good to hear. I have to get to work." Tom scanned his eyes over the table. "May I leave this food here?"

"Sure. Git going. I'll clean up and put the leftovers in the fridge."

"You sure I can't help?"

"Yes, I'm sure. You cooked. Cleaning up is the least I can do. Besides, the food was excellent and it's going into my fridge. I thank you again."

Tom started for the door with Alex right behind. He turned around quickly and asked her to be careful. Then, he wrapped his arms around her and drew her close to him. With one final look into her deep brown eyes, he kissed her gently at first and then a little harder. Alex returned the kiss just as powerfully as he gave it to her, until they ran out of air. With a quick grab of her tush, he laughed at her squeal, and left the house.

Alex sucked air into her lungs and gleefully turned around to the table. As she put the food away, she tasted a little bit of everything. Micky got to try a few more things also. After she was done, she picked up the victim list and was about to read it when the phone rang. "Yo!"

"Yo yourself." Cat grumbled. "Are you coming to get me or what?"

"Oh, my gosh! I forgot! I'm on my way." Alex heard Cat cussing and yelling as she hung up the phone. Alex threw the list into her purse and flew out the door.

Chapter 22

Alex flew into Cat's hospital room. Her friend was sitting dejectedly in a chair. "Finally. I'm glad you found yourself a man, but does that give you an excuse to forget about your old, injured, and helpless friend. Although," Cat leaned her head to one side, "it has been a long time since you've had breakfast with a man, and in your own home nonetheless."

Alex, who was looking out the window, turned sharply to look at her friend. "I know that news travels quickly but this is warp speed." She ignored Cat's helpless and guilt routine.

Cat gave Alex a wicked grin. "So tell me. How is he?"

"I'm sure I don't know what you mean." Alex replied all innocently.

Cat sneered. "That innocent act doesn't work on me and you know it. The man gives you a picnic at night and breakfast in the morning and you don't know what I mean. Shame on you!"

"Who in the world is your informant? Whoever it is needs to get a life. I mean, crap, does someone have my place set up with remote cameras or should I check my trees whenever I make a move?" Alex grumbled and glared at Cat.

"Beats me," Cat laughed.

"Yeah, I just might. Well, you ready to go or not?"

"Damn straight I'm ready. Everything's signed that must be. All we have to do is leave."

Alex filled Cat in on most of the details with Tom, arguments included, on the way to Cat's house. She helped her friend get comfortable in the living room. She was about to leave when she decided to check her answering machine at home via Cat's phone. Even though it was only a little after nine in the morning, there were two messages from Tom on the machine. Both asking her to contact him at the station.

Alex dialed Tom's number and was informed that he had just stepped out for a minute. The person said that he would leave a message for him that she had called. Alex hung up the phone, said good-by to Cat, and started to leave when the phone rang. Cat picked up the portable, yelled for Alex, and threw her the phone.

"It's Tom." She grinned and wiggled her eyebrows.

"Grow up." Alex chided her, but smiled to lessen the impact of her words. With Cat laughing in the background, Alex said, "Hi, Tom!"

"I've got some great news for you babe."

"I could use some. What's up? Solve the case?"

"Sorry, ah….no. However, you can open your store as soon as you want."

"Wheeeeeeeeeeeeeeee! That's totally cool! Thanks!" Alex turned her head away from the phone and toward Cat. In her peripheral, she had caught Cat wildly waving her hands in the air. "What?"

"You'd better apologize to the man."

"Huh?"

"You probably just blew his eardrums to kingdom come with that screech of yours."

Alex sheepishly returned her attention back to the phone and Tom.

155

"Uh. You there Tom?"

"Barely. Dang woman! I know that you're happy, but sheesh, I need my ears today." He chuckled as he rubbed his ear. "I'm glad I could be of service to you."

Alex could picture him grinning on that last comment. "I don't have any complaints. Well, you know where I'll be, if you need me. There's a lot of work to do. If I can't get the girls into work today, I'll be there all day. If I leave, then someone there will know where I'll be. Sound like a plan?"

"Sounds like a plan to me. One thing though, your cell phone must be off or something. I tried to call you earlier and only got your voicemail, that's why I left messages at your house also."

"Thanks. I turned it off at the hospital when I picked up Cat and forgot to turn it back on."

"See ya. Take care beautiful."

Alex turned to Cat, "Where do you think you're going?"

"With you. I take it we're open for business again."

"You betcha." Alex walked over to Cat and they high-fived. "Are you sure about going in?"

"Yes, just try to leave me here." Cat challenged. "Let's go!"

Chapter 23

Alex and Cat pulled into the bakery's parking lot. As she parked in her normal spot, she looked at her favorite tree. It's a Linden Birch tree. She loved the way it had leaves of two different sizes and two different shades of green. The tree is as tall as a two story house. The trunk of the tree is one piece until its about five foot high and then it splits into two thick sections that disappear up into the tree's fullness of branches and leaves. From time to time, Alex would find flowers in the split of the tree.

When Alex parked her car, she looked at the split in the trunk and smiled. She saw some flowers laying there. When Alex and Cat got out of the car, Alex went to the tree to get them. They were very pretty and smelled nice. Cat watched her do this, "I see a couple of daisies and the one flower looks like what I sometimes buy my mom at Easter time. I don't recognize the other one, what is it. "

Alex frowned slightly. "I know the one is a white hyacinth and you're correct on the daisies of course, but this other one has me puzzled. I don't know what it is. Maybe I'll call the flower shop later and find out."

"I still think it is strange that someone leaves you flowers like this. A note or letter would be nice. You always have to figure out the meanings."

"Just think of it as my guardian angel. Someone is thinking of me and cares. Who knows, maybe the person doesn't know how to write or is no longer capable of writing. As for the flowers' meanings, my aunt taught me a lot, I just don't remember it all. So I'm inclined to look at it as a memory challenge and a cool reminder of my aunt. I do remember that a daisy represents 'patience' and a white hyacinth means 'I'll pray for you.' I think someone is telling me that they care about me and to just be patient and things will work out. I'll just have to figure out the last flower."

Alex and Cat entered the store and went to work immediately. The first thing they accomplished was to clean all the stuff off the floor and put it in their respective places. They turned on the store lights, put out the open signs and flags, and filled the register with change. Even though the store had only been closed a few days, it felt like an eternity to them. Alex called her friend, Randy, at the local radio station and asked if he could announce on the radio that she was open. He put her on hold for a few minutes, so he could check with his boss. Randy reported that his boss was happy to oblige. Since Alex did a lot of advertising on WCTT, they were happy to help out. Randy promised to throw in a statement or two about her re-opening a few times throughout the day. He wished her luck and hung up.

Alex and Cat returned to the back room to check cake orders for the weekend. Cat called each number to make sure that the order was still valid. Most of the customers expressed their happiness at the bakery reopening; however, many had placed orders elsewhere to insure themselves of a cake for the weekend. Cat told them that she totally understood and that they would appreciate any future business from the customers. She made sure that she thanked each person for their past business.

"Alex, I have good news and bad news."

"Give the bad news first."

"We had two wedding cakes for this weekend, but they both canceled. They both said that they didn't doubt your innocence, but were afraid that you wouldn't be open for this week. I reassured them of your innocence and added that we would like their business in the future."

"Thanks. I kind of expected that, but crap. I can just picture the comments and jokes about their wedding cakes and whether or not the bride and groom will survive their first bite of life together." Alex sighed deeply. "What's the good news?"

"There are a few novelty cakes. Not as many as originally ordered, but there are some."

"Some are better than none. Please start on calls to next week's people."

"Sure thing." Cat hobbled off to start her task.

Alex looked around her kitchen, there really wasn't anything to do at the moment. She figured that she best finish talking to her employees. Alex ran back to the front of the store and asked Cat if she could hold down the fort for a while. Cat looked around and dryly commented, "I believe I can handle this throng of people."

"Ha. Ha. Ha." Alex returned. "I realize there's no one here yet, but there may be soon. Are you sure you can handle everything with your leg in a cast?"

"Yes, Alex. I'm not an invalid. I can still get around. Now git going."

On her way out the door, she stopped. Using her cell phone, Alex took a couple of photos of the flower she couldn't identify.

Chapter 24

Alex decided the best course of action was to stop at the park, think about the "case," and decide how to finish her questioning. Alex loved the park with its big beautiful lake. It was a gorgeous day, so Alex parked her car and got out to walk by the lake and think. She saw the tree where Tom first kissed her and smiled. She walked over and sat below the tree. Alex allowed herself a few minutes to reminisce about Tom. She hoped that when the murder was solved, Tom would still be around. It surprised her that in such a short time, she could become attached to the man. She had just about given up on such an idea. Not too long ago, Alex figured tht she might as well kick back and plan on a life of being a single businesswoman. This of course brought her mind back to her business and its current problems.

Alex thought back over the information in her head. She reached into her purse and got out the list of Abrahms' victims that Tom had given her. Alex's mood saddened as she reviewed the names. They were all too familiar to her, but three names stood out in particular: her sister's, of course, Taylor's sister (thank gosh Tom had warned her already or else she would have jumped to some major conclusions of his guilt), and one, that unless she was wrong, looked to be a relative of Jo-Jo's. She'd have to check into that. Of the two employees left to interview, Jo-Jo apparently had a family member who was a victim of Abrahms and Didi did not. Alex also remembered Jo-Jo's one kid had had some kind of infection recently that required him to take penicillin. She figured that the above alone didn't prove anything. She had a hard time picturing Jo-Jo- killing anyone. Here, of course, is where her trouble lay. Alex had trouble picturing anyone she knew, or anyone period really, killing someone in the manner that Abrahms had bought it. Using a cake to kill, sounded like a plan not only thought out, but thought out over a very long period of time. It's not like the person killed out of panic or rage or jealousy. Alex's skin crawled as she thought of the amount of anger and cold-bloodedness needed to pull off this crime. Her mind went over the events since the murder. In comparison to the original crime, the later attacks and vandalism seemed rushed and very messy. This made it seem as if different people completed the different crimes. But that was impossible, unless....conspiracy maybe? Alex rolled her eyes as she quietly berated herself. She had read entirely too many mystery books. To be fair, it was possible they were related. She shook her head as she thought it out. In her gut, she knew they were related. Maybe the murderer had planned the original crime for such a long time and had run through it so many times in his/her head, that doing it in reality was just another run through. However, reality had thrown in a "curve ball" that the murderer hadn't planned. That would explain the rush in the follow-up crimes. Alex looked across the lake without really seeing it. What was that "curve ball"?

Alex was jolted back to reality and the present when she heard someone scream, "Watch out!" She turned to look toward the noise when a body fell on top of her. After a few minutes of chaos and a few childish screams, her "attacker" rolled away from her. He got up with some heavy breathing and with a bright red face. With some shuffling of his feet, and without quite looking at her face, he apologized. Alex looked a little closer at the young boy. He stood around four foot tall and had a full head of tousled blond hair. She looked at his grass stained clothes and reached down to gently raise his head upward. She looked into his mischievous hazel eyes and smiled. "Your name's

Quinton, isn't it? Isn't your mama's name Jo-Jo?"

A big smile erupted on the kid's face, "Yes, ma'am." Before the shock disappeared from her face, Quinton turned and ran to whence he came.

When Alex's eyes turned from the disappearing kid and onto the oncoming adult, she smiled. "Hey! How are you doing?"

"I should be the one asking you that question, Alex. My kid hit you pretty hard."

"No, not really. I just didn't see him coming." Alex looked at her employee, one she also considered her friend. "You should be proud of him. He's one polite kid. He apologized and threw me for a loop." Alex chuckled. "I think what shocked me more than his tackle, was when he called me 'ma'am.'"

With a glance toward her playing children, Jo-Jo sat on the ground beside Alex. "Yeah, well, we try to teach the kids manners." With a grin on her face, she giggled and said, "And I hate to tell you this, but you are old enough to be called 'ma'am.'"

Alex cringed briefly and dramatically. "Argggh! Don't remind me." They were laughing for a few minutes when Alex got to cringe with real emotion as Jo-Jo screamed at the top of her lungs at one of her kids to stop doing some sort of action or other. Alex couldn't really comprehend what the problem was, because her ears were ringing something fierce as Jo-Jo got up to chase her kids. She shook her head a few times to clear her ears, and then got up to follow her employee. Alex watched as Jo-Jo managed to get two of her kids off of her third one. They had played "flesh pile" with the results of the youngest child being squished on the bottom. Jo-Jo examined her youngest child while he flustered about. He didn't think anything of his being pummeled and just wanted to get back to the rest of the kids. With one last swipe of her hand to remove some dirt, his mom double-checked his knee and sent him on his way.

Alex was invited to join Jo-Jo on their picnic blanket and she accepted. As she was getting adjusted on the blanket, Alex felt a rock under the left side of her tush and scooched uphill a little to get away from it. She smiled as she moved, remembering the last and real recent time she found herself on a picnic blanket. The thoughts of Tom put her back on track for questioning. "Jo-Jo, would you mind if I asked you some questions?"

Jo-Jo shrugged. "I don't mind. Is this about that guy's death?"

Alex indicated it was and gave a quick explanation as to why she was questioning everyone. As she talked, she tried to observe her friend's reaction. Getting a true reading was hard because the kids kept interrupting or otherwise gaining their mom's attention. "Do you understand what all I have told you and is this going to be a problem?" Alex hesitated apprehensively and then continued on. "I just want to make sure that you don't think I'm accusing you of anything, because I'm not."

Jo-Jo didn't respond immediately. She took a few minutes to watch her kids and make sure they were okay. She slowly turned her head to Alex and examined her face. Calmly, she said, "I don't have a problem with you asking any questions. I didn't kill the man nor did I take any active part in doing so, so ask away. But if I may ask first, how did you know to fnd me here?"

"I didn't. Originally, I stopped here at the lake to try to put my thoughts together. I planned on going over to your place next, so it was just fortuitous that you were already here. I didn't know you were here until your son bowled me over."

Alex was confused to see a sense of relief cross over Jo-Jo's face before it was replaced with a slight grin as she watched her kids playing around. "I was wondering if you knew anyone or overheard someone who was particularly angry with Matthew Abrahms?"

Disbelief and anger filled Jo-Jo's face as she answered. "Everyone in town hated him, including me……..and I know that you hated him too."

"Yes, I did. But what he did to us took place a long long time ago. I was looking for something a little more recent."

"Why?"

"Why what?" Alex asked bewildered.

"Why more recent? Didn't he do enough in the past?" She vehemently spit out.

Alex was taken back by the power in Jo-Jo's voice. "Definitely. But why would someone wait so long for revenge?"

Jo-Jo had a strange look on her face as she answered. "Many reasons. Maybe the person was incapacitated for some time. Maybe the person was out-of-state. Maybe the person lacked a weapon or the proper opportunity. The list of reasons can be endless. You had an excellent reason to want the bastard dead, Alex. Are you sure that subconsciously you didn't have something to do with the murder?"

Emotions of all sorts rushed through Alex. "Do you actually believe that?"

"I don't know what to believe anymore. I do know that everyone in the bakery had a reason for wanting that man dead. I know for a fact that you and Cat tried to get revenge for your sister's death years ago. Maybe now you two managed to get it right. I believe you know that the man also killed my sister. What you don't know is that he had stalked and assaulted her before he killed her. He didn't just kill her quickly, he mutilated her. He defiled her. He….." She broke off in tears and reached for a napkin.

Quinton ran over and stood defensively between his mom and Alex. "What did you do? Why did you make my mommy cry?"

Alex just stared at the little boy, she didn't know what to say or do. Her mind was still mixed up with emotions and information. Jo-Jo came to the rescue. She reached around her son and turned him to face her. "It's okay honey. She didn't do anything. Mommy's just a little tired and we're discussing a difficult subject. I think it's about time we go home." Jo-Jo smiled and wiped her face. She hugged her son. Jo-Jo asked him to round up his brother and sister and all their toys. He looked at his mom, smiled, and kissed her on her cheek. Before he left, he turned and stuck his tongue out at Alex and ran off for his siblings.

A small smile graced Jo-Jo's face as she apologized for Quinton's actions. Alex felt about as low as she could ever remember. "That's alright. He's just trying to protect you. I like his spunk. I'm sorry I'm causing you all this pain, Jo-Jo. I'm just trying to figure out what happened. I truly don't believe you are responsible for this murder. I can also assure you that neither I nor Cat had anything to do with it either. I do have a few more questions that I would like to ask if you're up to it. I'm asking everyone the same questions, so please don't think I'm picking on just you."

Jo-Jo looked around wearily. "You have as long as it takes me to clean up here and load the kids up in the van."

"That's fair enough." Alex got up as Jo-Jo did. She helped her employee start to clean up, but very slowly. She needed the time to finish asking questions. "Do you happen to have any penicillin at home?"

Jo-Jo hesitated briefly and then finished cleaning off the blanket. "Yes. I'm sure there's some at home right now. Things accumulate in the medicine cabinet for a while before I end up cleaning it out. With kids around, there always seems to be penicillin around. I swear, it always seems like one of the kids either has some kind of infection or just finished with one. I know I'm supposed to give the whole prescription to the kids, however, sometimes I end up with one or two tablets left over. But then, you wouldn't understand that Alex, would you?"

Alex was stunned into silence once again. She never would have believed this woman to harbor such nastiness toward her. She wondered what was really behind all the hate. She wanted to leave immediately, but knew she couldn't. She still had to ask at least one more question. Alex helped Jo-Jo pick everything up and head for the kids and the van. "Just one more thing Jo-Jo. What were you doing on Saturday between four fifteen and four twenty-five?"

Jo-Jo was quiet as they herded the kids to the van. Except for a few comments to her children, she remained quiet as they strapped the children into their car seats. As they were putting the stuff in the rear of the van, she answered the question. "Rick and I had taken the children to my mother's earlier in the day, somewhere around ten. We did chores around the house until it was time to get ready for the party. When we left the house, we headed straight for the party."

"You and Rick were together the whole time on Saturday?"

"Yes." She hesitated briefly. "Except when he went to the hardware store for a few odds and ends."

"Do you remember the exact time he was gone?"

"No. You'd have to ask him. I know it was sometime in the late afternoon."

"But you remained at the house the entire time?"

"Yes."

"What did you do while Rick was out?"

"I cleaned the basement."

"No one saw you or called you?"

"No one and no. Is that it?" She asked nastily.

"Yes. That's it." Alex tried hard to say politely.

166

Jo-Jo shut the van's back door and turned slowly to Alex. In a real low voice, so low that Alex had to lean toward her, she whispered with a tear running down her cheek. "If you and Cat had just succeeded, my sister would be alive today." With that she ran to the driver's door, got in, and drove away leaving Alex with her mouth hanging open and her eyes watering. Her sister! Alex did not even know that Jo-Jo had had a sister killed – let alone one killed by Abrahms.

Chapter 25

Alex sat in her papasan chair slowly stroking Micky's fur. She felt emotionally drained and physically exhausted after talking to Jo-Jo. She was heavy into self-pity when the phone rang. She decided to let her answering machine take a message; however, when she heard Cat's voice, she reached for the phone quickly and turned off the machine. "Cat! Sorry about that. What's up?"

"I thought you were coming back to the store. Did you forget something at home?"

Alex stammered, "Ah-h-h-h-h. No. I guess I just forgot. Is everything okay?" She asked suddenly concerned.

Cat listened carefully to her friend's voice before answering. "Yes. Everything's cool here. As we figured, there's not a lot of business." Cat hadn't liked the sound of Alex and was about to close the store to come see what was happening. "What's wrong, Alex?"

Alex sighed, "Nothing Cat. I guess I'm just bummed out a bit."

"Just a bit? Alex, you forgot to come back to the store and you say that you're bummed out a *bit*? What happened after you left the store? Did you interview Jo-Jo and Didi?"

"Just Jo-Jo. That was enough. To tell the truth, she put a huge guilt trip on me and unfortunately I left it take hold." She answered sullenly.

"It's almost five o'clock. Do you want me to close up now and come over?"

"What? Five already?" Alex was confused and a tad disoriented and Cat could tell it in her voice. "Ah…no. I don't want you to close up early. I'm alright. I'm just beat. I'll see you in the morning, okay Cat?"

"Sure, Alex," Cat replied to a dial tone because Alex had already hung up the phone. Cat was worried. Alex didn't sound good. She wondered what Jo-Jo could possibly have said to throw her friend off balance. Cat looked down at the cast on her leg and swore, then looked around quickly to make sure that there was no one around to hear her. Alex had dropped her off and had been scheduled to pick her up. She looked at her watch and knew that it would be impossible to reach Mike at this time. She was just reaching for the telephone when she heard a car door shut. Cat looked expectantly at the door when a sound behind her caused her to jump and swear again. "My, my, my, my, my Cat. You have some mouth on you. Didn't your mama ever wash it out with soap?" Tom chuckled. He raised his hands placatingly, "Sorry, I didn't mean to scare you." The look of relief that washed over Cat's face as soon as she got done swearing, caused Tom to tense up quickly. He didn't think this woman would ever be happy to see him, at least not for a good reason.

"Thank the Lord you're here."

"Why? What's up?" He looked around quickly, "Where's Alex?"

"At home." Cat got up to close the store. "And *where* ain't the problem." She quieted as she rang out the register.

Tom's gut started to knot up immediately. He didn't recognize the tone in Cat's voice and that bugged him. "Well, what is the problem?" He growled.

"Lock the door and turn the sign to close, okay?"

Tom rolled his eyes and counted to ten. He knew that he had to keep his temper in check. If it was an emergency, Cat would be pushing him out the door and screaming at him. He did as he was asked. As he turned to see what else needed done, he realized that he was alone. With a huff, he went to find Cat. He found her in the back room hobbling around and getting ready to leave. "You seem preoccupied. What's up woman?" He thundered and followed her out the door. He looked around and asked, "How are you getting home, Cat? Mike picking you up?"

"You're taking me home. On the way, I'll fill you in. Now let's go!" She commanded as she opened up his side door.

As Tom drove, Cat filled him in on what Alex had done that day or was supposed to do. She explained her call to Alex, Alex's response or lack thereof, and her worries for her friend. "Can you check on Alex? If yes, please take me to my house. If no, please drop me off at Alex's."

Tom stated that he would check on Alex. He helped Cat into her house the best he could, basically just making sure she hobbled without falling. He figured that anything more would just piss her off. He was sure her leg and other aches and pains were bugging her more than what she was letting on, otherwise, they'd be at Alex's right now. "If you don't call me by eight o'clock, I will be calling you." He nodded affirmatively and went out the door. He almost had the door closed when he heard Cat call his name. He popped his head around the door and gave her a questioningly look.

"Thanks." She said sincerely.

"No problem. You're welcome." Tom carried Cat's look of concern and apprehension and her sound of sincerity with him as he returned to his vehicle and headed down the road to Alex's.

Tom knocked on Alex's door a few times and had called her name a few more before he tried the door and found it unlocked. He opened the door and called out her name again as he entered. As his eyes adjusted to the slightly dimmer lighting in the house, he saw her sitting in her papasan chair. "Alex" he whispered as he approached. She was just sitting there staring into the corner where Georgy used to sit. Tears were rolling slowly down her face as she gently petted Micky. Music was softly playing in the background. "Alexandra" he said slightly louder as he sat on the sofa facing her. Tom was beginning to wonder if he should call a doctor. Micky jumped to the floor, gave Tom a nasty glare, and swaggered out of the room. Tom reached over and laid a hand on her knee. Alex's face slowly became focused and tuned onto him. She gave him a slight smile and inhaled deeply. "Thomas, how are you?"

"Me? I'm fine. It's you I'm worried about." He removed his hand from her leg.

Her smile deepened. She closed her eyes and listened to the music for a second or two more. Then she shook her head and wiped at the tears on her face. "I'm okay. I was wallowing in self-pity for a while before letting my mind wander into the past." She looked at the clock and was startled. "Look at the time." She started to get up while saying "I must look a fright."

Tom reached back over to her and gently stopped her from getting up. "Tell me what happened today."

Alex shook her head a little harder to try to clear the rest of the cobwebs. As she thought back to the beginning of this long day, she suddenly turned back to the clock, once again she started to get up, "Oh my gosh! Cat! I forgot…"

Tom once again stopped her from rising and interrupted her. "Don't worry. Cat's at home and the store is closed up for the day. She told me that you were acting weird and asked that I check on you. I must admit I haven't known you for long, but this doesn't seem to be typical of you."

He quieted as he heard a strange noise. He cocked his head trying to place the sound. "What's that noise? It almost sounds like a wolf howling?"

Alex started laughing. It felt good. At Tom's look of confusion and some alarm, Alex only laughed harder. "Don't worry, I'm not losing it. It's just that if you could just see your face. It is a wolf's howl. I have three cds in the sound system. One is plain jazz. One is a cello playing beautiful gospel music. And the other…." She looked at him and smiled broadly "is wolf jazz."

"What the heck is that?"

"It's a blend of jazz music with wolf howls and in some cases

171

growls."

He lifted an eyebrow, "That's weird. And this…." He wafted his hand through the air "calms you?"

Alex inhaled and settled back in the chair. "Yes. Calming might be one way of saying it. If I have a particularly trying day or I have a massive headache, I play this music to mellow out or clear my mind."

"Is that what I saw when I came in?"

Alex sobered quickly. "No. That was me screwed up. I interviewed someone today that messed with some deep emotions."

"Cat told me that you mentioned a guilt trip also."

Alex exhaled quickly. "That too, I don't know how you do it. Your job I mean. I actually felt washed out by the time I was done talking to Jo-Jo."

"My job can do that to a person sometimes, but most of the time it doesn't, because we don't allow it to. We're trained to separate ourselves or not to personalize it, or else we'd get burned out pretty fast. You have to remember that you are emotionally attached to this case and to all of the people involved. That's a lot of pressure. Normally, I'm not."

Alex smiled, "Normally?"

He returned the smile, "Yes, normally. This time I have to struggle to remain impartial and unfortunately I'm having trouble with that. Getting too close can cause one to jump to incorrect conclusions. One has a tendency to make the evidence fit a scenario instead of letting the evidence show the way." He settled back into the cushions as the realization that Alex was really okay sunk in. "Now, please tell me what happened to put you into such a funk."

Alex told him of her conversation with Jo-Jo. She asked Tom if he could check on Rick's whereabouts Saturday afternoon. Tom nodded and she continued on. Her voice got strained as she finished her tale with Jo-Jo's last comment. "She blew me away Tom. I know that she has two sisters. I did not know that she had had three. It just blows my mind about what I am learning. I thought I knew these people and I'm finding out how much I don't or didn't know."

Tom responded gently. "People only let you know what they want you to know. Some things are best kept in the dark. Some things are just too personal to share."

Alex slowly inhaled and exhaled. "I came home to just let myself return to normal and instead ended up thinking about my own sister and the way she died. She had been mutilated too. Oh, not in the same way as Jo-Jo's sister, but the casket was closed because of what the accident had done to her." She quieted again. When she looked at Tom, he raised his arms out to her and she went to him. She sat beside him on the sofa and sank into his embrace.

"You let your mind wander over the implications of her comment to you, didn't you?"

Alex nodded her head up and down on his chest. "In a way, she's right. If Abrahms had died when he fell down those stairs, a lot of people would have been spared a ton of pain."

Tom was getting a bit angry. "Alex. You ought to know better than this. 'Should've,' 'would've,' and 'could've' are a waste of time. What happened, happened. If indeed, you and Cat had something to do with that supposed accident, and he died, you two would have been arrested. You would not be here today enjoying the life you now have. Abrahms would have had two more victims, just not dead ones. You don't know what might have happened or not. You are not an omnipotent being. You're just human like the rest of us."

"Speaking of being human," Alex muttered as she moved her face up to his. She started to kiss him on the lips. Tom reacted strongly, his kisses forceful and full of passion. She slowly moved her hand to his groin. She felt him harden at her touch.. His hand slid up under her blouse and caressed a breast. "Make love to me Thomas." She whispered between kisses.

He kissed her a couple more times, but slowly shook his head while emotions battled each other inside it. "No. I'm sorry. I can't." He whispered.

Even though he spoke as gently and caringly as possible, Alex reacted as though she had been slapped. She pulled away and spit out, "You can't? Or you won't?"

He looked at her. Every cell in his body wanted her. He knew it had been a very long time since he yearned so badly for a woman, but he also knew now was not the time. His heart tugged hard as tears once again sprung from Alex's eyes and rolled down her delicate cheeks. "Now, is not good timing."

He winced at her reaction. "Timing? What the hell does timing have to do with anything? I though you said that you didn't have a girlfriend?"

"I don't Alex. I…."

She didn't let him finish. "Then what? Don't you find me attractive? Don't you want me? Am I misreading things that badly?"

Tom sputtered a few times. "No, you're not misreading anything. Of course, I want you. Couldn't you feel me react to you?"

"Yes, I did. That's why I'm not getting this. I don't understand your rejection?" She whined and that only made her more upset. She hated whining and she hated herself for doing it. Alex couldn't believe how screwed up her emotions were. What was wrong with her? "Get a grip woman" she mentally told herself. She was stronger than this.

Tom seemed to instinctively sense what she was doing. "Alexandra, please look at me." Alex looked directly into his eyes. "All I'm trying to say is…….let's wait. I want to make love to you with all my heart

174

and soul, but only when it's the right time. Right now, I know that you have some emotions to work through. I don't want to add to your problem. I want to be able to look back and know that this is something we both wanted and were ready for. I don't want your mind confused or looking for love for the wrong reason. I don't want us to look back at our first time together and remember this murder mess. Alex, I want out first time to be special, don't you?"

"Yes, I do." Sniffling, Alex replied after thinking through his words. She could feel his emotion and caring coming through as he spoke. She had to struggle to try to handle things as an adult, and not as a spoiled child upset at not getting her own way. "And you're right." Just then, the phone rang. Tom looked at the clock and motioned that he would get it.

On his return, Alex asked who was on the phone. "I forgot to call Cat. She was worried about you. I had agreed to call her at eight and forgot." He settled onto her couch beside Alex again and looked into her eyes. "I had something else on my mind."

"Does this mean you're leaving tonight?"

Tom gently pushed some hair out of Alex's eyes and smiled. "Not if you don't want me to."

"I really don't want you to go."

"Then it's settled. I'm staying. What do you want to do?"

"Cuddle?" As he opened his arms for her, she added, "Could you hold me all night?"

"Of course." He softly replied as she laid her head on his chest and they wrapped their arms around each other.

Chapter 26

Alex awoke the next morning in bed. She looked at the clock and her eyes took a moment to focus on the time. It was six o'clock. The time was right, but the alarm didn't go off. She was trying to figure out how she happened to wake up on time when there came a knock on her bedroom door. She panicked momentarily as she tried to clear her fuzzy brain to figure out who was in her house. Alex calmed immediately once she heard Tom's voice softly call her name. "Yeah, I'm awake." She quickly lifted the covers and looked down at her body. Alex blew out a sigh of relief as she noticed that she was fully dressed. She looked around her and her gut wretched a bit as she noticed that both pillows showed signs of being slept on. Alex shook her head to try to clear it. She'd never had a hangover, but she figured that she must be experiencing something like one. She couldn't remember how she got to bed. Slowly the bedroom door opened, Tom poked his head around and smiled. Quickly, he read her mental status. "Confused?"

"Definitely." She sat up and unconsciously ran her fingers through her hair. She knew she looked absolutely horrible.

"What do you remember last?"

Alex tried to concentrate. "Mornings aren't really my thing." She joked and then shut up as the memories came flooding in. Embarrassed, she looked at the sheets. "I believe I remember making a bloody fool of myself last night."

"That's funny." Alex looked up at Tom at his comment with a quizzical expression as he continued. "I don't remember that at all. I remember a woman who was in need of comforting. I'm just glad I was there to provide it; however, I'm sure that you would have managed pretty well on your own." He came into the room with a glass of orange juice and handed it to her. As he watched her drink the juice, "If you're wondering how you just happened to wake up on time, you can thank Cat. I called her last night and asked her when you needed up. By the way, she said that Maggie was going to take her to work today, so you're not to worry. I started breakfast, so if you want to get a quick shower, it'll be ready in about fifteen minutes."

Alex thanked him and meandered out of bed. She grabbed some clothes and disappeared into the bathroom. As she showered, Alex tried to remember the events of the night before. She shook her head as she remembered coming onto Tom and her reaction to his, now tht she thought about it, reasonable "rejection." She froze as she heard the door open quietly. Alex instinctively covered herself with her arms as she turned to look through her clear shower curtain. She saw a hand reach inside the room and place another glass of juice on the sink counter. "How did I get into the bedroom last night?" The hand hesitated and a voice floated through the steam in the room. "I carried you." She smiled as she watched that same hand disappear. She silently hugged herself with joy as the full impact of just what kind of man Thomas Andrew Baker was sunk in. She girlishly giggled as she thanked God for sending her such a decent man. She could only hope and pray that they could have a wonderful relationship. She refused to really think of marriage at this point. Why screw things up? Energized and renewed, Alex finished her shower and got dressed.

Alex finished her second glass of juice as she entered the kitchen. "Just in time," Tom smiled as he divvied up the food onto two plates. Alex looked at the ground and sheepishly spoke. "I've cried more in the last few days than I remember crying in my lifetime. It makes me uncomfortable to cry in front of people. It seems that every time I've cried recently, you've been there to see me. I hope you don't think that's all I do, as if I'm just one huge crybaby." As she finished speaking, her eyes raised to meet his.

Tom's mouth turned slightly upward at the corners as Alex spoke. He reached over their plates on the kitchen island and touched her chin. "I don't believe that at all. Besides, you're not all that huge." He chuckled. He got serious as he walked around the island and put his hands on Alex's waist. "There's nothing wrong with crying, Alex. It's a natural human emotion. I know what you've been going through. You have had plenty of reasons to cry. Believe me, I understand." He cocked his head to one side as he continued to speak. "Do you remember *everything* we discussed last night?"

Alex blushed deeply and tried to pull away. "Yes, I believe I do."

Tom tightened his grip and pulled her closer to him. He lowered his face to hers. "Don't be embarrassed. I meant what I said about making love to you. Another time, I'll prove it." Tom kissed Alex and felt his body react to her. He couldn't believe the power this woman had on him. For her, he would try to solve this case in the next few days, even if he had to do most of the work on personal time. He gently pulled away to give Alex some breathing room. "Shall we eat?"

Alex put her left hand on her chest and inhaled. "Wow!" she said to herself. To Tom, she merely said, "Sure."

Alex looked at Tom as she finished her breakfast, "What are you staring at?"

"You."

Alex looked slightly alarmed as she asked, "Why? Do I have food on my face somewhere?"

Tom laughed. "No, nothing like that. I was just thinking that no matter how much I learn about you, there's always something new to learn."

"Anything in particular?" She asked warily.

"Your bedroom ceiling."

"What about it?"

"It's interesting."

"I'm confused." Alex responded scrunching up her forehead.

Tom laughed. "I'm talking about the stars."

Alex joined in the merriment. "What? Oh! My stars. I like my stars." She responded slightly defensively.

"I didn't say I didn't. I've just never seen them before. I thought they were kind of neat. What exactly are they?"

"They're little pieces of glow-in-the-dark vinyl or plastic. I can take them down or move them very easily because they stay up by some form of static electricity. I have always loved the stars and this is a wonderful way to brush up on my constellations. My ceiling is covered with the northern hemisphere right now. This is the best way I found to sleep under the stars. I can do it all year round and one can't catch a cold this way."

"Or run into a skunk." Tom chuckled and she joined in.

Chapter 27

Alex arrived at the bakery bright-eyed and bushy-tailed. When she entered the main room, she observed both Cat and Maggie with their feet propped up on the one table, chawing down on some cinnamon rolls. When they saw Alex, Maggie swung her legs to the floor and bounced up. Cat did not change her position, the cast seemed more comfortable this way. They both shouted, "Alex!" together.

"Morning guys! Any problems?"

Maggie and Cat smiled at each other and said that they smoothed over any difficulties that they may have had. "Great! Glad to hear it." She looked at the rolls on the table and asked if there were any more.

Cat smiled, "Sure. But first, it's time for a group hug." One ran and the other hobbled over to Alex. Alex, who was never a really huggy person, was getting better at it and put her arms around her friends. After a second or two, they parted and went to finish the rolls off.

Maggie paused between bites, "Yo, Alex."

"Yeah?"

"How's Tom? I heard he spent the night."

Alex just about choked on her roll. "Where'd you find that out?" Maggie didn't say a word, she just smiled at Cat. Alex turned to her other friend and glared. "Just who is your news source? You have a leg in a cast, and you still know things at lightning speed. Just which one of my nosy neighbors is your pipeline?"

Cat just smiled a superior grin that turned into a fun-loving grin. She lightly smacked Alex's shoulder, "Think about it Alex. Maggie picked me up and Tom's car was in your driveway, you add it up. It doesn't take a genius to add two and two."

"Usually, for you, that equals five." Alex looked at them with innocent eyes. "Besides, couldn't he have just dropped in before going to work?"

"Yeah, right." Both Maggie and Cat responded sarcastically together with simultaneous rolling of the eyes. "And we're Mother Teresa."

"Besides, he did call me last night and ask when you normally got up in the morning."

"Oh, yeah. I forgot. He told me that this morning when I woke up." Alex looked at the glint in her friends' eyes, "Okay, out with it."

Maggie and Cat looked at each other and tried to look innocent, but failed miserably. "What do you mean, Alex?" Cat inquired.

"There's something going on between you two, now what is it?"

Maggie smiled. "Oh, that." She waved her hand to show it was nothing. "We were just talking about how serendipitous your new relationship is with this cop."

"What do you mean?" Alex was confused.

"Serendipitous means that…"

Alex interrupted Maggie with a snort and the roll of her eyes, "I know the definition dummy. What exactly were the two of you discussing?"

"We thought it was interesting how a Baker met up with an Applecake who just happens to own and operate a bake shop." Maggie smirked and started to chuckle.

Alex just stared at her friends. Her mouth was slightly slack-jawed. She rubbed her forehead with her hand, ran the hand through her hair, and groaned, "Oh, no! I never thought about that. Am I going to have to listen to jokes about names now?"

Cat and Maggie started laughing hard. "Of course, at least until we get bored with the subject."

"You two get bored? I don't think so."

Laughing, they all licked their fingers, cleaned up their garbage, washed their hands, and got ready for work After some solid hours of work, Didi showed up to help open the store. There were no Thursday or Friday cakes, however, the Saturday ones were baked. While the cakes cooled, the pans and baking stuff were cleaned and put away. Maggie got ready to leave, "You need anything else done Alex?"

"No. It's a light week. Go on home, I'll see you tomorrow."

Maggie waved and left for the day. Alex went into the office while Cat wrapped the cakes for later decorating. When Cat walked into the office, she saw Alex with her feet propped up on a pulled out desk drawer. She was tilted back in the chair with her hands behind her neck, a smile on her face. Cat started chuckling. In a sing-song manner she said, "I know who you're thinking about."

"Oh, really?"

"Oh, definitely. It's that man. Thomas." Cat pulled over a chair from the baking area and thumped her cast onto the desk. With a raise of her brows, her eyes twinkled. "He's good, isn't he?"

"Yes, he's definitely a good man. However, not in the manner you think. In what you're thinking, I wouldn't know."

"Oh, please! Give me a break, woman! If you don't want to kiss and tell, just say so, but it ain't worth lying about."

"I'm not lying, Cat." Alex seriously replied. She got up and closed the office door. "This is for your ears only. If anyone says anything to me, I'll know where it came from." Alex then proceeded to tell her best friend everything that did and didn't happen. "He's a wonderful man, Cat. I just hope I don't get burned."

Cat watched her friend and with all sincerity she said, "I can't believe I'm saying this about a cop. But, he sounds like a great man. I don't think he'll let you get away. And I don't think he'll burn you either." If he does, I'll kill him, she finished to herself.

"I know." Alex responded firmly. "I just needed to talk."

Cat got up to do some more work. "Anytime Alex," she put a hand on Alex's shoulder and left the office. Alex looked at all the mail on her desk, sighed, and "rolled up her sleeves" and got to work. She had just sorted the junk mail into the garbage and the real mail into some semblance of priority, when Didi entered the office. She looked up and grimaced. Didi was pale and shaking a bit. "What's wrong Didi?" Alex asked concerned.

"I don't feel well, Alex. It might be the flu or something. I was wondering if it would be possible for me to leave early?"

"Yeah, sure. I didn't hear too much noise over the intercom earlier, has it been busy? Sorry, I haven't been out to check."

"Oh, that's okay. There were only a few customers."

"I thought so. We can cover for the day. Do you need any more time than that?"

"No, I don't think so." Didi hemmed and hawed around for a few minutes. "Ah...one more thing."

"Anything, you know that."

"Is it possible to get a ride home? Carlos is at work. I don't want to call him if I don't have to."

"Sure Didi. Let me clear things with Cat and we'll be on our way."

Didi swallowed and gave a thin smile. "Thanks. I'll get my stuff."

On the way to Didi's place, Alex decided the timing wasn't the best in one way, but excellent in another way. "Didi, may I ask you a few questions? I realize my timing isn't the best, but you're the last of my employees to question." She quieted when Didi put a hand on Alex's thigh.

"It's okay, Alex. Really, I know what you're trying to do. Jo-Jo called and told me all about it. So you might as well ask me what you want to know."

Alex smiled. "Thanks. Do you know anyone who wanted Abrahms dead?"

"Yes." Alex's head swung over to look at Didi at her simple response. At Alex's questioning look, Didi continued. "Just about everyone I know. Including you. But do I know anyone who would have killed him? No."

"Where were you on the Saturday he died from four fifteen to four twenty-five?"

Didi rested back against her headrest as she thought about that Saturday. "I believe I was at home with Carlos. We had played some tennis that morning and some other athletic games. Afterwards, we took showers and a nap before getting ready for George's party. Then we went to the party."

"Cool. Then that clears us all. I wanted to show the cops that I was thorough and could clear everyone at the bakery. This way, they can concentrate on other people." Alex pulled into Didi's driveway. "Here we are."

"Thanks, Alex." Didi gave Alex another wan smile.

Alex waited until Didi was at the door and then jumped out of the car to follow her. "Just one more thing? If you don't mind?"

Didi unlocked the door. "Okay. Do you want to come in? I'd like to take a few aspirin or something. Hopefully, that and some sleep will clear whatever this is out of my system."

"Thanks." Alex smiled and followed Didi inside. Alex wandered around Didi's living room while she waited for her friend to return. She couldn't remember the last time she was in this house. Her face brightened as her eyes fell upon a huge aquarium against one wall. She walked over to see if she could identify the different types of fish. She smiled as she saw an elephant nose fish hovering in a fake cave in the back corner. She became just ecstatic when she noticed that Didi also had a knife fish. A small handsome whale, some beautiful clown loaches, and tri-colored sharks shared the tank with the knife and elephant nose. Alex took a double-take on a fish that was sitting close to the bottom of the tank behind some fake foliage. Alex had her face so close to the tank that she looked like she was kissing it when Didi came back into the room. "Alex? What are you doing?"

Alex jumped, she didn't hear the woman come into the room. "Aaah!" she shrieked. She turned around putting her hand to her heart, "Sorry. I didn't hear you. I was just looking at your aquarium. It's wonderfull! Except.." She stepped out of the way for Didi to come closer and pointed to the fish she had been observing. "I think you have a sick fish. Have you been having any problems?"

"A while back, we did. But nothing lately."

"Well, you might want to keep an eye on things. I think that fish might have body fungus. If you have any ampicillex, that should take care of it. You have some beautiful fish here, I'd hate to see the disease spread and possibly kill them."

"Thanks. I'll leave a note for Carlos. I like fish. I just don't know all that much about them. However, he'll probably have to go get the proper medicine. Jo-Jo called us some time back and asked Carlos about a problem with a tank. The pet store was closed, so she ended up coming over here and getting some of our stuff." Didi glanced at the tank briefly and then turned to Alex. "Was there something else that you wanted to ask? I really would like to lie down for a while."

Alex slapped her forehead with a hand. "Jeez! I'm sorry. Yeah, just one more thing. Do you have any penicillin?"

Didi touched her cheek with a finger while she thought about it. "We might. I haven't cleaned out the medicine cabinet for some time. I know some time back Carlos had a tooth pulled and he had a prescription for some. Whether he finished it or not, I'm not sure. You know how that is."

"Yeah, I know. Well, I'm sorry for taking your time. I hope that you feel better." Alex turned as she reached the door. "Take tomorrow and Saturday off, Didi. We can handle any business until Monday. You just rest and get your health back. Hopefully, business will return to normal soon and there will be plenty of work for everyone."

Didi smiled weakly. "Thanks a lot Alex. I owe you." She shut the door behind Alex and went to bed.

Alex smiled as she headed for the car. She was done talking to her people and they were clear, just like she thought in the beginning. She wondered how Tom was doing with Cliff and the case. She knew it was wishful thinking, but she hoped he had already solved it.

As per normal, as Alex passed Cassie's pet store, she turned to look at it. The sight of Cassie running through her store with arms flailing around above her had almost caused Alex to come to a dead stop in the middle of the road. A nasty screech and loud honk of a car horn from behind her startled Alex into action. She stepped on the gas pedal and pulled off to the side of the road. She mouthed a "sorry" to the angry driver, but he didn't notice because he was too busy giving her his middle finger and screaming. She looked to make sure the road was clear and made an u-turn to make her way back to the pet store. Alex stood outside the store looking in. She started laughing hysterically as she watched her friend run through the aisles of her store. She could hear Cassie screaming at some poor soul and cursing at another one. On one of her passes by Alex, Alex saw that her friend had a net in her hand. That at least told her a bird was loose. Cassie stopped quickly at the sight of Alex laughing. She stalked to the door. With a quick glance back over her shoulder, Cassie threw the door open. "Get your sorry butt in here. Don't waste time either."

Alex slid in the door as Cassie closed it. "Having a problem?"

"Oh, no." Cassie answered sarcastically. "I was just holding my daily exercise classes. I just love running around chasing aerial bodies. Don't you? It just invigorates one's body."

"Not really. I have enough trouble chasing things on the ground."

Cassie snorted as she searched around the ceiling with her eyes. "Not what I heard."

Alex chose to ignore that comment. "What are you looking for?"

"A Nanday conure."

Alex squealed. "Really? I didn't know that you had one."

"I just got it in not long ago. If we don't catch it soon, I won't have one again."

"We?"

"Alex, I know that you're more experienced catching these things than I am. Georgy used to get out on a regular basis."

"Micky helped. He used to let Georgy out so he could 'play' with him. What's your excuse?"

Cassie snorted again. "New employee."

187

"Keep snorting like that and I'll start looking around for a matador. It's not very becoming for you." Cassie stuck her tongue out at Alex as she continued talking. "You know as well as I do that you have to let the bird calm down. What's the rush?"

"There are some holes around here. If that bird finds one, it'll be out of here in a heartbeat."

"Oh, well. You can always write it off tax-wise." Alex matter-of-factly commented.

"Yeah, I know. However, this one's already sold. The buyer is coming this weekend to pick it up. Besides, wait until you see it. It's gorgeous! I mean his coloring is totally awesome!"

"Okay, you've convinced me. Where's the other net?"

Cassie handed her net over to Alex. "I'm pooped. Go get it cowgirl."

Alex laughed and started toward the center of the store. "Yee-haaa! I'm on my way to catch me a wild bird." Alex quieted and slowly turned as she scanned the ceiling and high shelves. "Gotcha, baby." She smiled as she saw a beautiful bird backing behind a squishy foam dog bed on a top shelf. She looked around and saw a small step ladder. Keeping an eye on the bird's location, she went and grabbed the ladder and placed it below the shelf. She quietly placed the net on a lower shelf. Cassie headed over with some thick gloves as she watched Alex quickly push the dog bed against the wall. Alex heard a squawk as she collapsed the bed around the bird. She slowly brought bed and bird down to her level. She tried to get a peek at the bird, to make sure it couldn't get away, without putting her eyes at risk from its beak. When she got back to ground level, Cassie took the bird from the bed with gloved hands. She spoke soothingly as she left to return the bird to its cage. Alex returned to the front of the store with the damaged dog bed.

When Cassie returned to the front, she shook her head when she saw the bed. "Now that's a tax write-off that I have no problem doing." She sighed as she took a seat across from Alex.

"Where's this new employee?" Alex asked as she looked around.

"Gone."

"You fired her? Or is it a him?"

Cassie looked guilty as she looked at her friend. "No. I told her to take the rest of the day off. I sort of read her the riot act."

Alex heard Jeffrey snort in the background and chuckled. "Snorting is catching in this store." She smirked. "*Sort* of read her the riot act?" Alex raised her eyebrows at Cassie.

Cassie shot a dark glare at Jeffrey before answering Alex. "Well…" She shrugged. "Maybe I yelled at her a bit."

Alex shook her head. "I do believe you're the queen of understatement Cassie. Does she still work for you? Is she still alive?"

Cassie laughed and reached over to smack Alex's arm. "Geez! Yes and yes. She'll be back tomorrow. She tripped all over herself apologizing. When I hired her, she said she could handle birds. Now, I find out, she meant parakeets and finches." Cassie rolled her eyes. "She's afraid of anything with a bigger beak that that."

"Give her a break, Cass. I remember our first experience with birds with dangerous beaks. Your uncle had to chase down the amazon parrot I let loose. At least this time, the bird didn't bite through the gloves and draw a gusher of blood." Alex looked down at Cassie's hands to make sure her statement was true.

Cassie rubbed her hands over her face. "You're right. I'll try to make things right with her tomorrow. That bird's special though. I let my emotions get in the way. Where you going?" She asked as Alex got up from her chair.

"To look at the bird of course."

Cassie jumped up. "Oh! Ahhhhh!"

189

Alex turned. "Something wrong? It's not dead is it?"

"No. It's just highly upset. But......I guess we can spend a few minutes." Cassie capitulated. " Let's go."

Alex and Cassie walked into the back room and approached the bird cage. The bird watched them approach and let loose with a long ear-piercing scream. "Wow." Alex said as she put a finger to her ear and shook her head. "That baby has some potent vocals. I believe he's even louder than Georgy was. Alex leaned as close to the bird as she thought prudent, so she could get a good look at his coloring. The general plumage on the body was green, with the coloring becoming more yellowish and pale on "his" underparts. The thighs were a reddish orange. The bird's chest and throat area were covered in a pretty sky blue color. The wings and tail were a blackish grey on the undersides, and an olive green on the topsides, with a beautiful royal blue on the tips. The nanday had a black head with a small white ring around each eye. They oohed and aahed over the bird for a few minutes, and then Cassie suggested they leave it alone for a while. On the way back to the front, Alex detoured to the fish department.

Curious, Cassie followed. "What's up?"

Alex casually shrugged. "Nothing really. I gave Didi some advice on her fish and I just want to make sure I'm right."

"Okay. Meet you up front."

"Sure." Alex looked over the fish stuff. She decided that she could use some medication at home. She picked up some ampicillex and ick guard and went to the front to purchase the items. After some more humorous repartee, Alex left the store for work.

As Alex approached the bakery, her mouth dropped open. The place was packed. In fact, there was no room for her to park in the lot. She went down the alley that separates her land and her neighbors' and pulled into the grass that abuts the parking lot. She took her time walking up to the back door. Alex was trying to figure out why the place was so busy. She dropped her stuff on the desk in the office and wandered up to the front of the store. She peered around the partition to the register. There were at least twenty people in line. Cat and Maggie were working in overdrive. Usually, when more than three people were in line at the register, one could hear grumbles and irritated sighs, but today everyone was smiling. Alex knew she should offer to help but couldn't shake the feeling that she happened into some kind of twilight zone. She quietly about-faced and slunk into the back room, taking cover in her office. She eased her conscience by turning on the intercom, telling herself that she would run out front if pandemonium broke out. Alex turned to her desk and delved into paperwork.

An hour later, Cat and Maggie closed the store and headed into the back room. Cat froze as she neared the office. She put a finger to her lips to indicate to Maggie to be quiet. She tilted her head and listened for a moment. After identifying the noise as a calculator, she swooped to the office and threw open the door. "Coward! How dare you hide? How long have you been back here?"

Chaos reigned instantly. Alex jumped and half fell from her chair. Her shriek echoed in the bakery. Her pen went flying through the air. Her heart felt like it was about to beat right out of her chest. As the sound of laughter made it through the sound of blood thumping in her ears, she turned and narrowed her eyes at her former friends. Tears were running down their cheeks from laughing. Cat was hanging onto the door knob to keep from falling over. Maggie was holding her stomach, bent over double. She decided it was easier to just sit, so she plopped down onto the floor. Alex had gotten so involved in her work that she had totally tuned out the outside world. The intercom and noises of closing failed to penetrate her brain. Cat's comment, however, had made it through loud and clear. "Swine!" Alex glared at her friend.

Once her friends had sufficiently recovered, Alex deadpanned, "We're quite happy with ourselves aren't we?"

Cat and Maggie grinned at each other and then simultaneously turned and grinned at Alex. "Yes, we are." They preened.

Cat added, "You know, Alex, your indignant act would be more effective on people who wouldn't know that you would have done exactly the same thing if roles had been reversed."

A sly smile appeared on Alex's lips before she could stop it. After a small nod of acquiescence, she asked if something in particular had caused all these people to show up. Irritation and anger filled the women's faces. "I'll say something happened." Maggie spit out.

"Some jerk called the radio station and asked if they would amend the on-air statement. The secretary said no problem and added the additional lines to the script without checking with anyone. She never told anyone what she did. In fact, the one deejay had announced our spot quite a few times before Randy heard it and pulled it."

Alex's gut knotted up as she asked what else had been added. Tired of Cat always getting to give the juicy news, good or bad, Maggie jumped in with the answer. She winced as she said, "That in order to build the business back up, all cake orders would be fifty percent off regular prices for the next week, including any wedding cake orders placed during that time period."

"What!!!!!" Alex screamed. "I can't afford that!!" Her eyes opened wide and she pulled at her hair, "People didn't actually believe that did they?"

"Unfortunately, yes. However....." Maggie raised her hands to try to calm Alex. "We took care of things." Maggie inclined her head toward Cat for her to take over with the details.

"We were majorly confused at first when people started pouring in asking for the discount. While we were trying to sort things out, Randy called from the radio station and explained what had happened."

Maggie cut in and continued. She smiled and nodded at Cat. "You should have seen and heard Cat, Alex. It was out of this world. She looked at everyone like they were crazy and asked if they were out of their minds. They knew the problems this place was going through. She assured everyone that this place would be exonerated from the bad publicity. However, the people would have to be nuts to believe that we could afford to sell cakes at fifty percent off. Maybe in the big cities that could happen, but not here. Of course, her wording wasn't quite as polite as I just said, but she got the message across. Cat raised her hands and whistled to get everyone to quiet and stop grumbling in order to give them a choice: they could leave the store with our apologies for the mix-up, even though it definitely was not our fault, or else they could order their cakes today and receive a two dollar discount with our apologies for the mix-up, even though it was not our fault." Maggie smiled at Alex. "Naturally, people took the discount and left on a happier note."

Alex just stared at her friends for a few minutes, her face blank. Cat and Maggie looked at each other and frowned. Cat waved a hand in front of Alex's face and asked if anyone was home. "Of course, I'm here." Alex smiled and knocked Cat's hand away from her face. "You guys did an excellent job. I don't know if I would have handled it as well. I believe I would have been severely ticked off."

Cat snorted. "Oh, well, we were that. But once we realized that we had to at least appease the general populace, we came up with the two dollar discount. Sorry, we couldn't clear it with you first."

Alex rolled her eyes and waved her hand again. "You did fine. I'll call Randy tomorrow and check up on a few things. I'm just glad I didn't have the station on earlier or I might have driven the car off the road somewhere. Well...at least it looks like we got the business rolling again."

Cat grinned. "I'll say. We got a ton of orders. None for this week though. The ball starts rolling next week. And just to let you know, when you see 'rad disc' on the cake order forms, it stands for the two dollar radio discount."

"That's quite alright. This week has had its share of excitement already."

"Speaking of excitement, Jo-Jo called up and said that she couldn't make it to work until Monday at the earliest. It's not like she asked or nothing, she just told me. If that's going to be a problem, I suggest that you call her and see what's up."

Alex rubbed her face with the palms of her hands. "No. That's okay this week. I don't really feel like talking to her right now, maybe tomorrow. If you two can help, we can get through the next two days in good order."

As they nodded their heads affirmatively, Alex asked if everything was set for closing. Cat mock saluted and said, "Yes, ma'am. Oh, and one more thing."

"What's that?"

"We had two orders for death cakes." Cat matter-of-factly stated.

"For what?" Alex asked, she couldn't have heard correctly.

Cat looked straight at Alex and repeated, "Death cakes."

At Alex's stunned and uncomprehending look, Cat continued, " A guy called up first thing today. He said that his ex-girlfriend won't leave him alone and wanted to know if we could send a death cake or a killer cake to her. What he was actually asking for took a few seconds to sink in, and I was really ticked when it did. I told him no, besides that's called murder and we definitely do not do that."

Maggie spoke up then, " The other call was from a woman. She says she's tired of her ex bugging her. She wanted to send him a death cake. I basically told her what Cat told that other guy and suggested she talk to her divorce lawyer or check with the cops to see what might deter him best."

Alex just shook her head. When was this going to end? Some people did not make sense. She hoped that they were joking but if not, was she responsible for telling the cops about this…what…possibly being asked to help kill someone? Do we know who they were?"

"No." Cat stated.

"Nope," Maggie responded with a shake of her head.

"If we get anymore, try to get the names of the callers, otherwise, let's let it go. Hopefully, your use of the word 'murder' scared them straight and reminded them of the seriousness of their request."

Maggie laughed. "You should have seen Cat's face when the guy first requested it. I thought she was going to throw the phone at the wall. At least, I was kind of prepared for the possibility of such calls when I answered that woman's call."

"Well, let's call it a day. Cat, am I taking you home or is Maggie?"

Cat smiled hugely, "Neither, Mike should be outside at this moment."

As Alex watched her two friends depart, she decided to make a quick stop on the way home.

Chapter 28

On the way to make her quick stop, she saw a sign that changed her mind. As she passed the lake in town, she noticed a sign at the "Community Connection" area. This area is located at the one end of the lake. It consists of three connected wooden rectangular bulletin boards with a roof overhead. Anyone who wants to advertise an event, be it big or small, that is open to the public can put a sign on one of the boards. One side of the one board is strictly for advertising yard sales and pet sales and such. Even at night, people can stop and check it out because there are lights in the roof's rafters that shine down on the boards. The sign that caught Alex's eye was one titled "Happy Plants Flower Shop and Greenhouse." It stated that it was a business starting up on a nearby farm. The grand opening was a month away but anyone could stop by and check it out. Alex decided that a quick check would be fun.

Happy Plants Flower Shop and Greenhouse was located about a mile outside the town. At the entrance to the driveway was a large eight foot wooden daisy flower. The petals were white and the center of the flower was yellow with a cheerful face. It had a single green stem that ended in a flowerpot. It had two leaves. One leaf was waving at you and the other leaf pointed you up the driveway. It was a very friendly and welcoming sign. Alex pulled up next to the main entrance and walked in. A bell announced her arrival. The building was far from complete on the inside, evidence of construction was everywhere. Alex saw that things were roughed out so that you knew how the general layout of this building would go. She walked up to a counter, stopped to see if anyone was around, and saw a blond woman approaching her.

"Hi! Welcome to Happy Plants Flower Shop and Greenhouse! My name is Heather. I apologize that we don't have anything to sell yet, but I can answer any questions that you might have."

Alex said hi and introduced herself. She indicated that since she had a bakery, she was sure they would be doing business together in the future. She indicated that she had seen their sign by the lake and was intrigued. "Are you the owner?"

Heather responded with a big smile. "One of them. My sisters and I have decided to go into business together. Willow and I lived a couple of towns over and we saw that this farm was up for sale. We all checked it out and fell in love with it. Three of us are here now and the other three are making arrangements to come and get settled."

"That's awesome! I sincerely hope it works out for you. I look forward to your Grand Opening. However, I was wondering something. Someone dropped off a flower for me and I don't recognize what it is. I was wondering if you could help me out, I have a picture of it along with me."

"Sure. Let me give it a try."

Alex handed over the photo and Heather studied it a bit. She shook her head slowly left and right, "I'm sorry. I don't recognize it. Let me check with my sisters."

In minutes, she returned with two other women. After Heather introduced her sisters Willow and Iris, Willow spoke up. "It looks like figwort."

"I don't believe I have ever heard of that one." Alex responded.

"I'm not surprised. It's mainly in Asia. Only a few species of it grow naturally in Europe and North America. Where did you get this?" Willow asked genuinely intrigued.

"Someone left if at my bakery for me without a note of any kind. I know this might sound weird, but does it mean anything?"

Confused, Willow asked, "What exactly are you inquiring about?"

Alex quickly explained about her aunt and the older woman's belief in flower language. Willow shook her head in agreement while Alex explained while Iris just rolled her eyes. Slightly embarrassed by her sister's reaction, Willow eagerly responded. "I totally understand what you're saying. I believe in the flower language as well as some of my sisters, however, as you can see, Iris is one that does not."

Alex looked at the three women and smiled a small smile. "What's up?" Heather inquired politely.

" I'm sorry. I don't want to be rude, but it occurred to me that your names are the names of flowers. Is it just you three or do you all have flower names?"

Willow giggled. "All of us have flower names. We all love flowers and gardening, so it sounded logical to go into this type of business. Each of us have our own expertise and interests that helps to round out this business perfectly. One of my areas is the knowledge of all kinds of flowers and the language of flowers."

Alex looked at the different women as she spoke. "I find this all fascinating. I would love to learn more about you, your family, and this business." Alex took note that Iris seemed a bit impatient but continued on. "But, I don't want to take up too much of your time and I also find myself in a bit of a time constraint. I was wondering, what does the Figwort flower usually represent?"

Willow waved her hand. "Don't worry about us. We have plenty of time before the grand opening."

Iris spoke up quickly and curtly. "Willow, just tell the lady what she wants to know."

Willow looked at Iris and smiled. "Yes, of course, Iris."

"Good. I'll be in the back working in the garden." Iris turned abruptly and walked out.

"I'm sorry, did I say something wrong?" Alex inquired.

"No." Heather replied. "Of all of us sisters, Iris is the only one that really needs to work on her ability to relate to others. She loves to garden. She loves to talk to her plants, which is good. It helps them grow better. However, people are not her strong point."

"That shouldn't be a problem. I prefer ability over personality. Not everyone is a people person. If the rest of your sisters are like you two, you will do well here."

"Thank you very much." Willow smiled. "And figwort means 'future joy.' Is that helpful?"

Alex thought briefly and returned the smile. "Yes, I believe so. Thank-you. Nice meeting you." Alex started to turn to go and then turned back, "By the way, did you know that the people who used to own this place had the last name of 'Flowers'?"

Heather chuckled, "Yeah, we know. Our one sister, Daisy, believes in omens and portents and such and said it was a 'sign' that we should buy it. She believes we're guaranteed a successful business."

"Do you believe the same?"

"I believe the location is great, the soil is great, and that and hard work will make us a success." Heather responded straight forwardly.

"I agree with Heather." Willow replied. With a twinkle in her eye, she continued, "However, I'll take help wherever it comes from, if you know what I mean."

Everyone had a good laugh and as Alex turned to go, the two ladies hollered after her, "Good-by and see ya at our opening!"

Chapter 29

Tom pulled up to Alex's place about eight o'clock. He had called to see if they could compare notes and if she could answer a few questions. One of the questions was if there were enough leftovers to feed them a good meal. She laughed and assured him that there was plenty in her fridge.

Tom knocked on the door and heard Alex yell to come in. When he entered, he was a little irritated that she had left her door unlocked. After all, how could she know who would be knocking at her door? He shook his head sadly as he realized that the past events had not apparently taught her anything. He stopped shaking his head when the scene in front of him pushed its way into his brain. A cozy fire was burning in the fireplace. Alex had spread out a picnic blanket on the floor in front of the fire. "Make yourself comfortable Tom. I'll be out in a minute." Alex's voice floated out to him. He kicked off his shoes and sat down on the blanket. Cushions had been thrown down on the floor and leaned against the base of the couch. He backed up against one of the huge pillows. Tom looked off to his side and saw a silver bucket with a bottle sitting in some ice. Two champagne glasses were sitting on a small silver platter beside the bucket. He eased the bottle out of the bucket and looked at the label. "Sparkling Apple Cider" was printed on the label. He popped the top off and poured some into one of the glasses. Hesitantly, he tasted some. His face showed his surprise at the enjoyable taste. He filled his glass about half full and stuck the bottle back into the bucket. He leaned back against the pillow and closed his eyes. He was just thinking how wonderful everything was when a sound caused him to open his eyes and he smiled.

"Comfortable?" Alex grinned.

"Very much so. Care to join me?" Tom replied with one eyebrow raised. He patted the floor beside him as he spoke. "Are we celebrating anything in particular?"

"Not really. I just felt like we could use some comfortable time alone without thought of any business problems." Tom watched as Alex slipped off her shoes and sat down beside him. She was dressed in what he considered a fancy casual style, who knows what the fashion world would describe it as, that suited her wonderfully; blue jeans that still have the "new" look about them, leather casual slip-on shoes, and a cream silk camisole under a loose-fitting unbuttoned cream-colored silk overshirt that was covered in mountain scenery and wolves. Tom sensed that somewhere under her seemingly calm exterior, Alex seemed a bit nervous. "You're absolutely beautiful." He leaned over and kissed her gently on the mouth. Feeling her tense up, Tom pulled away and settled back into his pillow and momentarily studied her face. "Want something to drink?"

"Sure, I'd like that." Alex replied softly.

Tom took his time pouring the juice to give himself time to figure out what was going on. He turned back to Alex and handed her a glass of juice. "Here you go." He tipped his glass to hers and tapped it gently. "To us?"

Alex looked deep into his brown eyes and felt herself tremble gently. She was nervous and knew he could tell. "Yes, to us." She gave a slight smile and took a sip of the juice.

Tom was a bit confused as he took a sip of his drink and watched her. "Alex, you seem a bit nervous. You want to tell me why?"

"I guess I'm just nervous about how you're going to react to something that I have to say to you."

He felt himself involuntarily tense up. "Then maybe you should just say it and we'll both find out how I'll react."

Alex blushed red as she looked uncomfortably around her living room. Her eyes settled momentarily on Tom's face before she lowered them to her hands. She put her drink to the side so she wouldn't spill it.

"I'm afraid that I have given you the wrong impression about me." She raised her eyes briefly to Tom's face again before looking down at her hands again. "I really would like to get involved with you and see if we have a future…"

"But," Tom said to gently help her continue because he hadn't a clue as to what she wanted to say or where she was going with this.

"But, I guess one might call me old-fashioned or something, but I don't believe in fooling around outside of marriage. The Bible says premarital sex is wrong and I agree. I don't consider myself a religious nut or anything, but religion is very important to me and I'm not willing to give in on this point." Alex stopped talking and took a deep breath and slowly let it out. "I'm embarrassed that earlier I asked you to make love to me. It was wrong and I was wrong. I'm really glad that we didn't do anything. I guess I was really out of it, so to speak. I'm glad that you had the wisdom to say no." Alex continued to look at her hands, she wasn't sure what Tom's reaction would be and was afraid to look.

Tom closed his eyes and felt himself exhale. He hadn't noticed that he had held his breath until just now. He smiled and reached over to take her hands. "Is that all?"

Surprised, Alex looked up at him. "What do you mean is that all?"

"Well, I wasn't sure what you were going to say. I thought maybe you were going to dump me, and weren't exactly sure how to go about it, or that you were rumored to be connected to some other incident that I might not like."

"Oh, oh, I'm sorry. I didn't mean to…" She stopped talking when Tom put one of his fingers on her mouth.

"Shush. Let me say something here. Okay?" She mutely nodded her head up and down. "There's nothing wrong with wanting to wait for sex. I don't have a problem with that, in fact, it's kind of refreshing to hear it. I will tell you one thing though, I don't consider myself overly religious, but I do believe in God and going to church. I am glad that you told me how you feel. And you're right about that earlier time, and I told you the timing wasn't right, so forget it already. I believe we have a future and I'm quite willing to see just how big of one we have. How about you?"

Alex felt like her face would burst if she smiled any bigger. "Definitely." She chirped as she leaned over and kissed him. They talked a couple more hours on numerous topics, just enjoying each other's company and the fire.

Tom woke Alex up at five o'clock by tapping her shoulder. Confusion crossed her face as she realized who was doing the tapping, Micky usually banged her other shoulder when he wanted something. Alex squinted her eyes a little harder as she looked at Tom.

He chuckled. "You did say earlier that you were not really a morning person."

Alex sat up in bed and shook her head. She looked down and noticed that she was wearing the same outfit she was last night, then she swung her head toward the clock. "What time is it?" Alex looked at Tom and point blankly said, "I'm confused."

Tom laughed uproariously at her comment. " And also a bit irritated," she added.

"That's for sure." Tom winked and swiftly brought her up to date. After they had talked last night, Alex had fallen asleep leaning against him. He had picked her up and put her to bed. Because of the hour, and the fact that he also was exhausted, he had slept on her couch.

"We need to talk about the case before I go to work. I hope you don't mind that I woke you up early."

Alex crawled out of bed, "No, I don't mind. Let me get a quick shower and wake up first."

"Sure." Tom got up and turned as he reached the door. "By the way, I already took a shower. I used my own toiletries, I keep a bag in my car because with my job one must be ready for anything, but I used some of your towels."

"No problem."

When Alex came into the kitchen about twenty minutes later, she found breakfast waiting for her. Micky was crying for food from Tom. Tom's attention was fixed on the fish in the aquarium. He looked up and smiled. "Morning, beautiful." He would have continued but a short snort from Alex shut him up.

"Who are you kidding? I look like death warmed over in the morning. It's a miracle you didn't go running out the door when you saw me." She explained at his quizzical look.

"Well, it did take all of my police training and willpower I could muster." He mockingly shuddered.

"Smart aleck." She returned back to him and stuck her tongue out quickly.

"Your repartee needs some work." He smiled at here and then turned his attention back to the fish. "Some of these fish are pretty cool, but I was curious about that hideous fish hanging on the back glass, what's he doing?"

She looked and laughed. "Everyone picks on that poor fish. His name is Freddie. It's a plecostomus. It's an algae eater and that's exactly what he's doing. Cleaning the tank. Haven't you ever had a tank?"

"As a kid, a long long time ago. But then it was goldfish, not tropical, and my folks took care of it, not me."

Alex and Tom settled in to eat and reviewed the case. Alex showed Tom her list of employees, possible motives, and their whereabouts at the time when she believed the cake was doctored.

"So, you believe that your employees are in the clear?"

"Yes, I do. What about your partner?"

"I know that Cat won't want to hear this, but I believe that Cliff is innocent of any wrongdoing in this case." He raised his hands to quiet any rebuffs momentarily. "There is no doubt that his car was used, however, he has witnesses to back up his whereabouts at those times. He's in the clear. The first time we believe the car was used, it was returned exactly as it was found. No damage to the body and parked where Cliff left it. The second time of course it had been damaged and moved. We're not sure why his car was used, except that it's older and easier to circumvent the ignition."

"So where does that leave you and the investigation?" Alex inquired.

"Mr. Abrahms had plenty of enemies and it's our responsibility to check out each one that we know of. His allergy to penicillin was well known in this town. Opportunity is still hard to place on most of the people. However, if one knows about glitter, than one could know or find out how to doctor the cake. Would it be possible to get a list of everyone who has ever taken a cake decorating class from you that involved glitter from you later today?"

"Sure. I just have to look in the computer, but how far back should I go?"

"As far back as possible. List the most recent first and then go back in time."

"There's quite a few. Not to mention anyone and everyone who has asked about glitter in the store. Some have seen its use in magazines and on TV. Some have just passed it in the store and inquired about its usage. Plus, one can purchase it through supply catalogs and other stores. I don't believe glitter can be traced back to any one store."

"Yes, however, this person knew how *you* applied it, therefore, I believe they got that knowledge from you directly or from this store and your employees. Am I right in my thinking that not everyone applies glitter in this manner?"

"To tell the truth, I don't know how most people use it. I don't recall any books or magazines showing the shakers, most show that hands or fingers sprinkle the glitter onto cakes. I picked up the technique in a class I took quite a few years back."

"Okay. But I believe the shop is the origin of the murderer's knowledge. Call it a gut feeling if you want. We can only get done by starting and this is the best place to start."

"Sometimes I wonder if this case will ever be solved." Alex stated somewhat dejectedly.

"No one said that it would be easy. Besides, it hasn't even been a week since the murder. Only on television do cases get solved in one hour or clues fall into an investigator's lap. Your store is open and you're out of jail. So relax and trust me to solve the case."

Alex smiled. "You're right. I do trust you Tom, but patience and I were never very good friends."

"No kidding." Tom spoke evenly. He laughed as he reached for his briefcase and pulled out a sheet of paper. "I also have some questions about the wedding cake form." Alex cocked her head to show her interest as he placed it in front of her. "What are these scribbles beside the cash amounts at the bottom of the page?"

Alex looked where he was pointing. The breakdown of the wedding cake costs was listed on the bottom half of the cake order forms, as were any and all payments. This particular form listed the cost of the cake, delivery and setup cost, and a refundable parts deposit amount. From the cost total were subtracted three amounts. The first was the initial non-refundable twenty dollar deposit that had reserved the date. This amount was deducted from the cost total when the cake was ordered or was kept if the wedding cake was canceled as a way to deter pranksters. The second deduction was a partial payment of the cake. The third deduction was the payment-in-full amount that reduced the balance owed to zero. "Those scribbles represent the initials of the person who took in that particular payment on the cake. If the person pays in cash, there are just initials and a date. If the person pays with a check, then there should be the date, the check number, and the initials of the store employee."

"Okay. So whose initials are these?"

Alex squinted and brought the paper close to her face for a few seconds. "I honestly don't know. It really doesn't look familiar to me. I know that it should, but it doesn't. This is where the original is needed. My scanner is not top-of-the-line and therefore doesn't do the superfine detail as clear as more expensive models would. I didn't think the difference in ability was worth all the extra money, but now I guess maybe I was wrong."

"Not really. How would you know that this would happen? You bought the item that you needed and its worked for you."

"Yeah. But this rots." She raised her head quickly and almost nailed Tom in the face. "Can any of your machines clarify this any better?"

"Nothing definite. If this was computer or type print, that was super small or faded in spots, we'd have better luck. But the computer boys say that with handwriting, especially scribbled initials, it's not that easy. They were able to give me a whole list of possibilities. All of your employees' initials match the possibility list."

"I'll tell you what. I'll try looking for the original again."

"That would be great. Call me if you find it."

"Sure, but how will the initials be of any help?"

"Don't know that they will." As Alex screwed up her face in

frustration, he quickly continued. "Don't know that they won't either. Sometimes the littlest detail closes the case."

Tom got up to leave. As they walked to the door, Alex hesitated, "Tom?"

"Yes?"

"Did you check out my ex?"

"Yeah, I talked to him." Tom replied noncommittally.

"And?"

"Right now, he seems to be in the clear."

Alex sensed that Tom was being hesitant and feeling a bit awkward or uncomfortable. "What aren't you telling me?"

"It's not my place to tell you. As I said, he's in the clear for now."

"Thomas, please! Tell me."

Tom examined her face as he told her the news. "He said that he came to town to try to patch things up with you. He wants to get back together with you, Alex." He watched her face go emotionless. "Is it possible? Do you want to get back with him?"

She grunted. "Fat chance! The nerve of the guy!"

Tom didn't even realize that he had been holding his breath, until after she got done speaking. He'd better snip this problem in the bud or else his complexion would soon have a blue tinge to it. "Are you sure?"

She looked up and searched his face. "Of course I'm sure. As far as I'm concerned, it's over and done with. It's been over since the divorce, if not before that. A snowball has a better chance of surviving in hell than David and I have of getting back together. I realize that you and I haven't known each other for all that long, and at the risk of scaring you off, I believe I love you. After our talk last night, do you have any doubt?" Alex refused to acknowledge the slight wave of panic sweeping through her body at the thought of his uncertainty.

208

Tom's face exploded into a huge grin. He crushed her body into his and kissed her deeply. "Not one. I definitely enjoyed last night. But let me warn you, that was your last chance to get away." Tom opened the door to leave and turned back to Alex. "I love you Alexandra Jean Applecake." He grinned and winked and was gone.

Chapter 30

Alex, Cat, and Maggie opened the store together in good spirits. Maggie came inside from setting out the flag and announced that she would be in the back decorating if anyone needed her. Cat suggested Alex finish up any paperwork or phone calls while she manned the front. Alex glanced down at Cat's cast and asked if she was having any troubles getting around. "Oh, I'm fine." Cat assured her. "Make sure the intercom's on. Have no fear, if I need help, I'll shout for it." Alex and Cat discussed what all needed to be done in the front store area and then Alex headed for her office.

Alex had just started on her mail when Randy called from the radio station. He apologized for the screw up. He reassured her that steps had been taken that should prohibit any such things from occurring in the future. After he had apologized for the umpteenth time, Alex told him to stop it or else (she wasn't sure what the "else" was and didn't particularly care either) and explained what Cat and Maggie had come up with as a solution to handle the problem. "No permanent harm done, so relax. However, I do have one question."

"Shoot."

"What script was there to add lines to?"

"I wrote a few lines for the other deejays to say on the air when I'm not here."

"Thanks. That's awful nice of you. I didn't expect you to go to such lengths. I hope it didn't take up a lot of your time."

"Heck, no. Hardly any at all, until the secretary messed up. She should have known better." He growled the last part. "Anyway, even that mess didn't take up much time to correct. I've known you all my life, Alex. I know that you're incapable of killing someone in the manner it was done. Besides, you do a lot of advertising with the radio station, and the station likes to help out those who pay their bills." With a chuckle, he hung up.

Alex booted up her computer and started to print out the customer lists that Tom had requested. Maggie yelled for Alex and she went out to see what she wanted. Maggie was waving a cake order in the air. With a look of doubt on her face, she queried. "Alex, I have a question about one of the cake orders that you took. Am I reading the colors right? Bright red, hot pink, pooh brown, mustard yellow and neon orange roses with lime green leaves?"

Alex rolled her eyes, scrunched her face, and stuck her tongue out.

"Yeah, you're reading it right. I asked the customer if I heard the colors right. She assured me I had and said it was some kind of inside joke." Alex shrugged, smiled, and returned to the office.

She started printing a few more lists out for Tom when she heard laughter coming from the decorating area and went to investigate. Cat saw Alex coming and asked, "Did you see the colors on this cake? It's gross." She made a gagging face and sound with her one finger pointed into her mouth.

Alex laughed. "Yeah, I saw it. I'm the one that took that order. Maggie had me out here earlier double-checking. It's an anniversary cake. I hope this doesn't mean that the wedding cake was done in these colors."

"Ohhhhhh, yuuuuuuuuck!" Cat wrinkled her nose.

"See, I told you." Maggie laughed back. "I'm trying my best to make the colors work, but these shades don't really blend well."

"It's some kind of inside joke. Whoever takes that out should ask about it."

"Well, as you always say, the customer is always right, no matter how wrong." Cat chuckled and shook her head while Maggie finished the cake.

Maggie glanced up at Alex and then did a quick double-take. "What's wrong, Alex?"

Alex closed her mouth and focused back onto her friends. "Nothing. I just remembered something." She made a quick turn and flew out into her office.

Cat and Maggie looked at each other and headed after Alex. They stood in the doorway and watched Alex stop the printer. She quickly pushed a few keys, looked up at them, and pushed a few more. Soon, the printer was at work again.

"What's up, woman? You ran out of the room like a woman with a purpose," Maggie inquired.

"Something Cat said got me thinking. I don't like where I'm heading, but that's tough."

"What did I say?" Cat looked at Maggie and then back at Alex.

Maggie shrugged. "Just that thing about the customer being right."

Alex pointed her finger at them. "That's right. And, so did the person who doctored the cake. Remember?"

"That's right, she did." Cat pointed back at her. "Oh….. "

"Yeah, oh…."

Maggie looked back and forth between the two. "I know I'm slow, but what? Oh… oh….what?"

Cat raised one brow at Maggie. "We use that phrase in here all the time. The first part is used lots of places, but 'no matter how wrong they are' isn't. That would point to one of us being the murderer."

Maggie looked at her friends. "Ohhhhhh. Oh, crap!"

Alex turned and grabbed the paper out of the printer tray. "When I saw you two come in, I printed a few more copies." She handed them each a copy of the Jordan cake order. "I would like you guys to see if you can figure out the initial scribbles on the bottom of the sheet. The first one, by the deposit amount, should be mine. I know my own scribble, however, the scanned version is definitely screwed up a bit."

They all went into the main decorating room and sat down. After a while, Cat said that the second scribble might be hers, but who can be sure. "These are really quite undecipherable." Cat threw her copy onto the table. "If I stare at those marks much longer, I'm going to have one huge head cramp."

Maggie laughed and tossed hers onto the table too. "Sorry, Alex. She's right."

"Yeah, I guess you're right." She picked up the papers and headed back to the office.

"I'm glad you have lots of aspirin in there." Cat shouted before she had the door closed.

After some more studying of the scribble, Alex threw the papers in the air and laid her head down on her crossed arms. Alex popped up quick and started to type on the computer again. She made a few copies of different scanned cake orders and grabbed their originals. Alex compared the original copies with the scanned copies, and then with one of the Jordan scanned copies. She still couldn't figure out who the scribbles belonged to. She stacked everything together, smacked the printer, and left the room. She returned briefly to grab the aspirin bottle and left for something to drink.

At five o'clock, Cat and Alex closed the store. Maggie had left at three. "What are your plans for the night?"

"Mike and I are going cruising on his Harley." She bragged. "He doesn't know it yet, but I plan on attacking him somewhere in the state game lands." She waggled her eyebrows and leered, "What're your plans?" She wiggled her brows again, "Tom?"

Alex smacked her friend's arm. "Geesh, Cat. You're such a pervert."

Cat laughed and headed for the door. "With Mike's job as a cross country trucker, he's not around as much as I would like. So, every chance I can get, I'll take. Well, what about you?"

"I'm staying here a little longer. Then I'm going home and vegetate."

"Not exactly noteworthy, but have a good time."

"Planning on it!"

"Ta!" And the door slammed shut.

"Ta?" Alex laughed and sat at the desk again. She looked at the mail on her desk and groaned. "I best get started on this stuff." She huffed.

She ripped open the top envelope and stared at the contents. "Darn! Darn! Darn-it!" Laying on her desk, was a bounced check and a slip of paper from the bank informing her that the check had bounced. "No kidding." Alex gasped as she realized who wrote this check. It was signed Matthew Abrahms. "You bastard!" She looked at the floor and stomped (after all, no way did that jerk make it to heaven,) "even in death, you're screwing me!" She looked at the top of the check for the initials of which employee accepted the check. She frowned at the scribble. "Who's mess is this? Honestly, I wish people would write legibly." She squinted hard. "It looks to be either Jo-Jo's or Didi's, but who knows. Curlicues were all over the place." She flipped the check to the back of the desk and leaned back in the chair.

Alex picked up the phone and called Tom. He picked up on the first ring. "Detective Baker."

"Tom. It's me."

"Hi! What's up babe?"

"You'll never guess what showed up in the mail." Alex took a few minutes to fill Tom in on the bounced check.

"That's great! Maybe it'll tell us something."

"Can you swing by and pick it up?" Alex inquired.

"Sure. How late do you think you'll be at the shop?"

"I'm not sure." Alex yawned.

"I have a few things to take care of here. When I'm done, I'll swing by the bakery on my way home. If you're not there, I'll stop by your place."

"Sounds like a plan."

"Sorry, I have to rush off. Take care and make sure you lock up. Bye!" Alex returned his "bye' to a disconnected line.

Alex got out a tablet and made two columns on the top sheet. She wrote Jo-Jo at the top of one column and Didi at the top of the other.

214

She planned on writing pros and cons to try to figure out if either could have killed Abrahms. They both knew the layout of this store and of the "customer is always right" phrase. They both knew what glitter was used for and how the decorators applied it. Each of their alibis were not the strongest. Jo-Jo could have run to the reception hall while Rick was out. Didi could have gone to the hall while Carlos was sleeping. They each admitted to possibly having penicillin around the house. And….as Alex thought, she glanced around her desk. She stopped as her eyes locked on to the fish medicine Ampicillex. She grabbed her box and turned it over. Ampicillex sounded a bit like penicillin. Her brow furrowed as she read the ingredients. Penicillin wasn't listed as one of the ingredients, but something called ampicillin was. She wondered if the two medicines were close to the same thing and if that could have been used to kill Abrahms. Alex made a note to have Tom check on it. In that case though, any one of her employees could have some. Each had a fish tank and each should have some Ampicillex in case it was needed. She remembered Didi said that they had had sick fish not too long ago. Carlos would have probably used Ampicillex to cure the fish. Therefore, Didi would have been able to get her hands on some. Something niggled Alex's brain again. She replayed her conversation with Didi and her mind clicked. Didi had said that Jo-Jo had come over and gotten their supply of medicine. Alex rubbed her forehead, her brain waves were getting into a traffic jam.

Alex grabbed the phone and called Cassie. "Cassie, quiz time."

"Okay. Shoot."

"Are ampicillin and penicillin related?"

"Man, start with the easy stuff why don't you? I thought you were calling with some more questions about football team colors." Cassie hesitated and then continued. "They sound alike, so it's possible, but I don't know. I mean I take it myself, when I get a cold or something, but that's only because my aunt, who had been a registered nurse, had showed me what fish medicine I could take and for what. I have a book here somewhere that might tell me, or maybe I'll 'google' the computer. I'll see if I can find out anything, alright? I'll call you back in a few minutes."

"Thanks." Alex started to hang up the phone when she heard something. She brought the phone back up to her ear. "Hello?"

"Alex? I'm glad that you didn't hang up yet. I wanted to ask you something."

"Sure. What?"

"If you're asking about Ampicillex because of the fish, why didn't you just ask me about straight penicillin?"

"What do you mean? Do you sell penicillin straight?"

"Yes, for fish. I thought you knew. Technically, anything you buy here should not be used on humans. But I use some of it, so I'm sure that there are others that do also. It's also cheaper than the human stuff. And you don't need a prescription to get it."

"So what you're telling me it that anyone could get their hands on penicillin."

"Yeah, I guess I am." Cassie replied.

"Thanks. When Tom gets here later, I'll pass on the information. He can check if there is any differences between the fish and human types."

"Cool. Glad I could help. See ya."

"See ya." Alex hung up the phone and just missed hearing the line go dead.

Alex got up to turn on some soothing music. As she settled back down, she recalled something Jo-Jo had said about everyone at the store having a reason to want the man dead. She now knew that Jo-Jo had lost a sister, but what about Didi? Alex grabbed her handbag and

216

looked for the list of Abrahms' victims. Neither Didi's name or maiden name showed up, but so what? Alex's "devil advocate" spoke up, Maggie's name didn't appear either, and she definitely had a reason. She made a note for Tom to check on that. Alex looked at the pile with the returned check on top and gasped. She must have have turned the pile around when she pushed an area clear for her tablet. The check was on top, but upside down. The scribble was more legible now. Sadness engulfed her heart, up to now, even though she was making a list, she didn't truly believe one of her employees capable of murder. "Oh, Didi." She murmured.

Alex had the receiver in her hand when a knock sounded on the door and made her jump. "Who is it?"

A muffled reply came back, "Detective Baker."

Alex relaxed and put the receiver back on the phone. She ripped open the door and excitingly spoke, "Tom, I just fig….." Alex quickly sucked in the end of her sentence when she realized who was at the door.

"What's wrong, Alex?"

She shook herself to try to relax. "Nothing, I was just expecting someone else. I must have misheard your response. What can I do for you , Carlos?"

"May I come in?"

Alex panicked. Her mind raced, "What to do? What to do?" Carlos made the first move and approached the threshold. Alex couldn't come up with a viable excuse to say no, so she backed up to allow his entrance while trying to think what to do. She nonchalantly turned her tablet over onto the returned check. "Sure." She hoped only she recognized the waver in her voice.

Carlos kept his eyes on hers. He tilted his head toward the desk and quietly asked. "What'cha working on Alex?"

"Orders and inventory," she shrugged.

"May I see?"

"You wouldn't be interested. Actually, it's quite boring. What brings you here tonight, Carlos?" Alex tried to calm herself. She wondered if Carlos could hear her heart beat as loud as she could.

"I want to know if I can pick up Didi's last paycheck?"

"What? Didi's quitting?" Confusion helped lessen her anxiety somewhat.

"Yes. I'm afraid that you upset her quite a bit, yesterday." Carlos moved closer to the desk. "I'd really like to see your 'inventory list' Alex."

"No! Ahhhhhhh, it's really none of your business. And now, that Didi's quitting, it's none of hers either. Honestly, Carlos, she was fine when I left. Just had a case of the flu or something."

"Honestly." He sarcastically sneered. "I'm afraid I must insist." Carlos may have only raised his voice a little, but Alex could feel the anger coursing through his body.

Alex inhaled slowly to steel herself and forced her eyes to stay on his. "Unfortunately, so must I. Please tell Didi, that if she comes next Friday, I'll give her her check or I could mail it to her. I need to consult my bookkeeper first. Now, if you'll please leave. I have a hair appointment in fifteen minutes."

"No." Carlos shook his head minutely and tried to compose himself. "I'll leave if you turn that tablet over."

"No, I won't." Alex said calmly.

Before Alex could even sense something coming, Carlos back-handed her across the face. She flew against the door to the decorating room. As stars cleared her vision, her knees shook as she watched Carlos flip the tablet over. She ran her tongue over her split lip as she felt for the doorknob and slowly started to turn it. Carlos scanned the

218

lists he saw and spun to face Alex full on. Alex read his movement and quickly opened the door to escape. She was almost to the basement door when Carlos tackled her from behind. Air whooshed out of Alex's lungs as she hit the floor, luckily she instinctively turned her head. Before she could recover, Carlos flipped her on her back. His knees held her thighs to the floor and he had a hand on each of her wrists. Panic seized her brain as thoughts of rape and worse flashed through it.

Carlos read the fear that shot through Alex's body. "Don't worry. I'm not going to rape you. I know what that can do to a person. I wouldn't wish it on my worst enemy." He seethed. He quickly brought her wrists together above her head. He used his strong left hand to hold both her wrists. He placed his strong right hand on her throat. He squeezed gently and held as he spoke. "Now, I'm not going to choke you either as long as you do as I say."

Alex quietly nodded her head minimally okay because she couldn't speak. However, nodding her head make her nauseous and she felt like throwing up. Pain shot into her brain as the nerves in the side of her face reacted to the blow from the floor. Blackness was creeping onto the edges of her vision. She tried to suck in more air.

Carlos loosened up his hold a tad. "Now, I'm going to give you a few moments to catch your breath. Then I want you to get up and walk back to the back room again."

Alex nodded very slowly once more and squeaked out, "-kay."

Carlos helped her up and she wobbled into the back. He pushed her into a chair and wretched her arms behind her. Alex could feel her wrists being tied with some kind of cloth, and in the back of her mind she pictured aprons. As Carlos came around to tie her ankles to the chair legs she realized that her guess was correct. She watched as he wound the cloth around her legs numerous times and finished off with knotting the strings together. Alex's heart sank as she concluded that the only way to remove the aprons from her legs was with a pair of scissors. Those strings were near impossible to unknot whenever they got tangled up in the dryer. She felt ill. Her head and chest ached. Alex's stomach was jumping around and she tried to mentally settle it. Carlos sat for a minute and stared at her.

"You just couldn't leave it alone, could you?"

"My store was in danger. I didn't truly believe any one of my people did anything."

He snorted. "Yeah, right. That's why you have a list with Didi's and Jo-Jo's names on it. Where's Cat's and Maggie's?" He blustered on without giving Alex a chance to respond. "I told Didi that you wouldn't stop. I told her she was an outcast here. I told her that you three would make sure that the truth was known if you figured it out. I knew you would. I tried to stop you." He halted with an audible click of his jaws.

Anger coursed through Alex as the realization of his comment made it through her pain-filled mind. "It was you that ran Cat off the road." Alex hissed at Carlos.

"Yes, I thought it was you. Imagine my surprise when it was Cat instead. I guessed she used up one of her nine lives." Carlos walked quickly to the office. Momentarily, Alex heard her music change to loud rock'n'roll. Carlos re-entered the decorating area and rubbed his jaw as he looked around. His eyes settled on Alex as he queried. "What did Didi do that gave her away?"

Alex's mind was sluggish from the recent events, "Huh?"

"I know you figured out Didi killed Abrahms. I heard you through the door before I knocked. What did my wife do that gave her away?"

"Oh, ahhhhhh, at the reception hall she made that 'customer comment' to an older woman who was working there. Only someone from here would have responded with that comment given the question

220

posed to her by the old woman."

"That's it? One little statement?"

"That's it. I forgot about it until we said the same thing here, earlier, about a weird cake order. Before that, I truly thought the murderer was an outsider."

"Well, I'm sorry you figured it out. Cause now I have to decide what to do with you."

Adrenaline shot through Alex at this statement. "What do you mean? I won't tell what happened. Just get her the help she needs."

Pain showed through Carlos' eyes when he looked at Alex. "If only I could believe you, I'd let you go. But I don't know you very well. And now, you're dating a cop. The cop investigating Abrahms' murder. A murder that you are a main suspect in. I can't trust you, Alex. I'm sorry. You'll have to choose between clearing your reputation and name and turning my wife over. I know how you'll choose. I have to choose between my wife and you and it's not a hard choice at all. I love her deeply. That monster beat and raped her years ago. What the assault left her, finding out that she couldn't bear any children afterwards, destroyed her. She's barely the person she used to be . Sometimes I wonder how she can appear to be so normal. I told her we could always adopt, but that wasn't the same thing to her. I thought she would eventually heal. I believe it would have worked too, until that night she worked here and he came in to pay off the cake. How could you, of all people, agree to make his wedding cake?" Tears glistened in his eyes.

Tears flowed freely down Alex's face. "Please, believe me. I did not know. If I would have known he was the groom, I would have thrown the bride out, you can bet on it, friend of Cat's or no." And before he could say anything, she continued. "Cat didn't know who the groom was either, I assure you. We hardly ever know who the grooms

221

are. That's the way the business is done. No amount of money in the world, would have made me make his cake. As you said, I have plenty of reason to hate him. Carlos, what happened the night he came in to pay for the cake?"

"That bastard came in the store five minutes before closing. After he was sure that they were alone, he tried to force himself on her again. That's what." Carlos spit out in anger. He started to pace and throw his hands into the air. "That bastard! He said that he remembered how good she felt the last time and wanted one last hurrah before he married. She started to scream, but he threatened her. He said that if she stayed quiet, he would marry and leave this pitiful town. But, if in fact, she did anything to mar his marriage, he would stay in town and 'do' her again. As many times as he wanted, because the cops were jokes and never could keep him in jail. Didi said they heard a car door slam. The possibility of a customer coming motivated him to leave before he could do more than press her against the wall. She doesn't remember finishing work, closing up, or driving home. She was and is a total emotional wreck."

"I wanted to kill the bastard, but she wouldn't let me. She said that if I got caught, then Abrahms would have succeeded in taking everything away from her and she would not allow that. She believed that he was leaving town and didn't want anything to stop him. By the next morning, she seemed okay. She said that knowing the man was leaving, helped her accept the past. No more seeing him around town every week. That afternoon, we made love and took a nap before going to the party. I didn't know she left the house until some time later. In fact, I didn't know anything, not a clue, until she told me late that night. She was upset that you were going to be convicted for something she did. She wouldn't have told me then, except I found her crying uncontrollably and insisted that she tell me what was going on."

"So, if she was a total wreck, does that mean you did everything afterwards?"

"Yes. I needed to protect her. Unfortunately, you were the best escape goat. You were all I had and I went with it."

"Why'd you wreck my bakery and put me in the closet?"

"I had to plant the glitter shaker with the penicillin. I didn't know where you normally kept them, so I wrecked the place to make the 'plant' more acceptable. I put you in the closet because I couldn't risk you coming to and recognizing me. On the way out, I saw the cake order form and swiped it."

"Then you wrecked my house." When he nodded, she choked as she asked, "but why kill Georgy?"

"I didn't start out planning to do that. Originally, I was just going to break in and plant some penicillin in your medicine cabinet. Nobody keeps those cabinets up-to-date except the anal retentive. I was relieved that you're far from that. On the way out, I accidentally knocked over a vase. You would have become highly suspicious of that. So I decided to cover my error with a fake burglary. I was on my way out when your bird started calling out my name. I have to admit, I freaked out when he started doing that. There was only one way I knew to shut that bird up and I did it. If it helps any, he managed to get me good. My finger was sore for quite some time."

"You deserved it." She grumbled.

"What?"

"Nothing." She growled. "He wasn't saying 'Carlos.' He was saying Garbo, as in Greta Garbo."

"Oh, sorry. That explanation sounds a bit off. I don't know much about birds. I thought he somehow recognized me and would tell you I was there. You see some of that kind of stuff on TV." Carlos got up and starting wrecking the bakery. He knocked things off the shelves.

223

Threw a few pans and chairs around the room.

"Stop!" Alex screamed. "What are you doing?"

"You were attacked before and survived. This time you won't be so lucky. The world's getting to be a dangerous place, Alex, even in small towns. You really should have been more careful about who you opened your door to."

"Would you answer one more question?"

"Sure, if I can."

"Why use Cliff's car?"

"Because it's old, and easy to hot wire. Because it's big, and I wouldn't get injured when I rammed your van. And basically, because Detective Taylor is an ass, and he deserved it."

"Makes sense." Alex agreed.

Carlos raised a finger. "That reminds me, where are your car keys?"

"I don't know. Why?"

"It'll make it easier to drive your car away that's why."

"Didn't you drive?"

"No, I walked. I wanted to be prepared in case you knew more than you let on. Which, unfortunately, you did." Carlos left the room and returned shortly with Alex's handbag and tablet. He dumped the bag's content on a table and smiled as he picked up her keys, "Thank-you very much. Now, I must finish and be off. I can't say that it's been fun, because it hasn't. It just something I need to do."

Carlos grabbed some cooking oil and squirted it all over. Alex screamed. "Don't! Please don't! I won't say anything!"

"You're getting redundant and I do believe, a bit scared. Though I don't blame you one bit. But don't worry, I won't let you suffer." He struck a match and tossed it onto the floor. Carlos watched the fire take and turned to Alex. She was crying, fighting her bonds, and looking around as the fire followed the oil. Carlos lifted a hand and gave her a

224

quick karate chop that knocked her out cold.

Chapter 31

As Cat and Mike pulled into the Slice of Life's driveway, Cat saw the tail end of Alex's car go around the back of the store. Mike turned off the motorcycle but Cat told him that she just saw Alex leave. Mike quickly restarted the motorcycle. As he rounded the store, Cat tapped his right shoulder and Mike turned right. They saw Alex's car up ahead. Cat squeezed Mike's waist to indicate to speed up but he shook his head no. With all the weird things going on lately, he wanted to be careful. Cat said Alex was planning to go home and that was the opposite direction. He decided to tail her from a distance and see what happened. Cat squeezed his waist a few times until he made a horizontal motion with his left hand to stop it. Maybe after today, she'd let him get the intercom system he wanted for this bike. He usually rode alone and didn't need intercom. He suggested it for when she rode with him, but she always had a reason for not wanting it.

They followed "Alex" to the mall and watched "her" park. Mike stopped his bike a little ways off to observe. Cat started to get off the bike but he laid a hand on her leg to halt her. He raised his visor, "I thought you said Alex was going home to vegetate."

"That's what she told me. She must have changed her mind. Let's go. Once I check something out with her, we can go ride."

Mike had kept his eyes on "Alex" while they conversed. As soon as "her" door opened, he halted. They watched Carlos climb into another car and drive slowly away. "Hold on!" Mike yelled. He goosed the throttle and flew to Alex's car. He jumped off with Cat right behind him. Mike looked inside and his heart leapt as he saw no Alex. He checked the door and found it unlocked. Mike opened the door quickly and reached down and pulled the trunk release. He ran to the back of the car and raised the lid. Mike swore with a mixture of relief and fear at its emptiness. What was going on here? "Back to the bike, quick!" Mike yelled to Cat. Cat and Mike jumped back on the bike as fast as her cast allowed her. She had to do a bit of a weird hop to get it over the bike. They raced back to the store.

After work, Tom drove to the bakery to see if Alex was there. No car. He decided he best check out the back parking area just to make sure. He didn't want to make a wasted trip to her house. He didn't see her car and started to continue on around. He was reaching for his cell phone when he noticed smoke coming out one window. "Damn!" he yelled as he slammed on the brakes. As he ran to the window and looked in, he called 9-1-1 to get help coming. His heart stopped as he squinted. Flames lit up the interior of the shop and outlined the silhouette of a person tied to a chair with its head hanging forward and down. The body was not moving.

Tom ran to his car and grabbed an afghan out of the back seat. He wrapped it around his arm and broke the glass window. After cleaning the pane of any dangerous shards of glass, he hoisted his way through. Tom ran to the still body. He panicked for a micro-second as he recognized the still form of Alex. He frantically tried to untie her but knew there wasn't time. Tom took a steadying breath to calm himself. He checked her neck for a pulse and rejoiced when he found one.

Tom picked up Alex, chair and all, and headed for the door. He knew it would not fit through the window he had just entered. He kicked open the office door and hurried through it. The outer door wasn't as easy. He put Alex down and quickly unlocked the door. He grabbed her and burst out into the open air. He started to fall but managed to stay upright. He felt Alex start to slip from his grasp and quickly compensated. Just then, he realized that he wasn't alone. He hadn't almost dropped Alex earlier, it was Mike Porter and Cat trying to help him ease her down.

Mike thrust a hand into his pocket and grabbed his pocketknife. He flicked it open and made quick work of cutting through Alex's bonds. Tom eased her to the ground and checked her vitals. He groaned as he tried again. No luck. He looked at Mike and received a nod. They started team CPR immediately. Cat hobbled around, helpless and frustrated, for there really wasn't anything she could do.

Sirens filled the air as Tom and Mike felt Alex respond to their CPR. They stopped working as she started coughing. Fire trucks and an ambulance pulled into the drive. Firemen flew into action to try to save the structure. The ambulance attendants ran to Alex and checked her out. Mike pulled Tom off to the side to explain about Carlos parking Alex's car at the mall. Tom had his eyes on Alex and the paramedics when Mike started to speak. As the implications of Mike's tale sunk in, anger pulsed through Tom and he quickly focused on Mike. Tom ran to his car to report in and request that surveillance be placed on Carlos and Didi until he called back in. Within moments, Alex was loaded into the ambulance with Tom at her side.

Tears ran down Alex's face as she looked at Tom. He read just about every kind of emotion in her eyes as she stared at him. She tried to talk but he stopped her and told her to keep quiet. He murmured that she was alright and would be okay. Tom noticed her split lip and his eyes narrowed as he realized how that probably came to be. He looked down at his clenched hand and consciously worked to clear his anger and relax. Alex would be fine and the suspects were being watched. He picked up one of her soot smudged hands and kissed it softly. His wonderment grew that he could love and care deeply for Alex, a woman he didn't even know one week ago. Tom gently wiped Alex's hair from her face as he tried to calm her when she croaked out the word "store" and tears flowed freely once more. He assured her that the firemen were doing all that they could.

He had managed to convince Cat to stay at the shop until the fire was doused. That way when she came to the hospital, she could give an accurate account of the damage and effort taken to put out the flames.

Alex was admitted for overnight observation. She had breathed in a lot of smoke and had two cracked ribs. Otherwise, she was just banged up a bit and bruised. Tom had contacted the station while Alex was being examined. The suspects were at home and seemed content to stay there. Tom said that he would check back in in about one hour. Once Alex was settled into her room, she was sedated and went to sleep. Tom waited until she was sleeping and then left the hospital. As he headed for the parking lot, he heard his name being called and turned to see Cat hobbling his way.

"How's Alex? Is she hurt bad?"

Tom filled Cat in on Alex's injuries and asked about the bakery.

"I stayed until the fire was put out and then caught a ride in. Mike is still at the shop. The firemen wouldn't let us in to check out the extent of the damage. They were able to get it under control relatively quickly. The fire chief believes the fire was kept out of the front room. Mike's hanging around for more info and then will come here. Where are you going?"

"To catch me some bad guys." He waved and jumped into a waiting police car.

Chapter 32

Alex woke up with a start and found a strange man in a robe sleeping in a chair beside her bed. She was starting to get nervous when the middle-aged man with a gray receding hairline and a slight paunch spoke in a gravelly voice. "Good early morning Miss Applecake. Please don't get upset. Detective Tom Baker asked that I stay here with you until he got back. He had to step out for a few minutes and didn't want you alone if you awoke in his absence. My name is Johnathan Whitameyer. I'm…" He trailed off as Alex spoke.

"Tom's usual partner." She smiled sheepishly at the gentleman.

"Ahhh. I see that Tom already spoke of me. He couldn't remember if he did or not. Please call me John. I would show you my badge but it's at home. I'm afraid these hospital jammies don't have any pockets."

"That's alright." Alex yawned. "Excuse me, John. I'm feeling a little out of it."

John laughed. "Yeah, I guess you are. Do you remember where you are? Tom said that you had awakened a few hours back and he filled you in on your present condition and the surroundings. He wasn't sure what all you'd remember if anything. He said you were a might upset when you awoke."

Alex slightly chuckled. "That's putting it mildly. I screamed like a banshee because of a nightmare apparently. The end result was that he was covered with coffee and so was part of the wall behind you."

John was laughing and holding his side to keep from shaking too hard. "Figures. I only got a very abbreviated explanation for his appearance when I showed up."

Alex squinted in the dim light. "Am I seeing correctly? Are you in a robe? What did you do? Let Tom borrow your clothes or didn't he give you any time to change?"

John chuckled again. He'd laugh harder, but found out that that wasn't a good idea. His side hurt too much when he laughed. "Neither. I'm still here after my appendectomy. I go home tomorrow. There was a minor complication following my surgery or I'd be home already. Tom called my room and asked if I could come down here." He spread his arms out in front of him, bowed his head, and smiled, "and here I am."

"I hope we didn't inconvenience you."

John waved her away before she could continue. He swiveled his head around and looked at the door. He leaned slightly toward her and whispered loudly, "Forget it. To tell you the truth, I was going bonkers in that room. They want me to get up and move around a bit anyway. The nurses just get irritated that I have a tendency to move further away than they like." He winked at her as he finished.

"Do they know where you are right now?"

"Yeah, I told them. Nurse McGillam actually smiled and thanked me for alerting them to my absence and whereabouts. I just had to promise not to do anything too physical just yet. Maybe give my guts another week or two to recuperate first." He settled back in the chair. "It's still quite early, why don't you try to get some more sleep."

"I'm sure that's good advice, but I don't know if I can sleep anymore just now. When I first woke up, I was tired, but I'm wide awake now. If you're tired though, you can go and get some."

"Nah. I'm not particularly tired either. Besides, Tom would kill me if I left before his arrival. How about some chess?"

Alex's eyes lit up. "You bet'cha!" She looked around and asked with some disappointment. "But where's a board?"

"While you were sleeping, I looked in the drawers of your end table. Sometimes there's a deck of cards or such. I didn't mean to pry, but I didn't bring anything with me. I did find a cheap, but still usable, chess set." He got up and fetched it and set it up on her movable table. She moved around until he could sit comfortably on the bed. "Are you any good?"

Alex shook her head. "Not bad. My friends don't like to play me though." She wiggled her eyebrows and grinned. "They say I always win."

"Do they now?" John's eyes twinkled as he chuckled and scrooched around a bit more. He sighed when he finally got comfortable. "That's better." He raised his eyes to Alex's as he continued, "I'm not squishing you in any way am I? What's wrong?" John asked with concern as he watched Alex's face change from surprise to curiosity.

"Why are you wearing a gun?"

John instinctively touched the gun with his hand. "You fell asleep before Tom could tell you everything. Didi is in a form of custody, but Carlos was not there when Tom and the guys showed up at their house. That's just one more reason I'm here."

"You mean, in case Carlos shows up here?" When John nodded in the affirmative, she continued, "what do you mean Didi's in a 'form' of custody?"

"She's lost it Alex. She's flipped. She's at the mental hospital."

"I'm sorry to hear it. Didi's a nice person." Alex spoke just above a whisper. "She didn't deserve such a harsh life."

"Who does?" John asked. "Now, if you say you are just a so-so player, but still seem to win all your games, what's your secret?"

Alex smiled. "You think I'm going to tell you? Let's start and see how we do. I'll tell you one thing, I play for blood. No pussy footing

231

around."

"Good. Exactly as I do. Take no hostages." They playfully glared at each other and started the game.

They were in the middle of their second game, when the door silently opened. Someone slipped into the room and closed the door. As Alex started to move a castle, she caught the movement in her peripheral vision and froze. John noticed her freeze and watched her hand shake and knock over a few other pieces. He froze momentarily and let his senses take over. He reached over to steady Alex's hand and watched her eyes. John very slowly adjusted his head and swiveled his eyes to see where she was staring. Alex steadied herself and drew strength from John's firm touch. He released her hand and moved his toward his gun. He took his gun out of its holster and laid it on the bed beside him. John waited for the person to come out of the darkness or make some kind of move. Alex starting shaking all over as the person slowly walked into the light. The intruder held his hands out to show that he was unarmed. "Stop right there." John ordered.

Carlos stopped. "Hello, John. I'm unarmed. I promise not to hurt you or Alex."

John winced as he turned around. "Why are you here then?"

"To apologize and try to explain my actions."

"Sit down in that chair Carlos. Move slowly and let me see your hands at all times. I am armed and will shoot if you do not follow my orders to the letter."

Carlos did as he was told. Alex watched him and didn't realize she was holding her breath until she exhaled as he sat. Tears were sliding down her face. He raised his eyes to Alex's. "I'm sorry I hurt you, Alex. I'm truly relieved that you were rescued. I only did what I thought I had to do to protect my wife. Mentally, she's gone Alex. She's had a total emotional breakdown. I left her with her mother, while I came here to apologize."

She nodded her head. "Now what do you plan on doing?" Alex asked with a waver in her voice.

Carlos tilted his head toward John, "Like I really have a choice with John here. The police station is my next stop." Carlos waited while John made the appropriate phone calls on a cell phone that Alex did not realize that he had had. "If its any consolation, that's where I was heading anyway. I just wanted to stop here first."

Just then, there was quite a bit of commotion as Tom hurried into Alex's hospital room with Cliff and a couple of uniforms behind him. Carlos was read his rights and led away by Cliff and the other officers. Tom shook John's hand and thanked him. "What for? This is the most excitement I've had for quite some time. Thanks for the game of chess Alex. Any time you need help or want to play chess, just give me a call." He winked as he shook her hand. With a groan and a wince, he was off the bed and on his way back to his room.

Tom sat on the bed and leaned over. He cautiously hugged Alex and gave her a long gentle kiss. She hugged him back a bit harder and felt Tom pull away. "What about your ribs, babe?"

She smiled hugely and throatily replied, "Who cares? I'm alive."

"That you are." He laughed and kissed her again. "And on some major pain drugs, I presume."

"Oh, yeah! I'm sure going to hurt when they wear off." She responded with a smile and a wink. "But, for now, who cares."

Epilogue

The next morning, Alex's room was filled with flowers and friends. Maggie and Cat wanted completely filled in on the events of the past night. While waiting for the doctor to come in to release Alex from the hospital, Tom related most of the facts with Alex filling in where necessary. Her voice still a tad raspy from inhaling all that smoke.

Didi was indeed at Tantebaum's, the local mental hospital. The full diagnosis wasn't in yet on her. She would need lots of help to recover, if indeed, she was strong enough to do it. Carlos was in jail pending a trial. He had been charged with numerous counts ranging from breaking and entering to attempted murder. Of the two parts of the bakery, the decorating and baking area had been extensively damaged, but the store part was basically safe. The store had smoke damage though. Alex sighed, "At least my insurance should cover the damage."

Cat smiled, "Yeah, now you can rebuild and have a brand new place."

"Yes. That would be the 'silver lining' of this dark cloud. Now would be the time to tell me if y'all want anything changed from the way it was."

Tom raised his hand, "Not right this minute though. You guys can make a list. Alex you should take it easy for a while yet." The doctor came in at that moment and agreed wholeheartedly. While he took care of what he needed to do to check her out, Alex's friends noticed a huge bouquet of red roses. They walked over to read the card and looked knowingly at each other. Alex finally had a man. The flowers were from Tom and the card was signed "Love, Tom."

"What are you guys doing?" Alex asked.

"Oh, nothing." They both chimed up and laughed. Cat made a show of putting the card back into the little envelope and replacing it into the bouquet. The whole room laughed when Alex turned bright red.

"How are you doing Caitlin? The leg feeling okay?" Dr. Chadsworth inquired.

"Doing good, Doc. Thanks for asking." Cat replied with a smile.

"You're free to go, Alex." The doctor stated, but then continued, "If you have any questions, or begin to feel funny in any way, call here and ask for me or just come in."

"Thank you Doctor Eric. I promise I'll call if anything changes." Alex replied.

Once Tom and Alex reached her house, he helped her out of his car. Tom followed Alex up to the front door. "The gang should be here soon with the flowers and food for a cookout. Why don't you go inside and get comfortable?"

"You're coming too, aren't you?"

"Right behind you." Tom responded.

Alex gasped as she walked in and found the gorgeous nanday conure from the pet store in her living room. His cage was placed exactly where Georgy's had been. They walked over to get a good look at the bird. "I hear you two already met." Tom chuckled.

"I'll say." Alex's eyes opened wide as she returned his grin and laughed. "So you're the customer who had already bought the bird."

Tom raised his right palm towards her. "Guilty. I went into the pet store to check out their birds. Cassie told me that you would like a nanday. Now, you know why Cassie was acting a bit weird. When she saw you come into the store, she just about had a heart attack. She was afraid that you'd figure out who bought the bird. Especially, after you insisted on going back to check it out."

"How was I supposed to guess that?" Alex inquired.

"I asked her to teach the bird a phrase and she was afraid it would say it while you were visiting." Tom stated.

"What phrase?"

"I believe you'll figure it out when you hear it." His eyes twinkled as he grinned.

"Thank you very much." Alex turned and embraced Tom. As they kissed, the bird spoke up, "Hey, beautiful."

57779449R00133

Made in the USA
Middletown, DE
03 August 2019